THE KILLER'S *wife*

THE KILLER'S *wife*

BILL FLOYD

**Doubleday Large Print
Home Library Edition**

St. Martin's Minotaur New York

This Large Print Edition, prepared especially for Double-day Large Print Home Library, contains the complete, unabridged text of the original Publisher's Edition.

This is a work of fiction. All of the characters, organizations, and events portrayed in this novel are either products of the author's imagination or are used fictitiously.

ISBN: 978-0-7394-9238-3

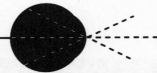

**This Large Print Book carries the
Seal of Approval of N.A.V.H.**

For Amy

THE KILLER'S
wife

CHAPTER ONE

1.

Don't I know you?"

I glanced up from the frozen foods case where I'd been considering the overabundance of packaged meals, narrowing down the choices according to Hayden's likes and dislikes, to find an older gentleman staring at me with his eyebrows raised. A healthy-looking type of guy, robust. Full head of salt-and-pepper hair, probably in his mid-sixties, wearing a casual pullover and blue jeans.

Distant alarm bells.

It was late, nearing midnight on a Friday; my favorite time to do the weekly shopping, because usually I could avoid these types of run-ins. I was no fan of idle chitchat with my neighbors, or anyone else in particular, if I could help it. Tonight when I'd entered the Harris Teeter, the big glass doors sliding apart at my approach, whisper soft as the airlock on a spaceship, it was as though I had the place completely to myself. That clean, lonely, safe feeling, exclusive to public places when they are emptied of the public. Of course I wasn't actually alone: the teenaged employees leaned drowsily in the checkout lanes, a couple of single men (second-shift types, non-professionals) wandered the beer aisle, trying to kill some time before returning home to their sofas. One of these guys was checking out my ass; I saw him staring after me in one of the parabolic mirrors that hang from the whitewashed girders in the warehouse-type ceiling. At my age, I could've taken it as flattery, but instead it made me feel exposed, so I pushed my cart a little faster. Most often, the clientele roaming the store at this time of night were all perfectly self-encapsulated, as unwilling to meet my eyes as I was to meet theirs. Which was exactly how I preferred it.

But now this older man was staring at my face, and his question wasn't posed rudely.

So I shook my head and said politely, "I don't think so."

"Leigh Wren?" he guessed.

I felt a measure of relief, and searched my memory for where I may have met him. He was familiar, wasn't he? A stirring in those pools deep down below, a single blip that wouldn't coalesce. My social engagements had been few and far between for longer than I liked to consider; mostly it was just me and Hayden and the office, and that was just fine, thank you, so I surmised that I must have met this man at some work-related function. I felt a moment's guilt at not being able to place him. Although, to be honest, there was nothing in particular to distinguish him; his kind was ubiquitous in Cary. I could even envision his SUV in the parking lot, a Jesus fish on one side of his license plate and a Bush/Cheney campaign sticker on the other.

"That's me," I answered. "I'm sorry, you are?"

I extended my hand.

He took hold of it, and his eyes changed. They flared and flashed. He took a deep, tremulous breath and commenced: "My name is Charles Pritchett. I've never had to use any other name than my own, because I've never been ashamed of who I am. Your real name is Nina Mosley, and on November 18, 1997, your husband, Randall Roberts Mosley, killed my daughter, Carrie."

The whole world telescoped. My hand went numb, as did all my other extremities, but I could feel the overt pressure Charles Pritchett was exerting, cracking my knuckles and pinching my fingers together. I tried to pull away, but he was holding on fast, his eyes like strobe lights now. He was shaking all over; I could see that he'd been rehearsing this very moment for a long, long time, and now that it was upon him he was having some sort of near-debilitating reaction, a galvanization that fired his every nerve. In his transport, he seemed capable of levitation; it was obvious that a Truly Meaningful Moment was upon Mr. Pritchett.

All I could think was, *You mean my ex-husband.*

But I couldn't seem to activate my voice. My throat was locked down against what could only be a horrible scream waiting to surge free if I dared to open my mouth. My teeth ached. I felt sick and panicked, withdrawing at light speed, receding toward a blessed and familiar disconnect. The half-full grocery cart, with its neatly bagged bundles of fruit (green grapes because Hayden hated the purple ones, too seedy) and vacuum-sealed sliced meats and cheeses, the health-food bars for me and the sugary cereals for my son, was forgotten. I was still trying to get away from Pritchett, backing up and bumping into the cart, which turned on its wobbly squeaking wheel and lodged between my butt and the cold glass door of the freezer. Pritchett followed, still gripping my hand, still speaking in steadily rising tones.

"It took me a long time to find you, Nina, and quite a bit of money, too. You look so different than you did the last time I saw you, at the trial. Your hair's a different color, and you've lost a lot of weight. Did you tint your hair so people wouldn't recognize you? I suppose I can understand that, wanting to disassociate yourself from your past. But I don't have that kind of luxury, you see," he said, his summation spat from behind clenched teeth. "I live with my past *every single day*, in *every single moment* that my daughter's not here. She's *gone.* I know what the police said, how it was all your husband, but you were never cleared to my satisfaction, not by a *long shot.* That's why I'm here now, Nina. I've come to expose you. I'm going to tear apart this tidy little fiction of a life you've made, and I'm going to show everyone what you are."

"Excuse me, are you all right?"

Another voice intervened, and I looked around to find the ass-watcher standing there, a bug-eyed checkout boy slightly behind him, both of them regarding Pritchett and me with some concern. The checkout boy seemed electrically charged, looking for some excuse to get physical and jump Pritchett, his adolescent head likely swarming with some fantasy of sticking up for the little guy. Perhaps Pritchett reminded him of a dominating patriarch in his own history. The ass-watcher was much calmer, holding his olive green basket of single-serving items loosely, a resigned and ready tension that suggested he'd been in such confrontations before, and come out on the winning end. Maybe he was ex-military. Or maybe just a bar scrapper.

Pritchett finally released my hand, but he kept right on talking, directing his commentary now to the would-be interventionists. "You know who she is? Who her husband was? I bet you'd remember his name." He jabbed a skinny finger at my face, his words coming in a barely checked avalanche. "Should we call the police, Nina? You want to report this 'incident'? Because I'd love that. I'd relish the opportunity to alert the local authorities as to who's been living in their midst for the past six years."

The ass-watcher had had enough. He set his basket down on the floor and stepped between Pritchett and me. I was still backing up, but couldn't tear my gaze away from the old man. Tears had sprung up in his eyes, the drear emotional weight he'd just jettisoned close to undoing him. The ass-watcher said, "I don't know what your problem is, sir, but I think you should leave the lady be."

The checkout boy called Pritchett a bully. Pritchett held up his hands, open palms outward, and backed off a few steps. In a steadier voice, he again suggested calling the cops. The overhead PA switched from a Commodores song to "Take on Me." On some quiet, murmuring level, I understood that from then on, whenever I heard that trite synth melody, it would be as a soundtrack to this moment of schism.

Pritchett called after me: "Where is Hayden tonight, Nina? You should keep a closer eye on him. I didn't keep a close enough watch over Carrie, and you know what happened to her. You know what he did to her."

That was enough to finally get me turned around, to send me running away from him, slipping and regaining my footing as I fled down the aisle to the front of the store. The automatic doors didn't open quite fast enough and I bumped into one of them. Tomorrow there would be a large bruise along that arm from the shoulder to the elbow. Right then I didn't feel it; right then my hand was still throbbing from where Pritchett wouldn't let me go.

2.

I'd made some jokes when they built the shopping plaza directly abutting our development, sour wit along the lines of how much more convenient it was than the one five miles farther down the road. Tonight I thanked God it was so close. A left turn out of the parking lot, then the stop sign at the entrance into Kensington Arbor, which I blew through without even tapping the brakes. Then a right, hugging the curb so tight I heard the tires squealing. In less that four minutes from the time I left the grocery store, I was parking my Camry in front of the McPhersons' house.

The street was quiet, the homes large and fashionably expansive, all built close together, with minimal yard space between. Moisture in the night air collected in shiny rings around the streetlamps. The front porch light was on at the McPhersons', but nothing looked askew from the outside. Then again, nothing ever looked askew in this neighborhood, this settlement of cookie-cutter single-family homes and town houses that had become our refuge. Our own place was three blocks over, a town house with a one-car garage and a nice patio out back where Hayden played. I didn't often let him spend the night away from home, but he'd begged all week and I knew I had the midnight shopping to do, so I'd relented and allowed him to sleep over with his friend, Caleb. A burgundy Yukon was parked halfway on the sidewalk. It was Caleb's mother's "old" car; the garage space now undoubtedly reserved for the Escalade Doug McPherson bought his wife for Christmas.

I softly closed my car door and then

slipped through the yard, glancing up and down the street to confirm that nothing looked out of place, although I wouldn't have even begun to know how to tell if something did. I'd only been to this part of the neighborhood a few times. Hayden had a cell phone with him and I'd considered calling it even as I fled the scene at the grocery store, but I hated to wake everyone up if no one was in any actual danger. And although Charles Pritchett might have a bone to pick with me, surely he wouldn't do something to my child. Surely that hadn't been as overt a threat as I'd taken it to be. Surely he wouldn't, not after what had been done to his own flesh and blood . . .

Where is Hayden tonight, Nina? You should keep a closer eye on him.

I looked up and down the street again. A few cars parked in driveways or along the street, but no silhouettes slouched behind the windshields, no one watched from darkened windows of the houses. The homes were crowded so close together they seemed like sentinels, or the walls of a labyrinth. I used to value such sensibilities, the idea that I'd found a fortress, but I'd always understood on some level that it could turn on me.

I simply was not ready for that to happen.

At the last moment, I decided against ringing the bell. The McPhersons already had their doubts about me, surely, but hopefully they were limited to wondering why I was single at my age and *She's so painfully reserved* and *Where's the boy's father?* and the sorts of things I overheard and dismissed from any number of acquaintances on a fairly regular basis. I could handle the isolation from my peers; in fact, I'd grown to value it, but my son needed friends and I didn't want to blow this for him. He was at the age where loneliness could become a preferred mode of coping, with alienation the next stop, and then by the time he was a teenager I'd have to search his closet to make sure he wasn't stowing an assault rifle in there.

I wasn't always prone to imagining the worst. It was a learned skill, a smart piece of involuntary conditioning.

Gabby McPherson gave me the short, house-proud tour the first time I brought Hayden over to play, but I was already familiar with the layout; I'd researched the floor plans to all the models when I was first looking into buying a place here. She didn't do anything original with the interior; the furnishings and arrangement were straight out of Martha

Stewart . . . five years ago. The living room where the boys were supposed to be setting up camp was around the side, and I stepped lightly through the yard until I could peek in the windows. God only knew what the next-door neighbors would make of me if they glanced out, but I could give a shit, really. I wouldn't have objected if a police car came cruising up the street—I had thought of calling them right off, but was already hoping that maybe Pritchett got whatever satisfaction he needed from confronting me at the store and that now he would leave us alone. Not that I believed it. My heart was pumping too fast; I could feel my pulse in my neck and it was difficult to swallow.

I would admit a grudging admiration for Gabby's taste in window dressing. She'd bought some fine, sheer drapes somewhere, but of course the boys forgot to close the blinds, so I could see right in. The living-room floor had been turned into a classic crash pad, sleeping bags unrolled on the carpet in front of the leather couch. Half-empty bowls of popcorn and soda cans crowded the coffee table. The plasma TV was on but no sound disturbed the window-pane, so I was guessing that either the volume was muted or else turned down low enough that it wouldn't wake the adults up-stairs. Caleb McPherson was lying off to the right, curled into a cashew, half-in and half-out of his sleeping bag, eyes closed. And there, sitting too close to the screen, propped up on his elbows: my baby boy. Hayden was being bad, watching some music video with twirling teens in skimpy clothes doing dance routines whose moves consisted of grinds and thrusts. I wouldn't let him watch this sort of thing at home—he was only seven, for God's sake—but I felt a wash of relief that he was all right, a physical sensation just like cold refreshing water poured over my head. A sob caught in my throat when I thought about how he'd stayed awake so he could view this trite, forbidden spectacle on MTV. He was only a boy, a regular, healthy boy.

He turned his head toward the window and I ducked down quickly. I made my way in a crouch back to the car, feeling ashamed and spotlighted, even though I know he hadn't seen me and there was seemingly no one else awake all down the silent street.

I locked my car doors and stayed right where I was. In the rearview, I caught sight of myself and made a severe assessment: I looked crazed. My light brown hair, usually tidy and shoulder-length, curled slightly at the ends in the more-or-less current style for a suburban mom nearing middle age, was mussed and frazzled. My smooth skin, which I considered my best feature, looked pale and drawn in the streetlight's harsh glow. And the eyes, the subdued emerald eyes that my girlfriends had always openly admired but which to me seemed too wounded, too vulnerable, an invitation to men telling them I was pliant, willing; now they seemed stark lifeless marbles wide with anxiety. It struck me that, for all the self-examination I did every morning in the bathroom mirror, brushing my teeth and drying my hair and applying my makeup, I rarely looked myself in those eyes. Even though I should have earned it by now, should have forgiven myself long ago. Then again, Pritchett obviously hadn't. I wondered if there were others who were still roiling inside, who'd never made peace in all the days since Randy had interrupted what should have been the normal, decent courses of their lives.

Deep breaths, I told myself. I wouldn't rouse the McPherson household; I wouldn't make any untoward scene. But damned if I was going to let the house out of my sight tonight. If there was one thing I'd paid so dearly to acquire, it was a sense of diligence.

Over the past six years, there had been times, I admit, when I would briefly forget who we really were. Hours, days, even as long as a week sometimes, when I just let go and believed that I really was Leigh Wren, and not Nina Leigh Mosley née Sarbaines. At times I let it slip completely from my mind that my name was ever anything but what it was now and that I'd had it legally changed after what happened with my ex-husband.

But such comfort never lasted long. Something always reminded me: a spree of atrocity on the evening news, a conversation at work, a legal nicety of some sort. And as soon as I remembered, as soon as I came back to the sharp, alert state that was now my default setting, I never felt any sense of relief that I'd been able to let go for a while, to put the past where it belonged. Instead I felt irresponsible, childish, and stupid. I felt selfish that I could have let Hayden down.

Charles Pritchett. He must have known where we lived. Must have known and must've waited for his chance to confront me, savoring it, my God that meant he was serious. That meant he wouldn't have gotten nearly enough satisfaction from scaring the shit out of me at the store; he had obviously undertaken a Project. Men of his sort charted their lives as a series of Projects, and mine had likely been a long time in the planning.

That realization, along with all its implications, made my head spin. I didn't have the luxury to get foggy, so I started jotting down notes on the little pad I kept in the glove box. Meaningless shit, I could barely even see what I was writing in the silver glow from the streetlights, but I needed something to do with my hands. I wrote random dates. I scribbled words and free associations. If I bothered to look at them later, I knew I wouldn't be able to decipher them. I crumpled the notes and tossed them on the floorboard.

I remembered Pritchett now, vaguely. He was wealthy, the one surname on the victims' list that the average person might have known by reputation for something other than having had a family member killed by Randy. He'd been the one to call press conferences before the trial, and there were rumors he'd even hired a PR firm to deal with the media on his behalf. I couldn't seem to recall his actually being in the courtroom, but that didn't mean much either; the most I'd retained from that ordeal were images: a few words other people said to me, some of the questions the prosecutors and the defense asked. I couldn't clearly remember my responses, although I was sure they were set down somewhere in the public record. In my own mind, the recollections from that time had been locked into a sealed vault and buried beneath layer upon layer, year upon year, of careful blockade. Back then, the prosecutors, having secured my unconditional cooperation, shielded me from the worst of the pretrial publicity, and I'd moved back in with Mom before the trial got under way, so I was out of state for much of the media circus that preceded it.

My main memory wasn't of the old man himself, but of his appearances on TV, pointing his finger at the camera and finding it difficult to control his emotion, which anyone could understand, given the circumstances. How could I have forgotten? Why didn't I recognize him when he approached me, why didn't his name come immediately to mind? I remembered many of the victims' names, probably most of them. I remembered one boy who'd survived by hiding in a guest room while the rest of his family was slaughtered.

After court, on the day he'd testified, I'd spoken to this sole survivor and found him broken, confused, nearly catatonic with guilt that he lived on while his loved ones had perished. Just another casualty along with all the other ones who'd lost their friends and family members to Randy's terrible compulsions. The majority of them hadn't attended the trial, and no one publicly criticized them for it. By the time things got that far, all their sons and daughters and mothers and fathers and brothers and sisters and spouses were long past help. By then it was Randy's circus, the last display to which his rotting mind could fully tend, the public revelation of what he really always had been inside. My partner. My mate.

Randy's festival of blood had lasted a decade at least, and probably much longer. I was there for most of it, and didn't have a single clue. Poor, ignorant Nina, sleeping with the Beast and caught completely unaware, even if some called me an enabler, even if at one point early on I'd been suspected of actually participating in the show, in Randy's foul harvest.

I swore, then and now: *I didn't know, I couldn't have.*

All these arguments, I'd never really had them aloud, never really been in the position to defend, and their logic had long rung hollow to my own ears. Of course there were clues. Of course I turned a willfully oblivious eye.

I kept watch there, in the car, all night. All was quiet, except for the dull echo of my heart.

CHAPTER TWO

When we had been married for about a year, Randy and I participated in a search party for a missing local boy named Tyler Renault. Tyler's mother and older sister had been found murdered in their beds two days earlier, and the rumors were flying. El Ray was a suburb of Fresno, and was usually spared the grotesqueries of big-city crime. One school of thought had it that the estranged husband had killed his wife and child, and indeed the police had questioned him several times, but hadn't yet taken him into custody. He maintained his innocence, but no one gave that very much credence. Another theory, most often whispered, was that the family had been the victims of a religious cult whose membership consisted of some burned-out youths that congregated in the trailer parks outside the city limits and sold meth to sustain their depraved lifestyles.

We didn't know the Renaults personally; their house was a few miles away from our neighborhood, and life had been such a constant rush since the honeymoon that we barely knew the people who lived on our own street. Randy's job as a compliance officer for Jackson-Lilliard Corporation, an internationally based chemical company that produced industrial dyes for use in everything from textiles to house paint, kept him traveling a good bit of the time, inspecting satellite plants, auditing their applications guidelines, and making sure they were all within the legal- and industry-standard parameters. And Shaw Associates, where I'd worked since we moved here after I graduated college, had already promoted me from assistant to the marketing VP to a business analyst's role, assessing their focus group/demographics-targeting procedures and trying to streamline them in a way to maximize profits and impact. So we hadn't gotten very much in the way of settling in accomplished since we'd moved here. There were still boxes in the garage that had never been unpacked.

But the crime was all anyone had been talking about, and when Judy Larson from the First Methodist called and told me that the police were asking for volunteers to beat the bushes for any sign of Tyler, of course I signed us up. Randy hadn't been thrilled at first, but he seemed to warm to the idea. Probably he conceded to going along just to avoid my recrimination, which gave me a smug sort of satisfaction.

Our designated search grid was a meadow just east of where Highway 1 cut through the edge of the suburbs. Along with seventeen other adults, mostly strangers, we walked in a staggered line through the waist-high stalks of yellowed weeds and thick undergrowth, swatting at the insects humming around our sweaty faces in the late spring morning, all of us looking for a body. Some sign of violence. The pair of uniformed city cops assigned to our group strolled up and down the line, calling Tyler's name through their bullhorns.

Randy strode confidently, an imposing figure in the hazy sunshine; at six-four he was the tallest of the men walking the line. He was in great physical shape, his wide shoulders and large chest filling out the Lands' End shirt I'd bought him for his last birthday. I sometimes still caught myself wondering how I'd managed to land him; he had sharp brown eyes and close-cropped black hair, olive skin and an expressive mouth; he was an archetype of what most women would classify as exceptionally attractive in a catalogue model sort of way. I'd catch them—alone or in pairs, older women and teenaged girls alike—at the mall or in a restaurant, following him with their eyes as we passed, and then I would become painfully self-conscious. I was shapely enough, at least I imagined so, but petite, and even our friends often commented on our appearance as a couple, Randy's robust physicality and my somewhat more delicate presence. If they were tactful, they'd say we complemented each other nicely; if not, they said we looked funny together.

We were somewhat acquainted with the people flanking us on the line that afternoon, by which I mean that we'd met them once or twice before and at least knew their names. Roger Adler and his wife, Georgia, were members of our church. He'd taught math at

the local high school for twenty years. She
was a retired accountant. Their children
were grown, and they seemed like the sort
of active, content people everyone dreams
of becoming when they retire. Randy had
commented in the past that they'd each
probably had cosmetic surgery, but I couldn't
tell. They both just looked "great for their
age" in that generic sort of way you associ-
ate with older couples in magazine ads pro-
moting vitamins and organic foods. Roger
walked beside me at first, Georgia on the
other side of him. He used a short stick he'd
picked up off the ground to swat at the bugs.
Often he paused and peered intently at the
aluminum cans or snack wrappers that were
tangled in the high grass. Georgia wore
short pants and her thick white thighs were
soon laced with bramble scratches. She pretended not to notice, but I could hear her
cussing under her breath. After a few minutes she switched places with her husband
so she could talk to me.

On the other side of us, keeping pace with
Randy, was Dalton Forte, a corporate lawyer
who worked out of a company headquarters
that shared space in the same office block
as Randy's employer. Forte was one of those

forty-somethings whose year-round tan and spiky hair would've been more at home on a teenager in some reality TV show: creepy or pathetic, depending on your disposition. He and Randy played racquetball at lunch sometimes, and today they soon fell into a comradely banter that was completely out of place, given the circumstances.

Georgia felt compelled to make the obligatory comment about how monstrous it all was, this tragedy that had befallen the Renault family. I'd been hearing the same clichés from everyone I talked to during the past few days: *it's so sad, so pointless, the work of a real sicko, they need to kill whoever did it on sight, skip the trial, save the state some money, it's a reflection of how modern life has become devalued* . . . on and on. As if anyone thought it *wasn't* a monstrous thing. But I'd spouted the same lines, of course, simply wanting to be on record registering my repugnance. Todd Cline, a policeman who lived down the street from us, had been one of the responding officers the morning Trudi and Dominique Renault's bodies were discovered (by the estranged husband, no less) and Todd had dropped some salacious and unsettling hints that went beyond what was in the newspaper. He said that certain things had been done to the bodies, things he wasn't at liberty to discuss, but it had been worse than anything he'd personally come across in eight years on the force. Certain things about their eyes.

Dominique Renault had been ten years old.

"I can't believe someone would do that, not even the husband," Georgia said, wiping the sweat from her neck with her shirt collar. "You never hear about something like that happening someplace like this."

An exasperated, theatrical sigh sounded from my right, and I cringed inwardly. Before I could slap him quiet, Randy piped up: "Actually, 'things like that' most often happen in places like this, if by 'someplace like this' you mean our comfortable-middle-class-idyll-convenient-to-the-highway-and-only-twenty-minutes-from-downtown. Three out of five homicides last year occurred in planned communities like ours, or in regular neighborhoods outside of the inner city. Of course, no one really lives in the inner city anymore, so 'someplace like this' is kind of a broad term nowadays, Georgia."

"I'm glad you were here to sort that out for us, professor," quipped Forte. "Your insights on exurban planning and crime rates are invaluable. Been listening to NPR again, I see."

Randy favored him with a "screw you" smile and pointed ahead of our skirmish line. Fifty yards farther on, the meadow terminated in a wall of trees. Up until a few years ago, it had most likely been a fairly dense stretch of forest. Now you could see gaps showing through to the other side, the bull-dozed and unearthed hillsides where a new housing development would rise up next fall. "I'm just pointing out that most of America now consists of places like this, and the crime rate has largely remained the same since the early eighties. Except for crack, of course, and I think we can all agree that the Renaults weren't killed as part of a drug deal gone awry. What you have here is either a classic domestic situation, or you have a troubled individual out there that did the deed. And who's still at large, I might add. In which case, the fact that the boy was taken instead of being killed at the scene might be an indication that he's still alive. Probably not around this particular meadow, I'll grant you, but there's always a chance."

I watched my fair share of true crime stories on TV, just like my husband did. Hell,
Primetime ran three such investigative pro-
cedurals every week, detailing everything
from the discovery of the crime through the
verdict. I assumed that's where Randy was
getting the information to make these broad
assertions. I know he'd never listened to
NPR a day in his life. When we were first dating, I thought it was charming how he'd hold
forth on practically any subject as if he'd
read extensively on it. So many guys his age
only talked about sports or money, it was
kind of refreshing. Over time, I realized that
he was grossly mistaken in many of his "informed" opinions, either quoting things he'd
heard in passing completely out of context,
or fabricating evidence for what were his own
already presumed conclusions. Still, he could
make it sound pretty good, and I learned the
hard way how much he hated to be challenged, reverting quickly to sullen pouting or
outright denial, so I usually just let it go. It
wasn't any big deal, when it was just me he
was spouting off to. But around other people,
it could be particularly trying.

This time I couldn't help myself. "I thought
if someone was abducted, their chances of

being recovered alive decreased with every day they weren't found." I said it quietly, making sure that no one outside our immediate vicinity would overhear.

"True enough," Randy allowed, cutting his eyes at me. "But if we're dealing with a psychotic type of person, someone who's out of control, 'in the throes,' so to speak, why not kill them at the scene? I mean, they're obviously not thinking clearly, but how then could they restrain their bloodlust and keep one of the victims alive? And why take the chance of moving them, of traveling?"

Georgia, her distaste for mutilation crimes duly noted, didn't like where her line of commentary had led. She shivered a bit and reiterated, "Well, it's just awful."

But now Forte's interest was piqued. "You said it yourself. Psychos who've reached the level of instability required to even commit such an act," he said, waggling his hand back and forth beside his head and smiling at Randy, "might not be making their decisions dispassionately. Reason has been abandoned. They might simply have been driven—by the voices in their heads or the little green men or whatever sick shit is motivating them—to take the kid along. Then again, maybe they're thinking more clearly than we'd like to admit, and think they can use Tyler as a bargaining chip if the cops hunt them down."

"Or they might just have not been quite done with him," Randy added, softly. He quickly continued, and I could tell he was really getting ramped up, ready to let loose. My unhappiness with this pattern was something I often decided not to think about, but while it was actually happening it was like a vise clenching around my stomach. I started to say something, anything, to switch the subject, but Randy overrode me with volume alone.

"If it was the husband, you might be right about his using the kid as a wedge with the authorities," he told Forte in a lecturing tone, suitable I supposed for arguing a point with a corporate lawyer. "But they've already talked to the guy several times, and I haven't read or heard anything along those lines. And it's not such a good idea, statistically, since hostage situations most often end up with both the hostage and the hostage-taker dead. Now, if this was indeed a crime driven by some sort of sudden emotional overload on the part of the husband, where he simply lost it, then in that case all bets are off. You can't predict the behavior of someone who's operating in a fog of hysteria. But let's go ahead and say it, the thing no one really wants to acknowledge, which is that a serial killer has struck, here in our own safe place. Profilers say that these criminals are often operating in ways that are not nearly as random or uncontrolled as those of people who commit crimes of passion. The crimes are planned in advance, down to the tiniest details and the most absurd contingencies, all based on some fantasy going on in the guy's mind. In the service of that fantasy, they become cold, analytical." He flashed that toothy smile at his racquetball partner. "Lawyerlike."

Forte was watching him sidelong, with embarrassment or an errant appreciation, I couldn't tell which. He said, "Thank you, Dr. Lecter," and then stepped on a mid-sized branch hidden in the tall grass. It flipped up and nearly skewered him in the face. He batted it away angrily and I applauded to myself.

"We watch too much A&E," I explained to Georgia, who was appraising us all with hooded eyes. She'd obviously decided that my husband's views on the subject were something she'd rather not indulge, so she started asking me about our plans as far as children were concerned. I mouthed rote words about how we wanted to get settled first, and we both had careers we were quite enthusiastic about, and so on. My husband took the time to spare me an annoyed look before he went back to rambling at Forte.

"Serial killers typically operate within a certain area around their home base, maybe into neighboring states but rarely farther than that. Part of the whole kick, whatever rush it is that rewards him, could be the terrorizing of the local population." He paused and stared up into the balmy blue sky. "All the rumors going around, the media attention, our little traipse through the field, even this conversation we're having, all this could serve his needs. The mere possibility that someone you see on the street could be that person, it brings an air of the surreal to our everyday lives and, like it or not, makes us that much more aware of our own mortality. We've all thought about that in the last few days, I'll bet."

Roger Adler, Georgia's husband, had been listening quietly, breathing heavily as he walked a little more slowly, behind the rest of

us. Now he said, "No offense, Randy, but I
have to call you on that one. It didn't used to
be that we'd think of murder as an event to
be appreciated for its cathartic value. These
were young children."

His wife started, "Oh, now, I'm sure he
didn't mean it that way—"

"No," Randy said quickly, and slowed his
pace a bit to let the older man catch up. "I
take Roger's point, and I apologize for couch-
ing it in those terms. I know that these were
human beings we're discussing. I know it's
real. I'm just postulating how we might be
unwittingly feeding this guy's ego." He turned
back to Forte. "The killer would get off on the
developing story, he'd read every article and
watch every newscast. All the while knowing
he can never share, never indulge in that last
thrill of renown, because if he's caught he's
effectively dead and his fantasy life dies,
too. But if he can control that desire for
recognition, what a sublime payoff he must
get from going through his everyday life . . .
The work, church, family, dealing day to day
with his wife and kids and neighbors and
none of them knows. If he's any good, none
of them even suspects, except on a level so
deep that they can't ever admit it or they'd

become instantly complicit . . . Think of the power that this sick bastard must feel. Everything taking place behind his eyes, this massive internal conflict being waged, a fight against these fantasies that in the end are so powerful he has to make them real, while to all the outside world he looks just like you and me. Shit, you're a lawyer, you're used to acting like you believe in things that demonstrably aren't true. Imagine undertaking a task on that level, with stakes that high. An ugly scenario, my friend."

Forte looked at me so he could pretend to be looking past my husband. He said, "Randy's a compulsive gambler, isn't he?"

"I look like I'd put up with that?" I asked, trying for sassy but feeling cold and a little ashamed by Randy's monologue. We'd almost reached the woods. All of us wore hiking boots that had been purchased at brand stores in malls, and that hadn't seen any real hiking in all the years we'd owned them. I got mine while I was still in college, right before I met Randy. I thought they made my legs look longer. "I bitch him out just for betting on your racquetball games."

"But he always beats me."

Randy wanted to say more, to further

demonstrate how his mind was so expansive that he could imagine the worst in a cold and curious light. In his career role as a compliance officer, he was paid to call everyone's attention to precise details; if the production procedures he assessed deviated to even a slight degree, it could result in lawsuits, federal intervention, and millions of dollars in fines against Jackson-Lilliard. So he loved to spin his little scenarios. But his shit talking today bothered me especially. I was, in fact, so annoyed with him that I could barely keep from yelling at him to shut up. What a scene that would've been. All the people in the search party alerted by raised voices and turning in our direction, only to witness a domestic squabble. I bit down on it and I guess Randy did, too, because he didn't bring it up again.

We searched across the length of the field and on through the thinning stretch of trees, up the opposite hillside almost to the edge where they were clearing the ground for construction. We found nothing, no sign of the lost child; the most interesting items anyone came across were an empty, rusted bullet casing and a young girl's dress, infant-sized, much too small and too worn for a seven-year-old boy like Tyler Renault.

His body was found a month later, twenty miles west of El Ray, dumped in a ravine off the side of the highway. His eyes had been gouged out, a pair of dice inserted in the empty sockets. The Renault husband was never charged; our neighbor Todd Cline, the police officer, told us that Mr. Renault had been cleared by DNA evidence found at the scene, which excluded him as being the murderer. But there was never anything in the paper about it, never any official update or word of progress. It would be years before anyone was charged in the case.

CHAPTER THREE

1.

I came awake to a tapping on my windshield.

How embarrassing. Doug McPherson was standing there in a Penn State sweatshirt and shorts, ready for his morning jog. Shorts—even though there was frost on the car windows, and my first sensation, apart from how humiliating it was to have been found dozing in my front seat, was that I was freezing.

I tried to roll down the window but of course the car wasn't even running, so I opened the door and greeted Doug. His initial look of concern had already shifted into one that gave me the benefit of the doubt.

"We were planning to bring Hayden by your place as soon as I finished with my run," he said. "But I guess you wanted to pick him up early. Everything okay?"

He thought I was sleeping off a bender of some sort. I recognized a fellow career enabler, and experienced an involuntary wash of warm, guilty gratitude.

I nodded. "Everything's fine. I was thinking we'd run some errands before the mall gets busy." I glanced down at my watch; it was six-thirty, barely even daylight. My eyes felt gritty and I probably had sleep lines across my face. I laughed at myself, for (mostly) Doug's benefit. "I just got up and put it in gear. Guess I should've had my coffee first."

Doug smiled benignly and glanced up toward the house. Gabby was standing in the front doorway, Caleb by her side, holding on to her robe and absently scratching his ear. Hayden was peeking out from behind them, blinking into the stark new day. I called out, "Good morning, guys. Figured I'd go ahead and get him so we could beat the Saturday crowds."

"What crowds?" Hayden said.

My mind still refused to kick in. Last night

came back to me and I quickly surveyed the street. No signs of trouble, nothing different from when I nodded off. "It's a surprise," I improvised, knowing I'd pay for it later. "The sooner you get moving, the sooner you'll find out."

Doug did his stretches, standing by my bumper and holding one leg up behind him, hopping in place a little bit and then switching to the other leg. The boys disappeared into the house and he said, "Go on up. Gabby'll fill you in on the all-nighter." He pointed at the car. "Looks like someone left you a note. Probably you were in such a rush you didn't see it before." Still making my excuses for me. I caught his last bemused glance as he bopped off down the street.

A small white envelope was wedged between my windshield glass and the wiper. I hadn't even noticed it. The morning air suddenly felt even colder. I snatched the envelope and shoved it into my jeans, afraid to touch it for too long.

Gabby's kitchen was painted a bright canary yellow, far too pastel, too Easter eggy. I couldn't imagine anything less than delirium resulting from extended exposure to such a degree of forced sunshine. That said, it smelled wonderful, and I gratefully accepted a cup of coffee while Gabby unfolded bacon strips onto a paper towel and popped them in the microwave. "They stayed up all night watching movies, as far as I could tell," she yawned. "The TV was still on this morning when we came down. Not to worry, we've got all the mature stuff blocked out."

I wasn't worried. MTV was probably the worst thing that came across their plasma screen. Gabby and Doug were stolid members of the Cary metaclass: conservative; grossly and happily misinformed on most any subject you could name; also kind, generous, and almost completely oblivious to their own snooty tendencies. Endearing, in a word, although not in a way that would distinguish them from anyone else you'd meet around here. I'd steadfastly encouraged Hayden's friendship with Caleb since they met on the school bus last fall. I wanted him comfortable in these environs, whatever their specific decor; I wanted this kind of secure, banal future for him.

He'd been in the den, collecting his things, and now he came into the kitchen carrying his sleeping bag and his little overnight suitcase, the one I had packed for him with a

toothbrush and a change of clothes. It was
apparent that he wasn't going to utilize either, but then again he wasn't supposed to
be coming home this early. His hair was
mussed, a general state of dishevelment
that damn near broke my heart in a very tender way. He and Caleb seemed to have developed some kind of unintelligible code,
and now they started vocalizing staggered
bleeping and buzzing noises at each other,
then nodding and cracking up as if they'd
perfectly understood.

"I told you, boys, none of that nonsense
while you're in the house," Gabby said absently. It was probably as harsh a tone as
she ever used on her son, which I found reassuring. She massaged her temples and
said, "I had a couple of extra glasses of
wine, overdid the Friday night thing. When
am I going to accept that I just can't indulge
like I'm still twenty-five?"

"I stayed up too late, too," I said. "Listen,
thanks again for having him over." I set my
coffee cup on the counter and bent down,
hands on my knees, to look at my son. "What
do you tell Mrs. McPherson?"

"Thanks, Mrs. McPherson."

She reached out and tousled his hair, and

I had to resist an impulse to slap her hand away. It was overly possessive, I realized, but I had a proprietary thing about him. No one else would have known it, unless they were watching and saw me tense up . . . Well, no one except perhaps for Hayden. He noticed way more than I cared for him to, and way more often than I liked.

We went out into the chilly morning and I let the car run for a moment, to warm it up. I asked Hayden about his night.

"It was cool," he said, fully awake now, wired and raring to go. "We played Caleb's PlayStation and his dad stayed up with us until like eleven o'clock."

"You shouldn't stay up so late."

"What's the surprise? What crowds do you want to beat?"

And since I didn't really have any surprises planned, I created something on the fly. After we got cleaned up and had breakfast and I dawdled nervously around the house, we headed off to Southpoint Mall for a matinee. Hayden, along with every other kid in the greater Triangle area—as soon became apparent—had been bugging Mom all week to take him or her to the latest Pixar/Disney movie. It was yet another one

of those digitized, talking-animal deals. Gag-
gles of parents and kids shuffled about the
theater lobby, everyone talking too loudly,
some of the children just staring wide-eyed.
A soft sort of spectacle that annoyed the
teenaged ushers but comforted the families
with its established, shared mannerisms. I
saw a few acquaintances from work and we
traded niceties briefly, politely, with express
interest. If you had asked me five minutes
later, I couldn't have told you a word that any
of them had said, or what I'd said to them in
response.

The film's plot was worn, the same movie
I'd been taking Hayden to see since he'd
turned five, it seemed like; even some of the
same celebrities were doing the voice-overs.
It was kind of nice to turn off my mind and
sink into the theater seating. Hayden barely
squirmed at all after the first few minutes.

Before it was halfway finished, though,
the seating started to feel vertiginous and
the little lights in the floor runners of the
aisles reminded me of landing strips rushing underneath a plane's wheels. I lost interest in the film, and instead considered
the envelope that someone had placed under my wiper blade. I had looked at it when

I first got Hayden home. Its contents provoked such a visceral reaction, such an
empty coldness in my stomach, that I'd immediately crumpled them and put them into
a drawer.

It consisted of two pieces of paper. The
first was a headline cut out of a newspaper.
NO LEADS IN SLAYING, POLICE SAY. The byline
was Memphis, Tennessee. The date was two
months ago.

But the coldness didn't abate, so I went
online while Hayden was taking a bath. The
Memphis daily paper from that time included
an article about a young woman who'd been
found dead in her apartment, no clues that
the newspaper mentioned, no witnesses who
reported any suspicious vehicles in the complex's parking lot. A distraught boyfriend had
been cleared as a suspect. The police were
asking for the public's input. A mention that
there'd been some mutilation of the body.

Along with the article was a photo of the
victim, a twenty-year-old named Julie
Craven. I studied her features for as long
as I could stand it: a chubby face framed by
a page-boy haircut five years out of style,
full lips, and a decent smile. Her defining
grace, a pair of sharp green almond eyes,

almost painfully beautiful to look at. I couldn't stop myself from imagining them removed, and some cheap trinket in their place. But the article didn't specify.

Attached to the headline, by a paper clip, was a separate piece of paper about the size of a fortune you'd get in a cookie at a Chinese restaurant. Written on it in block letters: BEEN BUSY?

He'd come and put the envelope there while I'd slept. He had been inches away from me. Did he look in my face, did he say anything?

If I flexed my fingers, I could still feel his grip on my hand as I tried to pull away. All that pent-up emotion he'd unleashed on me, the precise details of his recitation and delivery probably being recalled at this very moment with considerably more relish in his mind than in my own. Or was it disappointing, as those kinds of moments so often are? Was it not the performance he'd practiced? Did he not get the justified righteous rush he'd dreamed of all these years, visualizing the confrontation as he fell off to sleep?

It hit me then, sitting in a darkened theater surrounded by a crowd of oblivious viewers, all those children unaware as yet of what a boundless variety of dangers awaited them in their budding new lives, that Charles Pritchett must have been searching for me for *years*, seeking out the object of his contempt. It hit me that I'd been found.

2.

I first read about Cary in *National Geographic,* nearly six years ago. It was their featured "USA Town of the Week," or something like that. I was still living with my mother at the time, during the brief period after the trial when I still hadn't gotten any kind of bearings, and Mom wanted to keep us there, with her, for the foreseeable future. But it was obvious from the stares of people on the street and the way friends I'd grown up with spoke to me—alternately tentative or intrusive—that I wouldn't be able to stay in Tapersville. The small Oregon logging town where I was from, and where my mother still lived, was too small, too familiar—and not in a fond way. The people there wanted to believe in their own charity, a sense of stoic nonjudgmentalism, but of course in my case such restraints were washed away by the sheer prurient appeal of it all. Compared to the endless fog and rain, the grudging and ancient forest on the surrounding hills, and the logging trucks shuddering down the by-pass with hissing tires through all hours of the day and night, mine was the best story in years. Small-town folks thrived on scandal and tragedy, no less than those in the El Ray suburbs from whence I'd fled in the aftermath of the trial.

The specs in the Cary article were promising: an influx of relocated white-collar workers from the Northeast, drawn by companies like SAS and IBM, which had their headquarters in the nearby Research Triangle Park; affordable housing, decent schools, a low crime rate; three universities within a half hour of one another. The natives seemed grudgingly accepting, since the newcomers also brought a lot of money with them. I had immediately recognized it as a good place to be faceless, and to fade into the background, without necessarily dooming Hayden to the same fate.

I was seeing a psychiatrist at the time. Mom would drive me an hour both ways and wait in the car while I talked to Dr. Cannell about my problems. Dr. Cannell was probably a decent caregiver, well enough equipped to deal with substance abuse or depression or infidelities. But in our sessions, she usually only succeeded in making me angry, and I couldn't handle any more anger at that particular time in my life. When I told her I was moving, she said, "You're seeking a geographic solution to an interior problem."

"You're damn right," I told her.

"It won't help you until you've dealt with your own feelings of guilt."

"It's not my own feelings I'm thinking about."

And that was true enough. After Randy's trial was adjourned and the verdict ended his hopes of ever again torturing anyone outside of the California penal system, the same judge who'd granted my expedited divorce and name change also signed over a forfeiture of all marital holdings to me. It would be a while before I needed to work again. But I didn't have any more time to linger in one place.

When I moved here, I'd found out all the stuff the article didn't mention. That the new immigrants weren't only from the Northeast, but a great many also came from places like India and South Korea and Kenya. They spoke with wonderful accents, and most of them seemed to hold PhDs and work at multiple vocations. Job interviews were easy enough to come by; offers were another matter. The natives and newcomers alike were often rude and caustic, and the town itself little more than a dronescape of beige and off-white homes (they even had a municipal code that disallowed any garish exteriors within the city limits) repeated in development after development, peppered with disappearing woodlands. The kind of place where drivers couldn't be bothered to use their turn signals, even though the switch was positioned right there by the steering wheel. In other words, a place not altogether very different from El Ray.

I had done a decent job of disappearing, though, or at least I'd thought so until Charles Pritchett showed up. The company I worked for, Data Managers Enterprises, Inc., contracted data processing for several national companies: batch jobs collating trial product rollout results, phone lists, surveys, that sort of thing. I'd started in a cubicle and moved up to unit supervisor within two years. Now I had eight people working under me. While it wasn't anywhere near as engaging as my former career as a business analyst, it was just stimulating enough not to be tedious, just undemanding enough that I could always take personal time off to deal with any issues Hayden might be having. And I was as far away from El Ray and Randy and the past as I could get and still be in the United States.

But it wasn't far enough. I was almost ready to leave the office on Monday afternoon when Security called from the lobby to say I had a visitor. I asked who it was and the guard said some name I didn't recognize, followed by, "She says she's from the *News and Observer*."

"Tell her I've left for the day." I hung up and grabbed my coat. Most of my people had gone home already. Hayden was hanging out at the McPhersons' with Caleb. I had some reports left to run, but they didn't seem too pressing after the phone call. A reporter could only have been here for one reason: Pritchett had made good on his threats, and he was spreading the word about me. Which meant Hayden wouldn't be far from finding out . . . oh, God.

In the parking lot, a woman came running after me, calling my name as I approached my Camry. A man with a camera hung around his neck followed at the woman's heels, pausing frequently to snap photos. I got into the car and locked the doors before they could reach me, and the woman stopped a few steps away. The guy took some more pictures. The woman started talking and I could hear her through the closed windows, she was saying how they were going with the story regardless, and I might want to give my side, for the record. I turned the radio up and pulled out fast, nearly clipping her with my side-view mirror.

Randy's name was all over the national media when the story first broke. Yes, he was *that* Randall Roberts Mosley. The papers always use the full name for assholes like him, a respect you never see granted to the victims. No, assassins and psychos are worth knowing by their full titles, but not the dead. Randy killed at least twelve people over the span of a decade. If you watched A&E, there was a whole episode of *American Justice* devoted to him. I'd never seen it, but I caught the blurb in *TV Guide* or on the digital cable summaries from time to time. I didn't care to imagine how I came off in the hour-long summary of the unreckonable devastation that had spread from my husband's hand; I certainly wasn't a press darling during the initial furor. It might've had something to do with the dismissive way I'd treated the two big-name writers who wanted to get "my side of the story." Lane Dockery and Ronald Person had both called me several times; their agents and editors had called me, too; they all wanted me to go on the record. I had no regrets, though. It wasn't only myself I was protecting.

When I learned that Randy had killed again in prison, suffocating another convict during what the media suggested (without ever coming right out and stating it) was a sexual assault, it was on the scrolling ticker that endlessly unfurls underneath the talking heads on one of the twenty-four-hour news channels. I'd noted it merely as a blip at first, and when my brain registered what I'd read my whole body went electric. I rushed to my PC and read the story on CNN's Web site and I remember clearly my first and last real thought on the subject: *It should have been him. Damn it, it should have been him that died.* At that point it had already been four years since his conviction, and his appeals were predicted to hold up his execution for another five years. California was notoriously slow to execute the people it condemned to death. And now another inmate had attempted to take time into his own hands, saving the taxpayers any further cost. Instead, Randy had unintentionally avenged some other victims, the ones who'd died at his assailant's hands. I'd started shaking before I could get my computer shut down. I had gone and locked myself in the bathroom and had a quiet sort of breakdown, screaming into a wadded towel so I wouldn't wake my son.

That was when I decided to tell Hayden the Biggest Lie of All. It would be the crown on the pile of little lies I'd been telling him already. I'd been ducking the real story since he'd been old enough to ask the question.

3.

Tuesday morning at work, everyone was trying to look through me. The whole atmosphere felt different: the long rows of cubicles seemed more penal, the hushed ring tones suggestive of sanitized emergency, the omnipresent sound of fingers clacking away at keyboards like swarming birds.

I'd stayed home last night. Hayden didn't say anything unusual when I picked him up, so I guessed the press hadn't honed in on him yet. I had intended to address the situation with him, honestly I had, but I couldn't even begin to find the words. So I put him to bed early, then took a Xanax and lay in bed watching TV. I channel surfed past the local ten o'clock news broadcasts, afraid to look.

But now I could tell, just from the way people wouldn't meet my eyes. I had a unit meeting scheduled for nine o'clock, but at eight forty-five my boss called me into his office. Jim Pendergast was a pretty decent guy, marginally attractive and divorced for a few years. He'd made his availability known to me in subtle ways, without any overt pressure, but I couldn't get around the idea of dating someone at work. Not that I'd been out on a date for quite a while. A couple of years after we'd moved here, I had gone through a stage where I tried attending some singles functions but I always felt so stupid. The men were either sad or intimidating. And the Internet was just plain frightening. That was four years ago, and I hadn't really made any efforts since then. Hayden took up a sizable amount of my time, and I got my satisfaction from knowing he was well cared for; at least that was the excuse I used when the nights ran long and sleep wouldn't come. I told myself I didn't miss the romantic world and its attendant satisfactions and disappointments, not to a crippling degree. If I was ever going to take the plunge, Jim would certainly have been at the top of the list of probable targets. Alone at the top, actually. He was a native of the area, and I loved his accent, his hokey colloquialisms; I fully understood that I found him quaint, and I felt the requisite guilt. Jim was constantly out of the office, often caring for his thirteen-year-old son, who had learning disabilities due to an early bout of some childhood disease, I could never recall which one. Tack on some more guilt.

Also in his office was a representative from HR, one of those impeccably dressed girls only a few years out of college, who introduced herself as Susan Myers. I shook her hand and found myself marveling at its cool smoothness. My own knuckles cracked and flaked at the first shadow of winter, and it was already late January.

Jim suggested I sit down.

"I guess I know what this is about," I began.

Jim raised his eyebrows and picked up this morning's edition of the *News and Observer* from his desk. "You read it?"

I shook my head and he handed it over.

I hadn't rated a banner headline, but the article made the front page, just below the photo of soldiers returning to Ft. Bragg from a stint overseas. The accompanying picture was from yesterday afternoon, my face half-shielded from the camera as I climbed into my car. I looked harried, guilty. The headline: SERIAL KILLER'S EX-WIFE LIVING IN TRIANGLE. Beneath it: *Some Still Harbor Doubts About What She Knew and When.* I realized that I was holding the paper with shaking hands.

"You want to take a minute to read it?" Susan Myers asked.

I placed the front page back on Jim's desk. I smoothed my skirt. "I think I get the gist."

"I understand they came here looking for you yesterday," Jim said.

"Jim, this is something I never brought up because it's a chapter of my life I wanted to remain closed. I'm so sorry if this is causing trouble for anyone here."

Susan Myers started to say something but Jim cut her off. "Don't even think of apologizing to me. You've worked here for over five years without any blemish, and you've been an asset to me personally and to the company as well, on a thoroughly consistent basis. You'll always have a place here, and if the higher-ups say anything, I'll go to bat for you. But this guy . . ." He swiped disdainfully at the paper. "This Pritchett person. He seems to be on something of a mission. My suggestion to you is that you take a week off, get out of town, and let all the fuss die down. Something else will come along for people to flap their lips about."

Susan Myers had waited patiently, and now she said, "We agree that this is something that should be allowed to fizzle out. We've alerted the people in Security to turn away Mr. Pritchett or any media representatives who might show up here to harass you. But it might be less of a distraction for everyone if you took Jim's advice."

Suddenly, and for the first time since Pritchett accosted me in the supermarket, I started crying. Not because of any of the awful things that had happened, or the awful possibilities that I felt hovering in the near future, but simply because my big lug of a boss and this twenty-something girl were being kind and respectful to me. They didn't say, *But really, you can't expect anyone to believe that you had no idea that your ex-husband* . . . They didn't say, *You must have known* something *was wrong* . . .

They were both just considerate people, and obviously discomfited by the tears I could no longer hold back. Jim made himself busy looking for tissues, but he didn't have any, and ended up handing over the napkin from his breakfast, a biscuit and gravy that were still congealing in their foam container on his desk. He hadn't even had time to finish eating before he called me in. That made me want to cry harder, for some reason, but I managed to stifle it and I dabbed at my face, not making too much of a mess of my makeup. I apologized repeatedly, and both of them told me to stop it. I told them I wanted to at least finish out the day, if only because it would keep me distracted. Susan Myers seemed hesitant but in the end she agreed. She advised me to take care of myself and "go do something fun."

It worked all right for a little while, until I could no longer ignore the voices of the em-

ployees in my department. What is it about
cubicles that makes people think they can't
be heard? Such a fake insulation. The seven
women and one man in my unit, all of them
reliable and sweet and fairly hardworking,
were also, unfortunately, unrepentant gos-
sips. Celebrities, people from their churches
or neighborhoods, their coworkers . . . it didn't
matter. All were fair game for rumor and
innuendo, and throughout the morning I
caught bits and pieces: *Leigh isn't even her
real name . . . Well, it's her middle name at
least . . . She seems more like a Nina . . .
Can you believe what she looked like back
then? And her husband, I mean, I hate to
say it, knowing what he did and all, but the
man* was *pretty hot . . .* Which was the one
that finally sent me fast-walking down the
hall to the restroom, heads popping up from
behind the cubicle partitions to follow my
passage. I retreated to the farthest stall for a
real freakout.

Someone had left the front section of today's paper hung over the handicap bar beside the toilet paper dispenser. Although this
was a frequent occurrence, I couldn't help
but think it was meant as a message for me
specifically. After a long while, I picked it up.

In large part, the article was simply a recap of Randy's horrific crimes. It used the nicknames that the press had adorned him with at the time, before the killings were solved: Cross-Eye Killer, Harvester. There was a small side article with bullet points listing the victims by name, along with the dates of their deaths. Or, in the case of Wendy Pugh and Tyler Renault, the dates their bodies were discovered. The story described how Randall Roberts Mosley was eventually shot and captured on the front lawn of his very own home while his wife and infant son looked on.

Sensational.

There was a snapshot of me that I couldn't recall ever having seen before; it had to have been taken not long after our wedding, but certainly prior to my pregnancy, and my God I did look twenty years younger. In real time, it was only a little over half that, but I'd learned long ago that "real time" was largely a bullshit concept. Look at that carefree smile on my face, what a stupid fucking child I was, a stupid little girl with no concept of how time could go elastic and speed up or stop altogether. The text featured a brief mention of how "police were led to the house by a call from Mrs. Mosley, who had discovered grisly evidence of her husband's guilt." A last photo of me had been thoughtfully included, this one taken from the courthouse steps on the day of my initial testimony. The paper quoted police at the time saying that some suspicion had fallen on me because my picture was found on some of the fake ID documents Randy had hoarded, and my DNA was present at two of the crime scenes. Strands of my hair were identified but the police had quickly concluded that they probably came from Randy's clothes. The police never charged me with any crime, but that didn't stop the media from speculating.

I wanted to shake the paper and scream, *He wanted it that way! He set it up to cast doubt!* but of course that wouldn't help anything so instead I cried some more. Hot tears, shameful ones that vented not the least bit of relief.

The third part of the article was dedicated to Charles Pritchett, a summary of his daughter's death at Randy's hands. "I was always bothered by Nina Mosley's involvement, which was never satisfactorily addressed at the trial," he was quoted as saying. He spoke eloquently of his years of grief. He said he'd hired a private investigative firm to track me down. He now planned on sticking around until his questions were answered. "I hate to think this community has a person with her history living in its midst without even being aware of it," was Pritchett's penultimate comment. "There are a lot of families with children living here."

I wanted to hate him. He was very likely going to wreck everything I'd worked to build, to regain from the nightmare swirl of ashes Randy left in his wake. But Carrie Pritchett was only twenty-two when she died, the same age as I was at the time. She was a student, working on her degree in economics. She never got to be twenty-three. Randy gouged out her eyes and wedged smooth agate stones in their place, then left the disfigured body on the floor of her apartment, where some friends discovered it the next morning. They'd come looking because they were concerned that she'd missed an exam.

I heard the bathroom door open. I recognized the voices of two of my workers, Betsy and LaTonya.

"I'd feel better if she hadn't lied about it,"

Betsy was saying. "I mean, anyone could understand, if it wasn't your fault and all. But
the deception, I don't know."

"Shit, she's got a kid. Wouldn't you
change your name?"

"Yeah, I guess so. God, can you imagine?
Finding out the man you've been sharing
your bed with is a murderer?"

"A serial killer, girl. Ain't like he shot someone for money or something. I heard he was
all Ted Bundy."

I'd been trying to hold back but now a sob
caught me by surprise, a hitching sound that
echoed off the tile walls. I could almost see
them, pointing to the closed stall door I was
hiding behind and mouthing, "Oh, my God,"
their faces going red. They didn't say anything else I could discern, just flushing and
then some unintelligible whispers and they
were gone.

CHAPTER FOUR

1.

Randy often came home with random scratches and bruises, sometimes after business trips, other times when he'd only been gone for the afternoon. He liked me to trace them with my fingernails as we lay in bed, after lovemaking, idly watching the TV and neither of us in the mood to talk. Just touching seemed like enough of a connection during the first couple of years. I let my fingers linger. These weren't love marks, but his vague and often lame deflections when I asked about them were enough to set eddies spinning out somewhere in the deeper, darker currents of my heart.

"They were moving the machinery around the floor when I was in LA, and I got scraped up," he said one time when I inquired. "Our satellite plant, they're rearranging everything along some schematic Drew Holloway pulled out of his ass. Supposed to increase efficiency by four percent or some such bullshit. I think Drew followed the techs around for a month, counting steps or something. They're barely within specs."

Which didn't go far toward explaining why my husband would have a deep abrasion running from the hollow of his neck back across his left shoulder blade. Or why he, a compliance officer, a rules-and-regulations guy who never stayed longer on a production floor than it took to calibrate the machinery and audit the work logs, had decided to pitch in and assist with the reconfiguration.

The truth of it was that while Randy was away on his inspection tour of the Jackson-Lilliard plants down in LA, he made time on his last night in town to torture and kill Carrie Pritchett. She was one of several victims who put up a substantial fight, and years later the flesh that had been removed from underneath three of the fingernails on her right hand would be used to help secure his conviction.

I caressed his wounds lovingly. Sometimes I kissed them. He would become aroused, and turn, wrapping those thick arms around me, his rough hands already on my breasts. I used to love the sensation of being carried away.

Another time it looked like he'd been punched in the ribs. He told me some asshole knocked him over in the aisle of the plane while they were still on the tarmac in SeaTac, when said asshole tried to muscle his way past with an oversized carry-on. Randy and some of the other passengers nearly got into it with the asshole, and the stewardesses eventually had the asshole removed from the flight. "You should be glad you don't have to travel for work," he said. "You wouldn't believe the junior-league dipshits they're letting onto planes these days. This guy was some loser sales rep from Omaha, past his prime twenty years ago and determined to make everyone else suffer for it."

His stories were always filled with little details. This time he'd just returned from Calgary, his first trip to Canada. Two young women disappeared while he was in the city, but the news stories I was able to find, much later, never made mention of any suspects or any resolution. None of Randy's victims, alleged or proven, were from that part of the world. The women's bodies were never found.

But I can still see the shape of that bruise in my mind; it started just below the right armpit and extended down three or four ribs, purple and yellow in its exploded center, the approximate size of a balled fist.

2.

By the time I got pregnant with Hayden, I knew something was wrong, but by then I was frightened on such a fundamental level I was becoming obsessive-compulsive. True fear doesn't make you scream—true fear paralyzes, makes you afraid even to breathe. You are reduced to praying that the object of your fear will pass you over, not give you its attention—that's your last single hope. Think of your worst nightmares, the ones that leave your heart thundering too hard as you sit up gasping into the dark of your own bedroom;

you haven't come awake screaming, you've come awake just trying to take a breath.

Randy made me quit my job at Shaw Associates when we found out I was expecting; I'd put up something of a fuss, having recently been touted for another promotion, this time from analyst to the lead job in the marketing division, a position I'd been eyeing for some time. But he reminded me that we'd discussed the matter before the wedding, so I had to cede the point. Randy had always told me he aspired to the "traditional family" model, where he would be the breadwinner and I would look after the kids. It all sounded fine in a quaint sort of way, back when we were engaged, but then I'd discovered a fierce capacity for my job, and a rewarding sense of accomplishment every time I saved the company some money by improving their billing practices or finding a cheaper vendor. I'd stewed and pouted, but Randy held fast, and convinced me that a Rockwell-perfect home would be best for the child. He quoted developmental-psychiatry articles from magazines and journals that I suspected to be bogus, but in the end it seemed easier to let him have his way. He promised me I could relaunch my career as soon as the child started school.

With so many empty hours to fill, the fear crowded in. For a while I was able to tell myself that I simply had too much time on my hands. Our house was clean and spotless, no dust mote too diminutive that it could be allowed to settle on the furniture without my prompt attention. Six months in and I was going crazy. Randy noticed and told me I needed to ask the doctor what could be done about it, because I was getting all over his nerves with the constant dusting and polishing and vacuuming. "I feel like you're following around behind me, my every little move," he groused. "It's making me really *edgy.* You understand?"

I said I did. I blamed hormonal shifts. Meekness came more naturally to me by then than it ever had before in my life. *Don't attract attention.* I promised him that I'd speak to the doctor about it, then I retreated upstairs and closed the door to what had been Randy's office/storage room but was now being remodeled into a nursery. Our computer was still in there, next to the new crib. I logged on to the Internet and read the latest on the as yet unsolved killing of the Hughes family, Keith and Leslie. They'd lived in Bakersfield, only a couple of hours away. It happened over six

months ago but for some reason I kept reading about it. The initial reports said the bodies
had been mutilated, but never anything more
specific. I'd considered an anonymous phone
call to the Bakersfield police. "Was it their
eyes?" I would ask. "Was something done to
their eyes?"

I never called. Delicate tremors coursed
through my nerves day and night. I craved
sedatives, alcohol, sleep aids; I couldn't take
anything, for fear it would harm the baby.
Cleaning helped; circular motions, repetition
serving as a calmative blanket; actually
thinking about what might happen once the
baby was born had the opposite effect.

I watched Randy pose in front of the bathroom mirror. In our second house, the mas-
ter bath opened right off our bedroom, and
when I'd been quiet and he didn't notice me
watching, or when he didn't care enough
anymore to worry about what I might think if I
did see, he would flex and posture. He kept
his black hair cut close to the scalp, a more
conservative look than he'd favored when
we'd first met. I figured he must have been
hitting the free weights in his shed out back,
because his muscles grew more defined as

the years passed instead of less so, like he was aging in reverse. More likely he was self-conscious as middle age walked him down, and working hard to stave off any outward signs. A healthy vanity was one thing, but he was damn near narcissistic, especially with the scrapes and bruises. There was a full-length mirror across from the shower, and he assessed his wounds as if marking a tally. He fingered their contours with his eyes twin-kling. I can remember the shape of each con-tusion, the tiny scars that the deeper ones had left. I'd quit even asking about their ori-gins after a while. I simply noted them and catalogued them mentally and drowned out whatever they suggested.

A trio of shallow scratches over his left eye. That thin white thread leading from his neck back across his shoulder; you couldn't even see it when he was wearing a collared shirt. Another grouping of furrows marked his stomach and chest. Mostly the wounds weren't very deep and quickly disappeared, but a few turned out to be permanent.

The victims who resisted did so coura-geously. Keith Hughes was stabbed over fifty times before he finally succumbed. DNA taken from his fingernails would also prove damning to my husband in court. Jamie Hefner, Buddy Beckman, Daphne Snyder, they all got their licks in before Randy struck the fatal blows. I sometimes imagine him, against my will, standing over them while their lives ebbed away, him sucking it up like some vampire, panting and exhausted and elated with his accomplishments while human lights were extinguished so close at hand. Extinguished *by* his very hand and the tools he honed and wielded.

After they lay dead, he really went to work.

He came to bed and I loved him dutifully, distractedly, thinking of grouting the linoleum. What he thought of, I cannot say. He would place his hand over my eyes as he neared climax, pressing down hard enough that I saw stars exploding, comet trails and lava lamps bleeding across my eyelids. At first it freaked me out, and then, for a short while before I got pregnant, it kind of turned me on. Once I tried it on him and he firmly moved my hand away, held it down by my side as he slammed into me harder, those flat, packing sounds, stinging my thighs. Over time I grew to welcome the dark, fondly and then greedily, allowing it to take over, to block everything out and—*admit it, admit the worst, do tell*—hoping that one day the light wouldn't return at all. Too many things were exposed there in the light, too many things that were all around me now, so if I looked away from one there was another staring me right in the face.

Scars. He loved his own, nurtured them even. He only granted me mine, the interior scars that came with each of his little evasions and patronizing rebukes, chipping away at my pride and peace of mind like a prince carelessly throwing a kiss to some unremarkable commoner in a crowd of thousands, gone from his mind the next instant but haunting the recipient for all the longest nights of her life to come.

CHAPTER FIVE

1.

Hayden had often asked about his father, from the time he was old enough to understand that most of the other kids had one. When he was very small, I avoided the subject by telling him that I'd fill him in when he was old enough to understand. But you know kids; they get old enough long before you want to admit it. At that early stage, I might've actually intended to tell him the truth.

Right after Randy was convicted and sent to prison, he made several attempts to track us down. Letters would arrive at my mother's house, never addressed to me, but always to Hayden. I told Mom to throw them away without opening them, but of course she opened and read them. She said they gave her the shivers; Randy wanted to establish a relationship with his progeny. He claimed to have a legal right. And he may have been correct.

So I changed my name and moved across the country. Hayden didn't even know he was once a Mosley. By the time he was three, it had become obvious to me that the truth was exactly what I could never allow him to know, or at least not until he could handle it. I mean, how could you make those words come out of your mouth: *Your father was a killer who defiled and murdered a dozen human beings?* I had to tell him something, though. He was constantly falling into step behind adult men whenever we went out in public, reaching out to grasp the hems of their coats at the grocery store. I could see his eyes narrow when he saw fathers toting their kids on their shoulders while we were out at the park; he even seemed transfixed by men scolding their kids publicly in restaurants.

Eventually, my evasions sent him into tantrums. So, God forgive me, I improvised. I told him that he did have a father, but that his father had done some very bad things that made it impossible for Mommy and Daddy to live together anymore. I said his father stole money from people; I explained why stealing was wrong. I said his father was a dangerous man who would never be a part of our lives. I could see the deep wound in my son's eyes. I knew it was better than the reality.

Then came that story I saw on CNN, about how another convict had attempted to kill Randy and instead been killed.

The next time Hayden mentioned his father, I sat him down and told him that there had been an incident in the prison where his father was being held. I told him his father was dead.

I'd meant to do better. I thought it would end the conversation for good. But even as I told The Lie I could hear the searing bitterness in my own voice. I hoped it would deflect any further questions, and it did, but I could hear him crying in his bed that night. And I couldn't bring myself to comfort him. Always I had wondered: *Do those shots fired in our front yard in El Ray echo in his pre-memory?* He wasn't even a year old when it happened, but somewhere he must have retained it, down there wherever dreams come from. He'd always been a light sleeper, and he often talked in his sleep, too, child gibberish I could not understand but which nevertheless gave me chills up the back of my spine as I lay alone and awake and rest-less in my own room next to his.

Of course I knew that he would find out the truth at some point in the future. Of course I'd always acknowledged, to myself, that there would come a day, perhaps when he was in his late teens or even early twen-ties, when he would say to me, "Mom, I know that story you told me about Dad was a load of crap. I want you to tell me the truth." And by then he'd have developed into a stable, well-balanced person, able to cope with the shock of the reality without it forever skewing him or tainting him beyond repair.

But Charles Pritchett and the local media had decided, without my input, that today would be that day, and never mind that I was not prepared, not ready by even the most tor-tured definition of the concept of readiness. Never mind that my son wasn't ready, either.

2.

The school bus stop was a block from our house. Usually Hayden was under strict orders to go straight home and lock the door until I arrived from work. Lately, he'd been hanging out at the McPhersons more often than not, but today I parked my car at the curb and waited for the bus to drop him off. After overhearing the discussion in the ladies room at work, I went ahead and took the rest of the day. Jim had told me in no uncertain terms that he didn't want to see me back in the office for at least a week. He had told me to call him anytime I needed a sympathetic ear. He'd tendered both his home and cell phone numbers and I dutifully keyed them into my cell.

The bright yellow paint on the bus did little to disguise its prior history as conveyance for the NC State Bureau of Corrections; the school system bought a fleet of them from the state last year at bargain prices, and the vehicle had one of those blunt, ugly noses that looked nothing like the buses we rode when I was a kid growing up in Oregon. They hadn't even bothered to remove the mesh cages from over the windows, perhaps thinking it would keep the children safer in case of an accident. The effect was unsettling, though: sterile functionality crossed with overt restraint.

The doors opened with that pneumatic hiss. Seven or eight kids clambered off, hefting backpacks too large for them, a couple of girls cutting a streak down the sidewalk past my car, talking in excited tones about what Kevin did in third period. Another lone kid disembarked, talking into a cell phone. He couldn't have been more than eight. Still no sign of Hayden, and my throat closed up a little. But here he came, last off, listing side to side down the three steps, so obviously dejected that it was like he was having a hard time keeping himself upright. My heart clenched, seeing that gait, knowing what it portended even before he lifted his head and I saw the snot streaks down his puffy cheeks.

The bus driver watched him a moment, then looked up and spotted my car at the curb, me opening the passenger-side door and calling for Hayden to come on. The driver kept staring at me even as he pushed a button and the bus doors closed.

"Hey, champ," I said as Hayden climbed in beside me. He used both hands to pull his door shut. I told him to buckle his seat belt and he did so, moving like a robot. All my tears had dried up in my throat. *Be strong now if you're ever going to be, he needs you worse than you need anything, you're all he's got and if you go to pieces there's no one else around to pick them up, there's no telling what the long-term damage might be* . . . "How's it going?"

He faced me across the seat and his eyes were as cold as I'd ever seen them. Bottomless black glass. I swallowed and forced a smile and drove slowly back to our house. As the garage door was closing behind us, I turned to reach for his hand but he was already on the move. He had his own house key at the ready. He was through the door and up the stairs and gone before I could even retrieve my laptop bag from the backseat.

I found him in his bedroom, lying facedown on the comforter, crying helplessly. The curtains were closed and the only light came from the screen saver on his Junior PC, a soft blue geometric pattern that pulsed and twisted in place. I sat and stroked his hair. I began, "Baby—"

"It's true, isn't it?" he said into his pillow. It was very nearly a scream. "He's alive, and he's not just a robber. What everyone at school was saying about my dad, it's all t-t-true?"

No defense left. "Yes."

He turned over and his expression was very grown-up, which is always a disorienting thing for a parent to see on their child's face, but in this case it was worse, it was awful, because it was the very countenance of betrayal. I supposed that if he were an adult, this exact same expression would render him childlike in its nakedness. I couldn't help it, I felt the hot tears constricting the back of my throat and I swallowed thickly. His glare was pitiless. "You told me Daddy was gone. How could you lie about that?" he managed. "Yuh-y-you told me not to ever lie."

"Honey, I'm so sorry." I pulled him close and he allowed it but his arms remained limp at his sides. How many times could my heart break? How much longer could Randy—imprisoned and sterilized behind the meanest steel—keep doing this to us? "I didn't know how to tell you."

"Daddy *killed* people? For no reason?" He pushed away from me and repeated the second question.

I said quickly, "There's never a reason. Listen, Hayden, because this is important. Your father is a very sick man. You remember how sick you were when you got the chicken pox, back when you were in play school?"

He nodded solemnly.

"Your father wasn't sick like that. He was sick in his mind. I didn't realize it when I met him, because he pretended not to be sick, and it's easier for people who are sick in their minds to hide it than it is for people who are sick in their bodies. There are no sores or anything that would tip you off. He pretended to be just like everybody else, but really he wasn't. I didn't find out until years later, and by then I'd had you and I couldn't do anything to take back what your father had already done. I stopped him from doing it to anybody else, though, because I called the police as soon as I realized."

I heard echoes of my defense to Charles Pritchett, sounding just as lame. *Not my responsibility, not me, how could anyone expect the person who lived day by day with the madman to know anything about who he really was, his true nature? I mean, you can't hold me to such a standard, it's simply unrealistic, it's too much . . .*

But this was my son, and in this horrible moment of clarity I understood that what I had owed him all along was nothing less than the sad truth. "I was afraid of him, sweetie. I was afraid that if I let myself understand how sick your father was, and what he'd done to other people, then I'd have to give you up, along with everything else we'd . . . I'd worked so hard for. And later on, when you would ask me about him, I knew that I was afraid of what he might do to you if he ever got the chance, because he was so sick, and I thought it would be better for everyone if you thought he was gone."

He was holding himself at arm's length, watching me carefully with that betrayed face. But he'd stopped sobbing, and was attentive, trying to evaluate these concepts of insanity and personal responsibility. Usually, you wouldn't have to worry about getting these abstract kinds of ideas across to a seven-year-old. I realized suddenly that this was the first time he'd ever caught me in a lie. He would never ever look at me again in quite the same way as he had this morning. I could still remember the first time I caught my parents lying. My lip trembled. I swallowed and took a deep breath. I focused.

"Honey," I said, "you remember how when that mean boy stole your baseball in first grade last year, and your teacher asked who did it, and the boy wouldn't admit it but she found it hidden in his backpack anyway?"

"Brian Carter." My little man was all serious absorption now. Waiting to see if what
I had to say would be in any way independently verifiable.

"Brian, right. Well, you remember how I
told you that stealing was bad but lying
about it was worse? And how if he would
have just admitted it then the teacher might
not have punished him?"

Hayden nodded.

"Well . . . I told myself that if I didn't tell you
the truth about your dad, it might not hurt your
feelings so much. No one wants to know
something like that about their parents, and I
hate your dad for doing it to us, I will hate him
until the day he dies, and that's the truth." Hayden's mouth had fallen open; he knew "hate"
was a bad word. I *re*focused. "I only meant to
keep you from getting hurt. But you see how
the truth came out anyway, just like it did when
Brian stole your baseball? It's always like that,
which is why it's always better to tell the truth
in the first place, even if it's something bad.
I know I didn't do that, and I know I let you
down. I'm sorry. I was wrong to do it. From now
on, I promise you I'll do better."

I could see the doubt, the almost crafty cal-
culation running in tandem with his wounded

confusion. *She's lied to me all my life, how can I believe her now? What else has she told me that isn't true?* My coin long spent.

It was spooky, his silent assessment. I tried to salvage some degree of face, truly desperate that I might not be able to regain his faith. "How many times have I lied to you before?"

"I don't know, now."

"Fair enough. But you remember how I told you that Mr. Donahue down the street was breaking the law when he was watering his yard during the drought last summer? And you didn't believe me, because you said he was too nice and too old, and it was only water. But then you saw the police come and he argued with them and they gave him a citation?"

"Uh-huh."

"And how about when I explained that the boy on *Hey, Simon* wasn't really lost in the woods but that he was just an actor on TV? And then he came to the mall and signed autographs and you got his. I told the truth about those things, right?"

"Okay," he said. "I get it. But that's not really the same, Mom."

"I know."

"And Ashton at school said that if Daddy was a criminal then I was going to be one, too, because it's generic."

I bit down on the quick flush of anger that came along with that tidbit, and made a mental note to have a word with Ashton Hale's mother the next time I saw her. Assuming that she would still deign to speak to me. "I think Ashton meant 'genetic,' honey, and I've told you before not to listen to that boy. He's wrong, as usual. Genetics are the physical traits that mommies and daddies pass down to their kids. Plenty of kids have one bad parent or maybe even two, but they turn out fine when they grow up. And some parents who are good have bad kids. Genetics means you might have the same color hair or grow up to be the same height as your parents, but it doesn't mean you're going to act like they do. That's *always* your choice."

I remembered my mother tiptoeing around my father's infidelities. I remembered her lying to herself, and to me.

"Do I look like him?" Hayden asked.

And he stumped me with that one, because of course he did. Hayden got my fine brown hair, and if the baby fat didn't melt away he'd be stuck with my chipmunk cheeks, but everything else on his face was pure Randy. The sharp chin, the brown eyes almost black. The olive skin and a quick smile, too toothy for comfort when he was faking it. A certain way he cocked his head when he was trying to figure something out.

"Not so much," I said.

"Do you have pictures?"

"I threw them away. Now listen to me. What your father did was bad, the very worst thing a person can do. And he did it more than once. He lied to me and to everyone else but eventually he got caught and the police punished him by locking him up in jail. He'll be there for the rest of his life, and he'll never get out again." I thought about trying to explain state execution and decided we'd probably covered quite enough for this afternoon. I knew what I was about to say and part of me flinched away from it even though I could see Randy there in Hayden's eyes, plain as day—*oh, no*—and I was almost talking to him now, denouncing the father through my little innocent one. "I think it's what he deserved. Most other people think so, too."

"But if he's sick, why can't he just get better? Can't the doctors do anything?"

"There are some things that the doctors

can't fix, Hayden. And I could've forgiven him for his sickness, except he never even tried to get well. He knew the sickness made him do bad things but he never tried to stop. So you shouldn't think about him, as much as you can help it. I know that Ashton and some of the other kids at school might bring it up, but you're just going to have to do the best you can to ignore them. Soon they'll find something else to talk about and you'll still be the same sweet guy you've always been. You'll never be like your father, okay? I promise."

I must have had some credibility remaining, because his tears came back full force, and this time he was the one leaning into me, encircling my neck with those skinny, perfect little arms.

3.

I got him settled into bed early. Instead of giving me the usual good night kiss, he turned over and faced the wall and mumbled, "Love you, Mom." Not even half as convincingly as usual.

Maybe one day, he would learn to lie as easily as grown-ups did.

I was still shaky, but I didn't want to take any more pills. So I distracted myself by going online, looking up the most recent editions of the *Memphis Star*. There was only a short follow-up article about Julie Craven's unsolved slaying, this piece from a few weeks ago; police were still asking for witnesses to come forward. A spokesman said they were in the process of interviewing all the residents of the apartment complex where the victim lived, but so far there were no specific "persons of interest." Not for the first time, I considered calling the Cary police. I wondered if I could convince them that Pritchett's leaving the article on my windshield was a form of threat. He obviously saw some connection between the recent killing and Randy's crimes, and therefore to me, but I didn't understand it at all. People got murdered every day. Randy was behind bars, in maximum security on Death Row, three thousand miles away.

And when I turned on the ten o'clock news, there was Pritchett himself, being interviewed on Channel 11. The Features girl, an attractive reporter named Jennifer McLean, who'd briefly worked the consumer complaints beat before being moved into higher rotation, was asking him leading questions about his public campaign to disgrace me. He patiently, bravely told the story of what had happened to his daughter, while some archival footage from Randy's trial ran on-screen. They showed the outside of the apartment building where Carrie Pritchett's body had been found. I looked for similarities to the Memphis crime scene but didn't see any overt ones. Pritchett reiterated that he'd never been satisfied with the California police's conclusion that I hadn't been involved in Randy's crimes. Jennifer McLean seemed skeptical of his assertions, and she'd obviously done some homework. She told him she'd spoken with the local authorities and that they'd received no complaints about me. It was very strange to watch them this way, using my name so freely, the name I hadn't used in years; the sense of disconnect was so utter that I wanted to pinch myself. The interviewer asked Pritchett why he would spend all this time and money to come after someone who hadn't been a problem to anyone in the area.

"She changed her name, and she tried to hide," Pritchett intoned, with all the smug self-satisfaction of a religious fundamentalist.

"I can't hide from what happened. I don't think she should be allowed to."

My blood slowly came to a boil. The interview ended with McLean talking about how Pritchett made millions designing and catering celebrity shindigs in LA, then sold his business after his daughter's death. When she referred to what she called his "crusade," you could practically see the quotation marks, and I found myself liking this girl quite a bit. Most of the other coverage hadn't dared to question his motives, because he was, after all, a Victim.

For the first time in a few years, I found myself wanting, more than just about anything else I could think of, a freaking cigarette. I could actually feel one between my fingers. I could taste the smoke. The store was only a few minutes away, I could be there and back before Hayden knew I was gone.

But I'd quit smoking for my son. Not for the usual reasons, but because of the books of matches I found in the pockets of his pants sometimes when I was collecting laundry. The lighters I had found hidden in his desk drawer. The fact that he'd gotten them somewhere, and the fact that he'd hidden them.

He knew not to play with fire; I'd told him it was dangerous. I had caught him playing with matches once when he was only four years old, burning a whole book of them in our driveway, and it was one of the only times I'd actually spanked his rear. Except for during my pregnancy, I'd been smoking since I was fifteen. I started back before he was a month old. I only quit for good after I caught him burning that book of matches, seeing how his eyes narrowed and focused on the flames.

I tried to forget: he was Randy's child, too. That same blood moved through him. The same genetic derivations ran the synapses in his young mind.

All the books I read when I was pregnant, all of Randy's lurid true crime paperbacks, the ones I found in a box in his office and couldn't quit reading once I'd started in on them, they all suggested in one way or another that psychotics were genetically predisposed. Many of them came from abusive homes, which was always one of the mitigating circumstances that the savvier defense lawyers tried to have introduced at trial. Awful backgrounds of sexual perversity or martial punishments meted out by overbearing mothers or drunken fathers. But the true crime authors took pains to remind their readers that this only reinforced the idea that there was something fouled up in the physiology, hard-wired into the perpetrators: lack of impulse control, the damned deranging voices, the fantasies that couldn't be denied the way the rest of us block out the worst visions with which our minds surprise us during our idle moments.

The early signs: setting fires, bed-wetting, and the killing or torturing of small animals. I still discovered dampness in Hayden's sheets from time to time, long after it should've quit being an issue. As far as I knew, no pets had mysteriously disappeared from our neighborhood. But what if they did? Would I be able to look at my son without seeing ruin?

The shots in our front yard in El Ray, the neighbors watching and the cops converging while I held Hayden and screamed. The blood that fed the chambers of his heart. Echoes.

CHAPTER SIX

1.

We were lying around his apartment, him wearing a T-shirt and boxer shorts, me in only one of his T-shirts, the first time I saw the photograph. We'd just had our initial foray into actual sex. Three previous dates ended in some fumbling and dry humping, but this night I'd had quite a lot of wine, and holding back any longer seemed plain unfair to both of us. It was awkward, as such initial contacts usually are; both of us stayed neck to shoulder during the whole thing, facing past each other but close, really close, and it felt fine. He promised it would be better next time and I told him he didn't have a thing to worry about. The reassurances on both sides were nearly rote, but with the codicil that I actually liked this guy quite a bit, and it was the first time in a while that that had happened and he seemed to like me as well. We both recognized that tonight might not be the only night, but the first in a long string of nights. It was immediately comfortable on some fundamental level, and even the awkwardness of the intimacy quickly fell away into an easy, innocuous kind of conversation, good rhythms, neither of us forcing it, both of us secretly happy that it hadn't been any more disappointing than expected.

He lived alone, which was unusual for a twenty-three-year-old in our snug little college town. Most guys his age had roommates, out of preference if not necessity. My friends and I judged that most men didn't have the mental capacity for living alone; they needed to spout off to someone about stupid shit or else they got backed up, and turned weird. Randy seemed capable not only of handling solitude, but also of using the time alone to develop himself to an impressive degree. He was what HR types call a "self-starter." His apartment was tidy and fashionable without coming across as effete;

a gas fireplace and a couple of nice repro-
ductions on the walls, Impressionist ocean
scenes and rustic landscapes. He'd dropped
out of school his junior year, not from burnout
but because he'd interned with Jackson-
Lilliard, an international chemical company
that had a regional office headquartered in
Albany, an hour's commute north from our
campus town of Corvallis, and they'd offered
him a full-time position at a salary no sane
man his age would've refused. That's a
damned rare outcome for what had begun
as an unpaid internship; his mentor had been
extremely impressed with the way he'd carried himself and the amount of time and
energy he devoted to his work.

He was an extremely impressive sort
of guy.

When Dana had pointed him out to me two
weeks earlier, a face across the bar at Happy
Sam's, I knew right away that he was distinct
from the frat boys and the indie rockers and
the other types of posers who filled the classrooms and quads at school. It was there in his
carriage, his mannerisms of restraint, the way
he spoke quietly when Dana introduced us.
He made himself clearly heard without raising
his voice, even in the boisterous din of the bar.

A sharp dresser, not conventionally hot but put together just fine, ripped biceps and a thick chest under a tasteful Ralph Lauren shirt. Confident enough that he didn't have to take extra measures to impress anyone, he didn't sport any jewelry aside from what appeared to be a real Rolex. When Dana invited him to our table, he didn't offer to buy everyone's drinks; he just bought mine.

Now he returned from the kitchen to refill my wineglass. I was holding the framed photo I'd found on one of his end tables. "Is this you?"

He traded me a replenished glass for the picture, and a nostalgic, smoky sort of smile crossed his face. "That was in Alaska," he said, settling down beside me on the couch. "I went up there for Christmas break my sophomore year. Some guys from the dorm were going and I couldn't really afford it but in the end I decided, fuck it. I mean, when was I going to get the chance again?"

The shot was taken from a low angle, about waist high, and portrayed a silhouetted, featureless figure facing away from the photographer and gazing off into the horizon. The horizon was the most striking facet of the scene: a forested slope at dusk, dropping away beneath the first evening stars and a hint of rippling aurora at the very top of the frame, an orange hem of sprinkled light.

"It's quite majestic," I said, gently teasing. "But you should've turned around and smiled or something. It's a little too dour."

"It's dramatic effect," he chided me. "The lone figure against the coming night. When the sun starts going down, which is like at noon that time of the year, you really only have a short window between the daylight and when it gets totally dark. And it does, darker than you've ever seen." He sounded wistful, pensive; dramatic effect, I supposed. "Really dark, up there at the top of the world."

If that was not the exact moment I fell in love with him, still there was a palpable sensation in my chest as he said it. The moment could almost have been posed, just like the photo itself, but I didn't *feel* manipulated. It sounded like something he'd thought of before, pondered upon, and I felt awfully damned privileged, at that postcoital moment, that he would share it with me. I snuggled in close and he smelled good. I started kissing his neck, tasting salt and soap, and then we were going at it again. And it was better this time. It got better each time for a long while, right up until we got married.

2.

So let's suppose you're the young Nina Leigh Sarbaines, right out of Tapersville, Oregon, a logging town in the eastern half of the state, growing up among the big trucks thundering down the narrow two-lanes, the constant fog in the air like an unqualified gloom. The landscape all bright mossy greens and slate gray, that paper-mill smell that lingers over the town and that natives only notice after we've been away for a while. I wore flannel and triple-pierced my ears; I got a butterfly tattoo on my ankle. Certified full-time smoker by age fifteen, sexually active by sixteen, celebrity-obsessed and spending the money from my part-time job at the drugstore on gossip magazines and jeans jackets and accessories, but I managed to avoid the meth and the harder trouble that came with it, at least for the most part. Some of my friends succumbed, but I had starry eyes early on and didn't want to jeopardize my chances of getting out any

more than was necessary just to get by so-
cially.

Dad was the regional manager for one of
the trucking outfits, so we weren't as poor as
some of my friends whose parents worked
the mills or logged out in the expanses of
seemingly boundless woodlands (although
the interloping environmentalists from Seat-
tle and California were constantly reminding
us that they were diminishing by the hour).
Our house, though, was too small by half,
especially when Mom would catch Dad
cheating on her and the halls would practically scream with silence for weeks at a
time. I'd lock the door to my bedroom and
stay on the phone with my friends for hours,
or stare at my little TV, or listen to head-
phones, all those overwrought grunge CDs
that spun through my Discman. Mom never
did leave him; my father died of liver failure
my senior year of high school. He was never
a violent drunk, or particularly neglectful; my
memories of him are actually quite fond, for
the most part, and he treated me like gold,
spoiling me as much as he could afford to.
He bought me earrings and CDs and my first
car, an old Volkswagen Bug. I imagine this
was part of what made him attractive to

other women; when he was with you, you were the total focus of his attention.

I blamed Mom for the cheating; she could've left him at any time. The way I saw it, she brought most of her misery on herself.

My acceptance letter from Oregon State looked like a Golden Fucking Ticket.

By the time I met Randy, I was six months on the other side of my first "adult" relationship, which had turned out not to be so grown-up after all. Brad was a grad student in English Lit, one of those stereotypically gaunt and bookish guys, tall and thin with wire-rimmed glasses, shy around groups of people but garrulous when we were alone. Later I would think that one of the reasons I was instantly attracted to Randy was that he was damn near to being Brad's physical opposite. At the time I met Brad, though, I was still treading water in the backwash of the lingering grunge-rock romanticism that had defined my teens, and his pale intensity sent shivers right down to my core. We got to know each other through mutual friends when I was only a sophomore. It was a tempestuous nine months, high romance carried to an unhealthy degree: the early days sequestered in Brad's loft bedroom while his roommate practiced guitar downstairs. We didn't go out much, lost touch with friends and didn't care; we wanted it that way, immersed in our dyad. The feelings were so strong and, for me, so new. I'd had a few overtly delirious relationships in high school, but they'd always been tempered by the constraints of home and community and the knowledge, which I kept largely to myself, that I would be fleeing the scene as soon as it was economically feasible. With Brad, it was the great Meant to Be, the intimacy completely unforced, the sex so terrifyingly good that it left me in a sated daze for hours afterward.

Then came the nitpicking and jealousy and the vague, nebulous dissatisfactions, followed in short order by concrete manifestations: screaming fights, cheap, reflexive verbal barbs, and then drunken, maudlin reconciliations. Late night phone calls and weepy confessions. The two girls who shared my apartment advised me in no uncertain terms to drop-kick the fucker. Eventually came the strenuously resisted realization (on my part, at least) that it was never going to be good again, that those first heady four or five months were long gone, and what was left was only cinders turning to ash.

Brad was obviously an adolescent at heart, a romantic who would likely zero in on a romantic's dissolution. The probability was that sooner or later we'd do something severe, and perhaps even permanent, to one another.

It took another couple of months to break up, including several attempts at rapprochement that grew increasingly halfhearted on my part, increasingly desperate on his. I looked him up on the Internet a few years ago, during one of those early spells right after we'd moved to Cary, when I was still afraid of losing my entire history. (And at some point I did, but by then I'd realized that it isn't so hard to let go—there are advantages.) Brad has a wife and two children, and he teaches at a community college in Nebraska. I wish him the best; I hope he still thinks of me from time to time, and feels that same twinge I feel. Not exactly nostalgia, but more than fondness. The best kind of hurt, if there is such a thing.

So let's say you're me, only a year from graduation with a BS in Marketing and no real idea of where to go from there. Given to fits of impulsive behavior, drunken one-nighters with jocks or dropouts, I didn't make much distinction. They always left me feeling worse than before, emptier somehow.

Then, in swept Randy Mosley, at first simply another eye-lock across the bar and some sloppy kissing, an exchange of numbers, but he kept calling and so I went on a couple of dates, and what do you know? Turned out he was resourceful, commanding, self-assured, and seemingly knowledgeable on an array of subjects. On our third date, he brought me a pencil-shaded sketch he'd made of me, just a facial portrait, something in my eyes lacking and somehow unfinished, which I chalked up to his being artistically inept but touching in the effort he'd spent on it—and an aspect of him I'd have never suspected. Most important, perhaps, was his reaction when I got a little too tipsy and went all confessional on him, a mere two months into the relationship. I'd been acting as though Brad had been more of a fling than an actual love affair, but halfway through the second bottle of wine one night it all came flooding out. Randy didn't jump ship or quit calling. Instead, he said all the awful things about Brad that I really needed to hear. He never questioned what I'd been doing with such a loser;

he simply passed judgment and moved right along. Before I knew it I was sleeping over at his place, borrowing his clothes, letting him pay for just about everything.

Once I'd breached the dam with the Brad saga, I found myself confiding all sorts of shit to him that I'd never shared with anyone else, not even my girlfriends. We went away to a chalet in the mountains one weekend, and, while we lay naked on the overstuffed mattress, I told him about a friend of mine who'd died while we were still in high school. "I remember when my mom told me that Jessica was gone. It was so typical, Mom didn't even refer to her as Jessica, she called her 'Kay Flythe's daughter,' as in 'Mrs. Stancil just called and said Kay Flythe's daughter got killed in a wreck on Old Bridge Road. You knew her pretty well, didn't you, baby?' Like she hadn't met Jessica like ten times already." I'd actually been sneaking smokes with Jessica and her boyfriend, Greg, out behind the youth center just the day before. Greg lost control of his Jeep and flipped it, and Jessica wasn't wearing her seat belt. "Mom mentioned that, too, 'she wasn't wearing a seat belt,' like she had to make sure I got a lesson from it." Randy stroked my hair and didn't interrupt until I was done.

He didn't offer much about his own past, only random anecdotes that could just have easily come from any adolescent history: a best friend who'd betrayed him for a girl; other kids who'd picked on him because he was smarter than most, which drove him more deeply into solitude; the way his favorite dog had disappeared and then turned up dead, the victim of some sadistic neighbor. He mentioned an early abandonment, a series of foster homes, some abusive. And with a detail here and a detail there— Christmases where all his gifts turned out to be secondhand, a story about how he'd had to do a book report in front of his sixth-grade class with his eye still swollen from a smack his foster mother had administered—he intimated enough to let me know that he'd had it harder than most, so I didn't pry. I was amazed that he'd come out of it all so stable.

Jessica Flythe. That was my first taste, the first time mortality reared up and I understood how fast it can all go away. It was too real at the same time that it wasn't real at all, like a switch had been thrown and there was this low-frequency buzz in the back of my head all the time, blocking me from quite accepting that this girl would never again let me bum a smoke or help me adjust my top so that Greg's friend Zac would be most admiring. She had *ceased*; she was never going anywhere again, never getting any older, never resolving her issues with grades or knowing if she would be accepted into college.

My dad found me crying in our garage the day after Jessica's funeral. He sat down and patted me awkwardly on the back while I sobbed. He didn't offer any platitudes. He bummed one of my smokes, and said he wouldn't tell Mom if I wouldn't.

3.

Victor Haddock was an RA, one of the guys who oversees freshman in their dormitories when they first get to college. He was twenty years old when a seventeen-year-old named Randy Mosley moved into Freedom Hall on the Oregon State campus. Randy was there on a hardship scholarship, which he'd applied for following the deaths of his last foster parents, who'd been killed in a house fire a year earlier.

By all accounts, Victor was a friendly, capable mentor, who assisted several kids in adjusting to the pressures of university life. He was an outdoorsman, an avid kayaker and hiker who spent his summers in places like the Snake River Gorge or the Utah Badlands. The year before Randy came into his life, Victor had spent a month hiking the hinterlands of the Arctic National Wildlife Refuge in Alaska.

One of the first reporters who tracked me down after Randy's arrest, during that first week while I was still living at our home in El Ray, before Mom swept me back to enforced isolation in Tapersville, was a guy my age, who was kind and respectful and asked his questions politely instead of shouting them. So I let him into the house and spoke earnestly with him for nearly an hour before Mom came back from the grocery store and ran him out. I'd let the reporter take along a family album with some photographs. My reasoning was that we hadn't been married but a few years, and there weren't many photos in there anyway, and I didn't want them any longer. I was on a lot of sedatives at the time.

Randy's Alaska picture was in there, and apparently it struck the same sort of chord with the newspaper staff then as it had with me, several years earlier. Just the sort of effect Randy calculated it to have. So the paper published it as part of a background story on Randy, and by chance the CNN affiliate picked it up and ran the image nationally.

Victor Haddock's parents saw it and called the police. They confirmed that they had a copy of the very same picture, and that the figure shown in it wasn't Randy at all. Victor had gone missing during the summer school session the year after Randy lived on his hall. He'd been scheduled to fly out to Denver and spend a month with some friends, but he never showed up. Randy was enrolled in summer school at the time. The local police searched for Victor after his parents called them; for a few weeks there were copies of his student ID photograph papering campus, with MISSING PLEASE HELP written underneath, and contact information. But then the students returned in the fall and there was a whole new class of freshmen and the police soon had other priorities, like drunk drivers and date rape and the myriad dangerous and reckless behaviors of young people on their own for the first time. A file remained open. The Haddocks never gave up. But Victor's body was never recovered. To this day, no one knows what became of him. Randy never mentioned it during any of the interviews police conducted with him prior to or following his trial.

Dark up there, at the top of the world. Where Randy had only ever been in his mind.

CHAPTER SEVEN

1.

I wasn't answering the phone most days. It rang and I listened to messages and then deleted them. It was sort of sad and funny at the same time, since I used to almost jump out of my skin when the ringer went off, and then stare anxiously at the caller ID on my machine, hoping for a familiar name. For the past few years, it almost always came up as UNLISTED, which meant telemarketers or consumer surveys. Often I'd pick up and talk to the rep for a while, even if I had no intention of signing on to whatever they were offering, just to hear an adult voice. Those people didn't mind wasting your time, but they sure did get pissy when they realized you'd wasted theirs.

Now, the messages wouldn't stop coming. The newspaper called, and the TV stations. They wanted my side of the story. I could have told them very concisely that my side of the story was FUCK YOU, although I didn't think that would help my cause. Jim phoned from work, twice, "Just checking in. Just wanted to let you know you don't have to go through this alone." It both tweaked my dependencies and infuriated me; after all, what did he really have to offer? A patient ear and some awkward sex? Like he could even begin to understand. Then I remembered what he'd endured, with his sick child and his faithless ex-wife, and I got angry with myself. But I didn't call him back.

And then, Thursday morning:

"Hello, Ms. Wren? My name is Carolyn Rowe. My husband Duane and I run a private investigation service here in the area, and I'm sorry to have to tell you that we're the ones who located you for Mr. Pritchett. We were subcontracted by an affiliate company Mr. Pritchett had retained in California, and they turned out to be less than forthcoming about the reasons you were being sought. I'm calling you to offer our sincere apologies. We thought we had a pretty decent screening system in place to keep ourselves from getting into this kind of trouble, but it seems to have failed us in this instance, and you're bearing the brunt. I understand completely if you don't want to speak with us, but we have some information on Mr. Pritchett that we'd like to share with you, a few choice tidbits that might help get him off your back. We're just really, really sorry about what's happened to you and . . . well, that's all I can say, I guess. Here's our number—" I recognized the prefix for Clayton, a small bedroom community on the east side of Raleigh.

To tell the truth, I was curious as to exactly how Pritchett had tracked me down. He'd mentioned the private firm in LA during his interview, and I'd had visions of men in black sunglasses with walkie-talkies and satellite data. But that was bullshit. It wasn't as though I'd taken any extraordinary precautions against being discovered, aside from the name change and moving across the country: I only wanted Randy not to find us, and I had thought of his means as being limited. Now I realized that someone could track me by spending half an hour navigating the right Internet sites.

The message might have been a con, another draw from people who didn't particularly have my best interests in mind.

I looked in the phone book under Private Investigators (who knew they actually advertised?) and sure enough, there was the number, alongside a listing for ROWE INVESTIGATIONS. They didn't have an ad, just their title. I rested a little easier, but didn't know what would be the point of contacting them. Pritchett had money, recent history, and a valid grudge on his side. I had to let this pass over me like a storm, and then peak my head back out when it was clear.

If I didn't lose my mind first.

Then Hayden came home after school, and things changed again. He wasn't crying, but his face was screwed up so tight I could tell it was coming soon enough. I hugged him, and sighed. "Honey, I thought you were supposed to be going over to Caleb's."

"His mom won't let me come over anymore," he said, his poor eyes filling with rejection, that ugliest of hurts. "She says he can't be friends with me anymore."

Something in me went still and then hardened. I spent the next few hours trying to cheer him up, with little success. I thought of calling Gabby McPherson and telling her my exact opinion of her son, her house, her husband, and her shitty excuse for interior design. Instead, I picked up the phone and dialed the number Carolyn Rowe had left on the machine.

2.

We met at Pullen Park in Raleigh, on a Saturday afternoon. It was a public recreation area with playgrounds and ponds and a merry-go-round, and the day turned out to be sunny and bright, the sky that hard clear blue of late winter, with temperatures in the low fifties. Lots of people had decided to take advantage of the weather, and the park was busy. I got a table with an umbrella near the slides and swing sets, so I could keep an eye on Hayden. The Rowes, when they arrived, mentioned that they didn't have children of their own, which I soon surmised was their way of explaining why they got jumpy every time a group of kids exploded into screams or laughter. I'd forgotten how shrill large groups of kids

could be to the unattuned ear. Duane Rowe
joked that it was like a flashback to his days
as an uniformed cop, busting parties.

He was a short man, stocky and thick,
with a wrestler's kind of build. He wore a
Durham Bulls baseball cap, which he removed to shake my hand, and then promptly
placed back on his head. I was left with an
impression of a prematurely gray halo of
hair, cut short and patchy in places; I guessed
the cap was a routine fixture. A corduroy
jacket and faded blue jeans made him seem
both instantly affable and indistinguishable
from half the middle-aged men in the park.
His wife was his physical opposite, slim and
athletic, bleached blond and well preserved,
although her eyes gave her away as slightly
older than she was trying to look. Still, I could
imagine her being pursued by men in their
twenties and men in their fifties alike; a trick
not many of us could pull off. She managed
to sport the low-cut jeans worn by girls half
her age, without coming across as tacky. Several fathers were loafing in our vicinity, os-
tensibly keeping watch over their children, and
more than one of their heads swiveled in her
direction more than once. Duane seemed not
to notice.

Carolyn was also one of those Southern ladies who seems uncontrollably compelled to act a bit overly familiar; instead of shaking my hand, she hugged me quickly. "Oh, honey, I can't begin to tell you how sorry we are," she gushed, her eyes sparkling like she might cry right here in front of everybody. "You can slap each one of us in the face, pour a drink on our heads, whatever you want."

"Not necessary," I said. We sat at the table and I made a mental note of Hayden's location. He was playing with some kids near the swing set; a couple of them were talking amiably to him and they were all laughing. I reminded myself that they probably didn't recognize him, or know who his mother was.

"I like what you did with your hair," Duane said.

"Thanks." Yesterday, while Hayden was at school, I'd had it cut short and darkened a few shades. I was also wearing big sunglasses, and had yet to draw any untoward stares. "So . . ."

Carolyn sat beside me and brought a folder out of a worn leather tote bag that looked like she'd been carrying it around with her since she was a teenager. "Right off, let me tell you a little about us. Duane was a police officer in Baltimore for six years, then in a town called Reston, Virginia, for eight more. I was a reporter for the paper in Reston, and that's where we first met. When he decided to leave the force we moved down here, because I grew up here and my mom was sick at the time. She's better now, but we decided we liked it and we started up our business. Now we mostly do things like divorce, insurance fraud, those sorts of jobs."

"Following people around," I said.

Duane laughed.

"That's exactly right," Carolyn said. "It's less romantic than most people think, but I can see we don't have to disabuse you of that notion. Which is good. Now, as relates to you, we got a call from another investigative firm on the West Coast about five months ago—"

"You mentioned that in your message."

"I think Ms. Wren would appreciate it if you cut to the chase, darling," Duane observed.

"No, that's all right," I said. "It's just that it's all still kind of surreal."

"Well, anyway, Duane and I usually collect enough background information that we can screen out people who want us to locate someone for the wrong reasons. We don't assist stalkers, and we don't even work for insurance companies if they have a bad record."

"Which narrows the field a bit," Duane said with a smile.

Carolyn slapped his arm. "I'm trying to tell her what she needs to know." She looked at me. "Didn't he just tell me to hurry it up?"

I nodded, amused despite my best intentions.

"See?" she told her husband. "Now shut up until I'm finished. Okay. So Duane had a partner when he was still in Reston, a fellow who eventually moved out West. This guy works for this firm I mentioned, it's a lot bigger than our operation, obviously, I mean they've got like twenty investigators and a huge budget and all. Well, this guy called Duane and he made out like you were the target in a civil case and you'd skipped out and changed your identity in order to duck a subpoena. They already had your new name and everything, even your address. They just wanted us to establish if it was actually you, and get your routine down and let them know. We'd done some research on the Internet, so we knew a little something of your

history, and I can tell you I was kind of con-
flicted about it already at that point, but by
then we'd taken the job. And I figured that
maybe you'd done something wrong in the
time since what happened with your husband. Then Mr. Pritchett showed up and we
gave him our records and I suppose he used
them to sneak up on you. I heard he came
after you while you were shopping?"

"How did you know that?"

"Oh, we've had words with Mr. Pritchett,"
Duane said. "We called him and expressed
our displeasure with his little smear campaign in no uncertain terms. But my friend's
outfit had already cut us a check and Pritchett simply told us our services were no
longer required. He actually hung up on me."

"I love that you do your shopping late-
night," Carolyn confided, leaning over and
putting a hand on my shoulder. It was all I
could do not to flinch. "There's nothing like a
store when it's all empty, just you and the
Muzak. Do they still call it Muzak? Anyway, it
breaks my heart that he accosted you the
way he did. We never meant for it to happen
like that. Duane's had a pretty serious talk
with his friend in LA, too."

"This case has ended a couple of financially beneficial relationships," Duane said unhappily.

I wanted to like them. But when he said that, I responded before I knew quite what I was going to say: "I had to tell my son the truth about his father the other night. I had always told him he was just a petty criminal. And I'd told him he was dead."

Both of them were quiet for a moment, and we all looked over at the swing set. Hayden was going pretty high, his legs tucked in tight during the backswing to get the most momentum, his hair flying out around his head. The clouds had started to move in and the children were breathing steam, dissipating trails lingering momentarily wherever they went running by.

"Bless his heart, he is the cutest thing," Carolyn Rowe said mistily. When she turned to face me, though, her lips had gone tight and her eyes were cold. "After we realized what we'd been part of, we did some digging of our own into Mr. Pritchett's history. We have some ideas on how you might get him to let you alone."

"First off, though, you really need to give some kind of a response to the press," Duane said. "I know it sounds like bullshit, but if people don't hear your side, they assume that whatever's being said about you is true. Jennifer McLean has done the most extensive local coverage, and she's the only one who's actually interviewed Pritchett, so it would probably be most effective if we could get her to do an interview with you. It'll be tough, but once you can explain how you were as much a victim as Pritchett was, people will be much more likely to empathize."

"Hold up for a minute," I cautioned. "First, how did your friend in LA find me? Do you know?"

Carolyn sighed and Duane nodded. Duane said, "Your mother passed away last year?"

Damn. I knew it. "Last winter. She never even told me how sick she was, said it was just routine aging issues. It was stomach cancer. She left a note that said she didn't want a funeral because she didn't want me to come out there and attract attention."

"She must have meant well," Duane said kindly. "But both your real name and your assumed name were included in her will, and it was executed to your bank account once everything was liquidated. You signed in your own name."

It had been a two-week trip. I'd boxed up the house and hired some men to take the boxes to Goodwill. I avoided all my old friends and didn't leave the house but a few times. Hayden wandered the halls wide-eyed, sensing my disconnection and steering clear as much as he could manage. He played in the empty rooms with his handheld computer and stared at the photos on the wall until I packed them away. He asked who the people in the pictures were, and I told him I had to concentrate. I sold the house to the bank at a loss and kept only three boxes worth of memories, important papers, and photographs, Mom's file folder of all her editorials, clipped out of the newspaper. I didn't think about Mom much while I was there, spending my mental energy instead on damning Randy, over and over again.

Now I looked at the Rowes and told them, "I didn't know any better. I thought maybe everyone would forget about me. I always knew my mother would blow it at some point."

CHAPTER EIGHT

At first, Mom didn't seem overwhelmed at the joyous news. I asked her, "Did you hear what I said? You're going to be a grandmother."

"Yes, yes. I'm delighted for the both of you," she said, her distraction coming through clearly, even over the phone. "Tell Randy I said so. But I thought you were planning on waiting a few years. Have you told your people at work?"

"Mom, I just found out for sure yesterday." I was standing in the kitchen of our new home, a three-thousand-square-foot colonial with full basement and two-car garage;

except for its being the last house in the cul-de-sac (which added on another twenty grand to the asking price) it was more or less identical to the other homes in the neighborhood, located only a ten-minute drive across town from the house where we'd lived for the past couple of years in what we now referred to as our "starter home." The place was huge, with vaulted ceilings and a severely modernistic stairway leading off the entry hall to the basement and the upstairs. The kitchen was spacious enough that I thought I might get lost in it, the pantry closer in size to that of a bedroom than a closet. We'd both grown tired of the old house, feeling cramped and restless. As soon as Randy was offered a promotion to district chief, he said he wanted to go all out. I thought he was probably suffering some sort of intimidation factor from the higher strata. All his new coworkers had families, as opposed to the class of swashbuckling, fresh out of business school, wannabe players who'd made up much of his last team. I'd secretly hoped he wasn't feeling pressure from that angle yet; I figured I still had a while before the Mosley family expanded to fit our new space.

But I'd been feeling rotten for the past couple of weeks and, deep down, I knew why. My feelings were ambivalent, the shock of what the doctor had told me that morning still sinking in, as were about a million other corollary issues: the lifestyle changes that would soon be demanded of us, the financial restrictions we'd have to impose on our- selves, the baby-proofing of the new house, and on and on. The whole notion threatened a mental overload.

Mom, as usual, was being a great help.

"Honey, I don't mean to sound unim- pressed," she said now. "I do think it's won- derful. As you well know, I've been cheering for this since the day you got married. You're the one who kept raving about how much you loved the work you were doing and how you thought you could really accomplish some things before you had a child, and I guess I just got used to thinking that way, too."

She'd been cataloguing it, and now she was having the last laugh. I was being shifted into a matronly role quite before I was ready, and of course I'd been quite vo- cal about my feelings on the subject for the past few years. I never hesitated to tell Randy or anyone else who asked, "Not quite yet." Randy always said, "Before we're forty,

maybe?" and I ignored his sarcasm and
agreed that was fine. Before this morning,
forty still seemed like an abstract concept.
Now I was realizing that I'd be that age about
the time my child got his or her driver's license. I felt sick all over.

Mom went on gloating, describing at
length the troubles she'd experienced while
she was pregnant with me. The sore feet,
the aching back, the stray spasms and sudden fits of weeping. "You know, they say that
you'll have the same sort of pregnancy your
mother did, so I can't say I envy you the next
eight months."

Ever since Dad died, she'd come out of
her shell, to put it mildly. She bloomed, and
became something of a maven around Tapersville, volunteering at the youth center
and teaching Sunday school and writing op-
eds for the *Tapersville Dispatch*. To be honest, I only thought of her as having "bloomed"
when she wasn't pissing me off; the rest of
the time I thought of her as hypercompulsive.
She called several times a week. She cri-
tiqued and demeaned pretty much every
facet of our lives, which I found baffling,
since, as far as I could tell, we were living a
version of the American Dream so damned

near perfect that it was almost cloying. Right now I was feeling the emotional nerve memories of every crack she'd taken at me from puberty onward. *Hormones*, I thought, trying to make excuses for her. *She was always like this with you because she knew Dad loved you better.*

I was pregnant and she was menopausal. Yes, it looked to be a fine period we were embarking upon.

"I'll have to move down there for a few months after the delivery," Mom continued. I had a vision of her spazzing around in the house where I grew up, the phone cradled between chin and shoulder, watering plants with one hand and typing on her computer with the other. In the background, I could hear something that sounded very much like keys tapping. "Randy will just have to suffer through it. He'll be thankful that I'm there after the first few days. What do you want to bet?"

"I know he will."

Randy was unfailingly polite with Mom, but outside of her presence he made no secret of the fact that he couldn't stand her. His defense was that he was only derisive toward her because he knew how self-conscious she made me feel, how all my shortcomings, real or imaginary, came to the surface after a few minutes in her company. The truth of it was that the two of them simply had opposi- tional personalities. Mom was possessed by too much flurry, not enough focus; she drove him to distraction if he was in her presence for more than a few hours at a time. He was a laser, concentrated, and she scattered his at- tention. I used to try and referee, but they didn't need me, so now I was mostly just an interested observer.

I got up off the stool where I'd been sitting, and paced the hardwood floor while Mom jab- bered on. Randy had erected a spice rack in the door of the pantry. I opened it and admired the polish. I turned the jars of cinnamon and parsley and tarragon until they were all facing the same way, their labels nicely lined up. I never used these flavorings; most of our din- ners were premade, which I didn't mind a bit. Catching myself, I turned the paprika so that it faced backward. *See, there—I'm not OCD.*

"Are you going to keep working all the way up to your due date?" Mom asked. "I mean, I'd just begun to think of you as a careerist, and I know how you like to have things planned out in advance. This seems like an awful big one to just spring on yourself."

She'd been into her thesaurus again; ever since she'd started writing her little "Heard Around Town"–type column, she'd developed an annoying habit of slipping what she considered fifty-cent words into her conversations, most often awkwardly. No way, during all the time I'd lived at home, would she ever have used a word like "careerist." Next thing I knew, she would be advising "synergy." I toyed with the idea of bringing up Dad, which was the only guaranteed way to cut the conversation short. But that would be a cheap shot, and I considered myself above it, even if Mom wasn't. "We were planning on waiting, Mom. But the Pill is only ninety-nine percent effective, and I guess I'm one of the exceptions that proves the rule."

Quietly, my husband's voice surfaced from the next room. "It's time. It's time for you to have our baby."

Mom was saying, only half jokingly, "Well, maybe you should think about suing those Ortho Tri-Cyclen people. The pharmaceutical companies, they always settle, they only want to keep themselves out of court and avoid bad press."

"Yes, Mom, a married woman conceiving

is bad press." I belatedly registered my husband's comment, and looked around the corner into the den. Randy was reclined in his leather chair, one of the treats he'd bought for himself with his most recent bonus. I thought he would be staring at me, willing me to get off the phone before he got exasperated simply from hearing my end of the conversation. It had happened before. But his face was buried behind a newspaper, not the local one, but a copy of the *Chicago Tribune*. I froze in place and my mind stuttered to a halt. He'd been in Chicago for business last week, and I'd found that same issue of the newspaper among the items in his suitcase when I was collecting the dirty clothes from it. Some awful carnage was splashed across the front of the section that he was reading now: FAMILY BUTCHERED IN CALUMET CITY, SURVIVOR HID IN SPARE ROOM. The piece had caught my eye when I was going through his suitcase, and I shuddered to remember the details that leaped out when I'd read it. A father, mother, and daughter had been killed during a home invasion in the suburbs. The paper speculated that the crime may have been the work of a "ritualistic murderer," because of certain nonspecified

mutilations that had occurred. The younger
child, a boy whose name the paper had
declined to print because of his minor status,
had survived by hiding in a guest room during the attack. He'd briefly been hospitalized
for shock, but had then been released to the
custody of some family relatives. Unimagin-
able.

I saw the headline now and it struck me
that my husband was holding on to last
week's paper from another town and I distractedly wondered why he was rereading
an issue he must've picked up at the airport
on his arrival or departure.

Ripples crossed the surface down there;
currents eddied. Something sunk quickly into
the dark, heavily weighted.

"Did you tell Randy they offered you the
promotion?" Mom was asking.

Shaw Associates was going to make me
head of the entire marketing division, which
was nearly unheard of for someone who'd
been working there less than a decade, and
especially for a woman. I'd nailed a couple of
important projects and made the company
some money and cracked the fabled glass
ceiling. It was a small-time advertising operation, only thirty salaried employees and a

couple of commissioned salespeople, but things were going well. I hadn't told Randy about the promotion yet. I only got the offer last week, and by then I'd already scheduled an appointment with my doctor.

"I know you hate me to follow in your footsteps," I told my mother, "but I'm going to have to be thinking about more than my own best interests from now on."

"Plenty of women work full-time and are full-time mothers. I think I did a fine job with you, naturally, but I could've done it and held down a nine-to-five."

"I know you could have, Mom." Trying to head off the lecture, and suddenly I felt exhausted. Bone-deep weary. Her banter wore on me quickly in those days, as did a whole lot of things, actually. My patience felt just about spent, even though there was nothing really taxing it. I went to the window and stared out at our backyard. It wasn't huge, but a considerable upgrade over the postage stamp we had at our old place across town. Randy had bought a riding lawn mower to keep it trim. There were two oak saplings that, given a decade or so, might become quite lovely. For now, their shade barely crossed the cement birdbath. Then, at the back of our property line (complete with gray slat fencing), Randy's toolshed. At our old house, he had a room downstairs in the unfinished basement that was strictly off-limits to me, his "man room," as he called it, where he worked out with his free weights or gambled online or whatever. I'd only asked him about his solitary pursuits a couple of times, and when I'd teased him about his ambiguous responses, it was enough to bring on a tirade about personal space and how essential it was to someone like him, who spent much of his time among people whose company he didn't necessarily enjoy, but was obliged to tolerate as part of his job. So I quit inquiring and now he had the toolshed, which he proudly claimed to have converted into a tidy, fulfilling workout space. It was a ten-by-ten prefab outbuilding, basically, and I wasn't the least bit jealous or interested in what he did out there. That's what I'd told him.

He installed a padlock on the door anyway.

"We talked about it before we got married," I said into the phone. "Randy always said he wanted me to stay home and raise the kids, and there are more than a few studies out now that confirm that what you and

Dad did was right. It's the best way to give your child a chance to be happy and successful." I caught myself talking like a brochure. "Anyway, it's only a few years. I'll go back to work after the kid is old enough for school."

"Unless you have another one."

I had some rather sharp thoughts on that subject at the moment, but then I sensed someone behind me. When I turned around, Randy was standing there, leaning against the counter with his arms crossed. He made a snide little wave.

"Mom, I need to go. Randy says hi."

"Well I really, really am very happy for both of you. You know I can't wait to spoil that child, and I look forward to many years of doing exactly that. Neither of you will be able to stop me." She was trying to be cute, and even though it only made me more tired, it was finally worth an unforced smile. I told her I loved her and hung up.

Randy spread his arms wide and beckoned. "Come here, Mama."

I knew how much it meant to him. His own childhood was such a wreck, by any standards; from what little I'd been able to piece together from his reticent remembrances, his own biological mother was a drunk who abandoned him at an early age. He grew up in a series of foster homes and state-supported boarding schools, until he'd been able to struggle his way clear at sixteen. He worked shit jobs until he earned an academic scholarship. I felt a lancing, familiar slash of guilt at how annoyed I'd been with my own mother just now, when all she'd ever shown me was devotion. Even if that dedication was warped behind the veneer of her plasticine rage at my father, at least neither of them had ever left me on my own.

So I let Randy hold me, and I squeezed him tight. I tried to realize the sensation of the tiny life growing inside, something that both of us had made together.

Outside, some blue jays were fighting and raising a ruckus in the birdbath. For some reason, I suddenly thought of the Renaults, the family whose murder had caused such a sensation last year. The crime had never been solved. *Where was the outrage?* I thought. Why hadn't people demanded answers? Punishment, accountability?

Now came a clenching in my stomach, fierce and—although I was surely imagining it—almost sentient. I knew that neither

Randy nor I could ever again be so lazy with our lives, our incomes, any of it; it was essential that we never let our guard down, or pretend ignorance of the very real menace that went abroad in the world.

I tousled Randy's hair. He led me upstairs into the cool evening, away from the windows and the screeching outside.

CHAPTER NINE

Channel Eleven's Jennifer McLean was polite and cool until about halfway through the interview, when she sabotaged me. Up until that exact moment, I actually felt like it was going pretty well.

The Rowes had spent much of the last two days prepping me, asking the sorts of questions they thought I'd be answering, fine-tuning my responses so I wouldn't come across as either defensive or disingenuous. To them, my giving a public response to the allegations against me was essential before I could begin to rehabilitate my reputation. They let me use the enclosed back porch of their farmhouse to conduct the taping; it was out in the rolling countryside east of Raleigh, a forty-minute drive from my place. There was no way I was going to let cameras inside my own home. They hadn't started camping out there yet, still waiting, I supposed, to see if the story would garner more interest, drive ratings, get hits on their Web site . . . however they gauged those things. I didn't want Hayden to have to deal with them. We scheduled my interview for Monday afternoon, while he was in school.

Duane and Carolyn set everything up, and I was already feeling too indebted to them by half, afraid of how quickly I'd become dependent on them. I could actually talk to them about what was happening to me. I hadn't known how badly I'd wanted to tell someone.

The reporter and her crew arrived around lunchtime and spent an hour setting up their equipment among Carolyn Rowe's huge potted palms and flowering cacti, trying to work around the elaborate system of sprinklers and lights in the glass-walled porch/terrarium. Carolyn called it her "Florida room." Any other time I'd have been impressed with the profligate evidence of Carolyn's green thumb, but the camera crew asked if I wanted makeup, and when I arched my eyebrows in the Rowes' direction Duane said, "Maybe a little around the cheeks. The lights make you look paler than you are." His diplomatic way of telling me I looked ghostly.

I heard one of the crew asking Jennifer McLean if the Rowes were my PR reps or my lawyers. "They're private detectives," McLean said quizzically. "I'm still trying to figure out their angle."

That made two of us.

Then they sat us down at the glass-topped patio table, one camera behind McLean and another behind me, so that both our reactions would be captured, and she started with a succinct recap. She could have prerecorded this portion, but I figured she wanted to measure my response. The Rowes had presupposed this introduction, so I was able to keep my face perfectly neutral as McLean said, "Randall Roberts Mosley, known in the press as the 'Cross-Eye Killer' for the way in which he mutilated his victims, terrorized a large swath of the West and Midwest during a spree that lasted well over a decade. Between the years of 1988 and 2000, he is believed to have killed at least twelve people, and perhaps more. Mosley was eventually captured at his home in El Ray, California, thanks partly to information provided to the authorities by his wife of four years. Mosley was convicted in 2001 and remains on California's Death Row, awaiting execution.

"As Channel Five News reported last week, Mosley's ex-wife has been living in the Triangle for the past six years, working a respectable job and raising the killer's son, who was only six months old at the time of his father's arrest. Nina Mosley has had her name legally changed, and she's severed all ties with her old life. Her identity was exposed by Charles Pritchett, the father of one of Mosley's victims, Carrie Pritchett."

Now she shifted her eyes away from the camera and smiled at me. I'd watched her on TV for years, and I knew she'd come across as engaged and professional, with a serious demeanor, her sharp attention and soft cheeks in full flare for the camera. "During my interview with Mr. Pritchett, I asked him about why he would want your identity exposed after all these years, when you seem to have simply tried to move on with your life, like any of us would after such a devastating ordeal. What do you think his motivations are?"

I breathed deeply. This was something I'd rehearsed, but I meant it, too, and my grave, earnest tone was genuine. "I can only imagine the grief that Mr. Pritchett and all the victims' families endured. My heart goes out to them. I remember them in my prayers daily. Not an hour goes by that I don't wish I could've done something to prevent what happened to their loved ones. But Randy fooled me the same way he fooled everyone during those years, from the people he worked with to the members of our church. No one suspected him."

"Mr. Pritchett points to the fact that some of the falsified documents recovered from the home you shared with Mr. Mosley were made out in your name." She smiled prettily to show me she meant no harm, she was simply meeting her obligation to present both sides. "I believe there was a collection of driver's licenses from several states, and some passports with your photo but an alias in place of your real name. And your DNA was recovered from two different crime scenes."

"That's correct. But as the prosecutor explained to the jury during the trial, people who live together carry each other's DNA around all the time, in this case probably as hair strands on my husband's clothing. He might've picked some up from a suit he was wearing, or from driving one of the cars we shared. Then he either purposefully or inadvertently left the strands at the crime scenes."

"And the fake IDs?"

I tried to appear contemplative for the camera. "I've thought about that a lot. I don't know what was going on in Randy's head, and neither did many of the psychiatrists who later interviewed him. There was never any complete agreement on whether he was a sociopath, or clinically deranged, or faking. In any case, serial killers are known to have complex fantasy lives that drive them to do what they do, and those fantasies often have little or nothing to do with reality. In Randy's mind, he might've thought he could compel me to flee with him if he was found out, maybe by using our son as leverage. Whatever he imagined, it turned out to be incorrect. I contacted the authorities the minute I discovered that something was wrong. As soon as I was sure, I called it in."

McLean was nodding. I felt like I was doing well, and when I cut my eyes over to
where the Rowes were standing, they both
gave me the thumbs-up.

Then the reporter asked, "Do you remember a man named Lane Dockery?"

For a moment, my mind went blank. I recalled the name, sure enough, but hadn't
imagined it coming up in this context. Duane
Rowe was frowning. "You mean the crime
writer?" I asked.

She nodded. "He showed some initial interest in doing a book on Randy's case,
didn't he?"

"A couple of people did." Lane Dockery
and another hack named Ronald something-
or-other. I did recall that Ronald didn't sell
nearly as many copies of his stuff as Dockery did of his. "I told them both I wasn't interested in taking part in any of that. I turned
down some money, actually."

"Would it surprise you to learn that Mr.
Dockery was known to have been looking
into your case again recently, with an eye toward completing the work he'd started on
during the time of the trial? And that, as of
six weeks ago, he's been officially listed as
missing by his family?"

I knew I was making a face, and could almost feel the camera tightening in on me. "I had no idea," I stammered, and while that was true enough I could see from McLean's look that somehow I'd been scored on. "Why would he be writing about it all these years later?" I wondered aloud.

Carolyn was moving into my view, slashing her hand across her throat, telling me to quit talking.

"I don't know," McLean said. "We only discovered this information recently, when researching our facts for this interview. We called Mr. Pritchett to ask if Dockery had been in contact with him, and Mr. Pritchett claims that he had not. Mr. Pritchett suggested that perhaps some new information had come to light that sparked a renewed interest on Mr. Dockery's part."

I composed myself. "I wouldn't have any idea what that might be."

McLean shrugged more with her mouth than her shoulders. "Maybe Mr. Dockery had located you as well. His family said the investigation is ongoing, but they haven't heard any news in several weeks."

She was goading me, so I only nodded.

She wrapped it up by asking how all this

attention was affecting my son. I said,
"We've learned a thing or two about who our
friends really are. But I'd prefer to leave him
out of this, if we can."

McLean agreed that we could. The cam-
eramen cut off their equipment and started
packing up. McLean reached across and patted my arm. She told me she had a young
daughter of her own, and that she'd edit out
the last question.

Dockery," Duane said with the air of uttering
a curse. The crew had all gone, and it was
just the three of us sitting among the terra-
cotta pottery and the hanging razor leaves.
He looked at his wife. "We need to do some
more research here," he said, then turned to
me. "So, he hadn't been in touch with you?"

"I haven't even thought about him in
years." I wanted a cigarette so bad I was
thinking of rolling up a palm leaf and lighting
it. "I need to go. I have to be home when my
son gets out of school."

Carolyn was downcast. "Let me come
over and buy you a drink this weekend," she
said. "I promise to be good company, and we
won't even talk about any of this crap. We'll
just let loose. I'll even pay for a sitter."

I had to admit, it sounded like a nice idea. I thought I was opening my mouth to tell her so, but instead I started telling her about the note Charles Pritchett left on my windshield. I told them about the dead girl in Tennessee. My voice kind of caved in when I said, "I'm really terrified, you guys. I'm really afraid for my son."

CHAPTER TEN

I could feel his heartbeat inside me.

Lying on our bed, a paperback in one hand, the other flat against the smooth bulge of my stomach, the tiny nascent life pattered away, sometimes alarmingly fast, but mostly as a steady background noise. A doubling of my own pulse, something I'd also become more attuned to over the past six months. It was one of those things I'd heard pregnant women talking about before, an absurdly beautiful plus to go along with all the minuses of swollen feet and backaches and general impatience. No one could ever understand it if they hadn't felt it for themselves. Even when I put Randy's hand over my stomach, so he could sense the baby's heart racing beneath my skin, he would recite the appropriate dewy-eyed platitudes, but I could tell that the physicality of it freaked him out. I almost thought it repulsed him in some strange way. His palm was always sweaty, and it never lingered any longer than I held it in place.

That feeling, that sense of connection with something both inner and Other, had washed away my initial reticence. My chest felt like it might spring wide open with joy sometimes, although these feelings were frequently followed immediately by a strange, sourceless panic that restricted my breathing and prompted palpitations. *Bad for the baby*, I'd think, resorting to the deep, measured breaths they trained us for in Lamaze.

This particular night I was distracted, because you can get used to anything, even the magic of renewal and Life capitalized, and because Randy was making more noise than usual as he prepared for bed. He had the bathroom door closed, but I could hear him in there, splashing water around in the sink (in a fashion that I knew would leave the linoleum dangerously slick in large puddles), gargling and rinsing twice, knocking over the soap dish, cursing, setting it loudly back in place.

My schedule had changed significantly since I quit working, and it was bothering both of us. I'd started staying up later, restlessly pacing the length of the house at all hours of the night, and then sleeping away half the morning. I was shopping compulsively, mostly buying things for the baby, then rearranging them and reconsidering and often returning items to the store. Nothing satisfied. The nursery down the hall was overflowing with toys and baby-monitoring gadgets. I'd repainted the walls in there twice during the last two months, vacillating between pale blue and sea green. The baby manuals I'd been consulting differed on which color scheme would most stimulate young, fresh minds.

Through the door, I could hear it as Randy ran the ultrasonic toothbrush around his cheeks, no doubt bent over the sink and slobbering tendrils of foam. I never understood why he couldn't just keep his mouth closed while he brushed; I did. He was obviously trying to get a reaction out of me, his clattering ruckus some childish ploy to get attention, but I was seriously involved with Part Three of Ann Rule's *The Stranger Beside Me*, and even though Randy had succeeded in breaking my concentration, I wasn't going to give him the satisfaction of knowing it. Ah, marriage: the most ancient contest writ petty and immediate, nightly fought to a draw in bedrooms across the world. No advance, no retreat, no surrender.

Randy came in wiping his face with a towel. Without looking up from my book, I reminded him to cut off the bathroom light. He looked back, annoyed, like it was an accident, then hooked an arm into the bathroom and swiped at the switch.

"Not so hard," I said. "You'll break it."

He didn't respond, opting to simmer and grind his teeth as he climbed into bed. He made a show of adjusting the covers, fluffing his pillow, lying on one side and then the other before finally reaching over and turning off the lamp on his bedside table. By that point I was completely distracted and I laid the book down across my stomach and waited until he was done. He sighed heavily, theatrically.

"If you've got a problem," I said, with a surplus of saccharine patience, "why not just say so?"

He flipped over and glared at me, then his expression softened and he shook his head. He tried on the wounded-boy face, a mask with which I had some degree of familiarity—he wanted something. "I'm sorry, this schedule has got me pissy. Your hormones are seriously testing me. I have to get up for work in six hours, and you're not even sleepy."

"You're the one who wanted me to quit my job."

"I didn't know it was going to keep you from sleeping."

"Honey, if you think your schedule is off now, wait a few more months until you have to be waking up three times a night to feed the baby or rock him to sleep or change his diapers. And I told you before, I can go downstairs to read if it's bothering you."

"But I'd miss being close to you," he said suggestively. Or snidely, I couldn't tell them apart anymore. I didn't crack a smile and he reverted to his default mode of dour martyr-dom. He tapped his fingers on the paper-back tented across the hump in my midsection. "You've been reading a lot of that type of mess lately, too. Should I be concerned?"

"I found a whole box of these in your old office." In the first few months after my diagnosis, we'd used the weekends to move all the things from what we used to call Randy's "office" down the hall (although really it was only ever used as storage) into the guest room downstairs, and recast the office into a nursery. When I was cleaning out the office closet, I discovered a big cardboard box filled with these "true crime" books, mostly yellowed paperbacks, many of them used copies, with prices ranging from fifty cents to a couple of dollars stamped across the spines. Randy at first seemed embarrassed that I'd found them, then claimed to have bought them all from library clearance sales. I'd never known him to even visit a library, or if he had a card.

The majority of the stock concerned one serial killing spree or another, many of which I'd heard of but others that were completely new to me. The covers were typically lurid: blood spattered across family portraits or booking photos of the monstrous perpetrators. Nearly all of them contained ten to fifteen pages of photographs

inserted halfway through the text: school-
book portraits of men who later went on to
vivisect living human beings in stark base-
ments; crime scene photos of bodies lying
in ditches or bedrooms, reliably pixilated or
altered just enough to retain their prurient
appeal without offending the squeamish.
The blurbs on the back covers were more
often from members of the law enforcement
community than from critics. The Ann Rule
book was about Ted Bundy, but there were
also unofficial case histories of the Green
River Killer, John Wayne Gacy, and Richard
Ramirez. Lane Dockery had written two of
the books, one on Jeffrey Dahmer and another on an illegal immigrant who hopped
trains near the Arizona border and was suspected to have killed scores of women in little towns out in the middle of nowhere. I
faintly recalled the media furor that book had
caused on its publication, with some critics
labeling it as racist. As far as I could tell,
most of the freaks were your average American males, and all I'd known of them before
reading these trashy books was what I'd ab-
sorbed in an osmotic, pop-culture-echo sort
of way.

But for some reason, I was now totally

devouring these things. I'd read six of them cover to cover since a couple of months into the pregnancy. I was an emotional wreck, something Randy and I both attributed to the hormones; so easy to write it all off, my mind always full of worse-case scenarios for the world my son would inhabit. (And we knew at that point that it would be a son; the sonogram had confirmed it and while Randy made no secret of his happiness, I had to admit I was a little disappointed at the time.) Some vague unease was compelling me to face the worst in humanity so I would know what ugliness was possible, and be able to watch out, stay vigilant, to keep him safe. A murmuring ceaseless buzz at the back of my head drove me to it, some strange half-remembered, half-suppressed dreams of the Renault family, their newspaper photo portraits come to life and pursuing me down the hallways of sleep, trying to tell me something but I shut my ears and *ran*.

Randy glanced at the cover of the book and shrugged. He offered the same excuse he'd given me when I first found the box: "I went through a phase."

"I can see why," I said, with some unforced enthusiasm. "These things are like junk food.

Total page-turners. I can't even remember hearing about most of this stuff."

He turned back over. "Well, be careful. Like junk food, they'll make your teeth rotten. You should at least take a break, read some chick-lit."

"You'd prefer me all clingy and over-wrought?"

He conceded that point with a muffled chuckle. "I just don't want you giving yourself nightmares. You've been sleeping pretty restlessly, when you finally do nod off. The other night you got me up at four-freaking-thirty. You were yelling something I couldn't understand. I woke you but I'll bet you don't even remember it, do you?"

I shivered. I hated the idea that I was awake but not aware, because he was right; I had no recollection of it. He could be fabricating it completely, but why would he? To make a point about my reading habits? Maybe, but I felt that twisting in my stomach that told me maybe he wasn't lying, maybe I had been awake and talking to him but I didn't remember it at all. The lack of control involved was frightening to a nauseating de-gree, like a blackout drunk, or being under anesthesia.

I looked at the book and then folded the corner of the page I was reading. I closed it and placed it on the bedside table.

Randy's good night kiss was perfunctory. With the lights out, I lay there in the dark, feeling that heartbeat inside me. I thought of Ted Bundy, sitting at the phone bank beside the young Ms. Rule. Did he consider killing her? Did he think for a moment that his secret pursuits would launch her into a successful career? How these psychotics haunted people, skewing every life they contacted, even those not directly affected by their appetites. The last one of Randy's books I'd read was called *Black Dahlia Avenger*, and had actually been written by a man who came to believe his father was a serial killer. Imagine: your own father. I shivered in bed and wondered, for seemingly the millionth time: *How do they keep it a secret?* How could they manufacture a facile life so opaque and cosmetically sound that even those closest to them didn't know?

CHAPTER ELEVEN

1.

The vice principal of Hayden's school called me at home. Thomas Beasley managed to sound solemn and officious over the phone, even though I'd met him several times in the past and found him to be something of a pushover. It was a good thing he worked with grades K–5; he would never have succeeded in his role if he were dealing with teenagers.

But a call in the middle of the school day was always a bad sign.

"Ms. Wren," he said, "Hayden got into a fight with a couple of children today. We need you to come down here for a conference, if it's at all possible."

"Hayden's never been in trouble, the whole time he's been there," I said quickly, defensively, my hackles raised. It was true and Beasley had to know it. Hayden hadn't ever before been a disciplinary problem, and I couldn't even imagine him using his fists against another kid unless he'd been seriously pushed, backed into a corner . . . "He must've been provoked."

"I'll be glad to share the details with you in person. We have Hayden here in the office right now, so you'll get to hear his side of the story. When can we expect you?"

I patted on the bare minimum of makeup, just enough to lessen the shadows beneath my eyes, then tied my hair back and made the ten-minute drive over to the campus of the Cary Elementary Learning Center. It wasn't the most expensive private school in the community, not by a long shot, but it was a step above the public school, which, thanks to some strangely twisted redistricting, would've required Hayden to take a twenty-minute bus ride every morning to the other side of town. The grounds here were nicer than those of most municipally funded schools, too; a testament to the yearly tuition rates. Beige and tan buildings with pebbled facades stood grouped around the central hub of the Admin offices. Classrooms on the left- and right-hand sides, a state-of-the-art gymnasium and auditorium extending out behind. A security guard took my name at the entrance. I explained that I was expected, but he made me wait while he radioed the front office. I understood, as I was clearly intended to, that this little show was supposed to make me feel more secure about my child's safety while he was on school grounds, but I was in no mood to show the requisite appreciation.

Inside the building, through the glass-wall partitions, I could see the receptionist and a couple of teachers hanging around the main office, along with a single kid who looked like he'd rather be just about anywhere else, sitting in the waiting area and swinging his legs back and forth nervously. I went in and gave my name to the receptionist. She stared at me a moment longer than was necessary, a look I'd become accustomed to seeing anytime I left home during the past week: *Didn't I see you on TV recently? Oh, yes . . .* The receptionist said, "It will only be a moment. They're just about ready for you."

The principal himself was so often away at various conferences and districtwide functions that many of the parents didn't know for sure if he actually existed. Most of us dealt—when we had to deal at all—with Thomas Beasley, whose nominative role as vice principal seemed to include everything from disciplinary matters to scheduling parent/teacher conferences to the cafeteria menu. I'd often felt sympathy, if not outright pity, for him in the past; at the moment, I was feeling neither. When his office door opened a few minutes later, I had some choice and blistering words at the ready. It wasn't Beasley who exited first, though, but an entire nuclear family unit: mama, papa, and child. As soon as I recognized the boy being bustled along by his father, I felt my stomach lurch; the kid's face was hidden behind a wad of bloody paper towels, but that curly red hair was familiar to every parent who had a child at the school. I knew the Hale family more by reputation than any real kind of acquaintance, but that reputation alone was enough to make me more certain than ever that my son had not been in the wrong with regards to this altercation. Behind those paper towels smirked one of the only verifiable hellions to walk these hallways.

Since the school year had commenced in August, Ashton Hale had been caught uploading porn onto the computers in the library (yes, a seven-year-old), lighting off fireworks in the parking lot, and driving more than one of his teachers to considering another line of work.

Andrew Hale, the father, was a pale, flabby exec from one of the Research Triangle Park companies, the kind of IT guy who'd been troubleshooting network systems since twenty years ago and had fallen ass-backward into a small fortune doing so. He barely met my eyes as he shuffled quickly past. What sounded like a smart comment came from behind the paper towels as his son rolled his eyes at me. It was a good thing I didn't understand the muffled words, because I was surely in a mood to respond to the little twerp. I made do with the mother, Jerri, a cosmetically perfected suburban prototype Alpha Mom who was clearly in a state of high agitation, and who sent her men on brusquely ahead of her. "You two wait in the car," she said, squaring her shoulders. "I want to have a word with Leigh . . . well, Nina. I'll catch up."

"Hello, Jerri."

Beasley was now leaning out of his office door, eyes skittish, obviously hoping there wouldn't be a repeat of what must have been quite a scene in his office. He looked like he'd just been ejected from a roller coaster. He started, "Mrs. Hale, I need to see Ms. Wren and then—"

"We'll be done in a moment." Jerri shifted her eyes back in his direction just long enough to flash-fry him.

He sighed and ducked back inside, leaving the office door open.

"The school nurse says my son may need stitches," Jerri announced, her lips thin, an expression that probably took about two seconds to cow her husband, but to which I was utterly immune.

"I'm sorry about that," I said, trying to maintain my composure and not slap her silly right there in the waiting room. I thought of how scared Hayden must have been, sitting in Beasley's office while this woman huffed and puffed. "I'm sure Hayden wouldn't have done anything unless he was protecting himself."

Her sudden laughter sounded more like a gag reflex. "The very idea. I've already spoken with my attorney, and if the school doesn't take appropriate action, well then he'll be contacting the administration promptly. Your son could have very seriously injured Ashton. I'm not kidding, Ms. . . ." She threw up her hands. "I don't even know what to call you! Perhaps you'd be better off finding Hayden another school until he can deal with all this . . . trauma he's being subjected to."

As though I was the one subjecting him to it.

"That's enough," I said, nearly whispering. I took a step forward, close enough that I could smell her perfume. Whew—some people would buy anything if it came packaged in a shapely, postmodern bottle. "I'm going to get my information about what happened from Mr. Beasley, who I'm assuming knows a good deal more about what went on between our boys than you do. If Hayden deserves to be punished, you can rest assured that I'll punish him. But you'd also best believe that if I find out Ashton was provoking him, you'll be the one hearing from a lawyer."

Her affronted laughter sounded much less natural this time, significantly more forced. I savored it. "You're a piece of work," was her final comment, and she left the school walking angrily on her tiptoes, like she had to flee quickly before she was levitated by the sheer force of her umbrage.

This was the manner in which twenty-first-century parents worked out fistfights between elementary school boys: by threatening lawsuits.

Beasley's interior office was cluttered with file cabinets and potted plants. Diplomas hung on the wall, along with a photo of Beasley as a football coach in one of his prior livelihoods. A woman I hadn't met before was sitting beside Hayden. He wouldn't even look up to meet my eye. I checked him for bruises and cuts, and didn't see anything obvious. The woman stood and extended her hand, introducing herself as Rachel Dutton. I shook it quickly and tried to evaluate her presence; a heavy woman in a pantsuit, it was difficult not to be disarmed by her; she put me almost immediately at ease, as though she were a defense attorney inclined to see my side of things—which I rightly guessed was her role here. She had striking almond eyes, iridescent green, and sharply intuitive. The way her short brown hair was cut to frame her face seemed designed to highlight her aura of intelligent calm.

I took her seat beside Hayden and lifted his chin with my hand. He stared at me defiantly. I said, "It's okay, buddy, I'm on your side," then looked up at the two adults. "Let's hear it."

Beasley fussed with a stack of papers on his desk, briefly and helplessly eye-fucked me, and then said, "Hayden's fourth-period teacher, Mr. Drake, said that some of the boys got into a shoving match while they were in the hall on their way to the computer lab. Apparently Hayden got the best of the ensuing fisticuffs. You saw what happened to Ashton. One of the other boys has a swollen ear from where Hayden hit him, but the school nurse says he'll be all right."

I put my arm around my son, and he squirmed, staring out the window past Beasley's shoulder. I asked him, "What did they say to you, honey?"

Rachel Dutton, leaning her substantial, comforting rear on Beasley's desk, cleared her throat and said, "Ms. Wren, we've had some talk going around lately about what the news has been saying concerning your family's history. I realize that none of this is your fault, or Hayden's, but people do run their mouths. Kids, especially. All the same,

Hayden needs to learn some restraint where hitting people is concerned."

"They were calling you names," Hayden said quietly, glancing up at me and then quickly back out the window. "They said you should be in jail with Dad. Ashton called you the b-word."

"Hayden, you just can't listen to people like him," I said. I faced Beasley and Dutton. "Why didn't the teacher do something to stop it before it escalated? Why isn't Ashton being punished?"

"Apparently, Mr. Drake wasn't aware of what was going on until the shoving actually started," Beasley answered. "Now, look, Ms. Wren, usually we'd just have the boys apologize to each other and shake hands. But given that Ashton did get his lip pretty well busted, I'm going to have to take some sort of punitive action."

I was shaking my head before he'd finished his sentence. "Oh, no, absolutely not. Not unless there's 'some sort of punitive action' taken against the Hale boy, too, and whoever else was verbally abusing my child. I know Hayden got his licks in but you can't seriously just let the others off scot-free, not after what they were saying."

"Well, it's his word against theirs, and there were several of them."

"What, more than two?"

Beasley sighed. "We think there might have been at least five boys involved in the altercation."

It was my turn to laugh ruefully. "Five kids ganged up on my son, and yet he's the one who's going to be punished?"

Beasley looked admiringly at Hayden for a moment. "Well, he was the one who came out unscathed."

Unscathed, I thought. I was about to blow my top, but Rachel Dutton smartly intervened.

"Ms. Wren, Thomas and I were discussing this before you arrived and I think we've come up with a workable solution. We suggest keeping Hayden after school for two weeks. It would officially be termed as an in-school suspension, but he wouldn't miss any of his lessons and he'd be staying in my classroom for the after-school portion of the day. He could use the time as a sort of study hall."

Beasley's gratitude was overt. "Rachel has experience working with troubled kids. She often keeps kids after hours . . ." He saw my face and quickly backtracked. "Not that we're saying Hayden is troubled. We just think he's acting out, and might benefit from a little extra attention right now."

"And it would keep Jerri Hale from calling in her lawyer."

He shrugged. "She wouldn't only be coming after us, Ms. Wren. I'd think the last thing you need right now is any kind of legalistic entanglement."

I wanted to lose it, right then and there. Just tear all the neatly stacked papers off Beasley's desk, kick over his file cabinets, break that coffee mug with its NC State logo over his bald, officious little head . . . Rachel Dutton saw what was welling up inside me as clearly as if I'd already risen from my seat, and her kind, understanding expression was almost more than I could handle. I swallowed and ran a hand over Hayden's hair. "How's that sound to you, Iron Mike? I could pick you up and you wouldn't have to ride the bus for a couple of weeks."

He shrugged miserably. "It won't stop them from saying bad things. Next time, they just won't let anyone hear them."

Beasley leaned across his desk. "Son, I

can promise you those boys won't be giving you any more hard times if I can help it. I'm going to have each of them in here, in this very office, and I'm going to have a serious talk with them about their own behavior. What we need is a commitment from you to tell one of the teachers next time, instead of resorting to blows. Okay?"

Hayden shrugged and I said, "Honey . . ."

He said, "Okay."

That pretty much settled it. A bell rang and the hallways filled with chatter as we went out the front doors. It was three o'clock and all the buses were lined up at the curb, idling and lacing the air with that smell that seemed like two parts exhaust, one part rust. When we were in my car, I told him, "You can't let them get to you. If you do, you'll have to be fighting all the time."

"I'm already going to have to be fighting all the time, Mom."

2.

By ten o'clock, when the evening news aired, I was so emotionally spent that I couldn't even work up much ire against Jennifer McLean.

Our interview was over before I really registered anything that I'd said, or how I'd come
across. And I didn't really give a shit; I simply
wanted all this to end, to go back to the
anonymous and tidy life I'd worked so hard to
put together in the years since Randy's trial. I
wanted Hayden to go back to making friends,
to believing his father was just some loser
who didn't deserve our time or thoughts.

Impossible. I knew it, but in a way I was
glad to be out from behind the lies; at least I
would no longer live in dread of the day Hayden found out the truth. It had come and
gone, and the consequences were what I
had to deal with now.

Carolyn Rowe called just as the news was
going off. "Wasn't as bad as you thought it
would be, was it?" she said with a forced
perkiness that didn't fit her in the least.

"The Dockery question came across like
she wanted it to. She made it sound as if I'd
had something to do with his disappearance. I looked guilty."

"But you're not. You actually looked like a
decent person who just wants her life back.
More people than you think will identify with
that."

"I guess a private investigator would know more about that than most."

She laughed. "Which brings me to the reason for my call. I'm heading out of town for a few days, to chase down a couple of loose threads. I should be back by the first of next week, though, and we'll want to get together if that's okay. Maybe you and Hayden should get out of town, too, go rent a place at the beach or something. There shouldn't be anyone down there this time of year."

And it sounded nice, so I told her I'd think about it. After we hung up, though, I thought of the miles of empty, bleached sand, the steely look of the ocean under winter skies. If desolation was what I wanted, I could stay right here and save myself a hotel bill. Outside my bedroom window was an endless array of architecture repeated, kit houses for kit people, whose judgments after seeing my interview on TV would be as rote as their kitchen color schemes.

CHAPTER TWELVE

I think we've found a few things that might help get Pritchett off your case," Duane said.

We were sitting by the window in a Champs restaurant, looking out at the open-air promenade that ran down the center of Southpoint Mall. The crowds were light in the early weekday afternoon, mostly salespeople seated in the courtyards smoking or talking on their cell phones. A jogger bopped by, thumbing his iPod. The Rowes had come to my house, taken one look at me, and told me quite soberly that I needed to get out for some fresh air. Not only had I not gone to the beach over the weekend, I'd stayed locked

down at the house, watching children's films
on DVD with my son. Neither of us had
talked all that much and I kept telling myself
it hadn't been dismal, but I'd been ready for
him to go back to school on Monday.

And then, damnedest thing; as soon as
he left on the bus, I missed him.

Carolyn Rowe looked as poorly as I felt.
She had dark patches around her eyes and
her mouth was drawn. Her bleached blond
hair was tied up in a haphazard knot at the
back of her head, loose brittle strands sprung
loose at every angle; she seemed worn and
harried. For the first time I thought she
looked older than I did.

I unfolded one of the heavy napkins and
took out the utensils, then started refolding
it. They were both watching me. "Okay," I
asked. "What do you have on him?"

Duane was pleased. "Atta girl," he said.
He pulled a laptop out of the shoulder-slung
bag he'd brought along, and powered it up.
The waiter came and took our orders. Duane tapped on some keys and turned the
computer so I could see the screen. He
scrolled past a booking photo of some hulk-
ing man with a shorn skull, who had one of
those faces that seemed crammed into the

comparatively narrow space between a cleft chin and a rippled forehead. The man was glaring into the lens. Following that was a load of data written onto standardized templates, several pages worth.

Carolyn smiled at me and said, "Ever seen a rap sheet before?"

I shook my head.

"That's actually just a summary. His actual sheet would take an hour to upload."

Duane left the forms showing on-screen and clicked on another window. This one was a document, verbiage only, again several pages in length. Duane scrolled past information until I saw Randy's name. At the bottom of this page was a date—this past Saturday's—and two more names. One was Carolyn's.

"Who's Alfred Odom?" I asked, squinting to make it out. I looked up at Carolyn. "Where have you been, anyway?"

"San Quentin. Al Odom is the man whose rap sheet summary you just saw. He's on Death Row for the murder of a department store security guard nine years ago, and I've interviewed him twice during the past few days. He acted as the middleman who passed along Charles Pritchett's hit money.

Odom paid another prisoner named Lars Lindholm to try and kill Randy in prison."

"Oh." I barely remembered Lindholm's name, although I should have; he was Randy's thirteenth victim, the man who'd died attempting to murder him. It hadn't received much press at the time, beyond what I'd seen on a nightly news summary, the impetus behind that unfortunate lie I'd told my son. "Did you see Randy while you were there?"

"I requested a meeting but he declined." Carolyn watched my face carefully. "I know I should've asked you beforehand but I didn't want you stressing on it. Anyway, there wasn't much I could do after he refused to meet with me. I have no proof of his being involved in any new crimes, so there's no legitimate investigation I could claim to be a part of. I'd have thought he'd like the company—he's been on Death Row for, what? Six years? Those guys are separate from the general population so they don't get much socializing time. Still, he might've heard through the grapevine that I'd been talking to Odom. News travels fast in lockup."

I stared out the window. A security guard lazed against the wall of the Barnes & Noble, tracking a tall, lithe salesgirl as she strolled past. "Aren't you scared, going into a place like that?" I asked Carolyn. "Aren't you scared for her?" I asked Duane.

"Terrified," she answered.

"Which is the only reason I let her go," Duane said. "She's got the sense to be wary. Al Odom wasn't directly paid off by Pritchett, but he's the one who gave Lindholm his assignment. Lindholm was awaiting execution for strangling two teenaged girls, so I guess Randy inadvertently did one good deed in his life. The original payment passed through another man—a prison guard—before getting to Odom. Odom is willing to go on record, basically because he thinks he can get the guard in trouble. Apparently there's been a falling out of some sort."

Carolyn picked it up. "Everyone took a third of the payment apiece, except Lindholm didn't know that. He thought he was getting over fifty percent. Typical jailhouse accounting. I didn't approach the guard and I don't think we'll have to. I think if we tell Pritchett we know this much, he'll back off."

"What if this Odom guy just made it up?" I asked.

Duane shrugged. "Still, I'm pretty sure it would give us enough leverage. It would taint his cause in the public's eye, either way. And although I can't quite prove this, either, I think he used his company's own cash to finance the whole thing. The exact amount that Odom named as the payoff was listed in Pritchett's books for that quarter as having been spent on some mobile freezers that turned out not to function at all. Believe me, it was a fairly substantial write-off."

"All this information in five days?" I said.

Carolyn shrugged, mock sheepish. "We're very good."

Duane frowned. "None of it would stand up in court. We wouldn't want things to get anywhere near that point, if you know what I'm saying."

I knew. There had been some surreptitious hacking on Duane's part, and God only knew what kind of story Carolyn had told to get access to the tiers at a maximum security prison. I asked her and she said she'd played it straight the whole way; the warden had been the one to point the way to Odom. He'd suspected the con's involvement in Randy's attempted murder, but had never been able to prove it.

"And he's had plenty of problems with Randy—fights with other inmates and guards, repeated trips to solitary confinement. He also mentioned something else I thought you should know about." She raised her eyebrows at Duane and he nodded for her to continue. "The warden has suspicions that Randy is carrying on some sort of illegitimate relationship with someone outside the prison; all his mail, except his exchanges with legal representatives, is read, and apparently some of the content is rather disturbing. The warden wouldn't show me any of the letters, he said they'd need a warrant in order to hold them back or make copies, but the content he described is striking, especially with regard to Pritchett and Lane Dockery. The name on the letters is 'CB Taylor.' Ring a bell?"

I shrugged. "No."

"The address is a PO Box. We can't investigate the identity of the person Randy has been communicating with, because that would require a warrant as well, and as yet there's no proof that any crime has been committed. But apparently the letters include references to 'the caterer's house,' and 'the writer's house.' That's what tipped the warden that there might be some issue of concern, particularly after the attempt on Randy's life."

They both watched my face while I considered it. "So Randy bears a grudge against Pritchett and Dockery. Considering that one tried to have him killed and the other tried to exploit him, that's no real surprise. Randy is what you'd call the vindictive sort." I tried to laugh but it came out sounding choked and strained.

Duane asked, "And you have no idea who he might be in contact with?"

I shook my head. "I can't even begin to imagine. There are plenty of sickos out there who get fascinated with people like Randy. I mean, aren't there women who seek out imprisoned killers for relationships, things like that?"

Carolyn nodded hesitantly. "That's not nearly as widespread as you might have heard. This is an angle we need to be thinking about, though. I hate to think Randy's got an outside actor working on his behalf."

"I can't think of anyone I know who would want that task," I answered. Although, given my own experiences with Pritchett and Dockery, the vindictive part of *me* wished that actor success.

She'd promised to share whatever information she uncovered with the warden as soon as her client approved. "If that's cool with you," she finished.

I nodded absently, trying to get my bearings. "So Pritchett spent all this money to have Randy killed and he failed. And then the old bastard came after me instead?"

"It wasn't just the money," Duane said. "Odom thinks the old guy was actively trying to recruit someone to do the deed for years. Rumors had gone around among the prisoners that a contract was being offered, but unless someone's got some measure of reliability or trust with the inmate population, no one's going to take them up on it. Too big a chance that it's a setup. We think there were several 'goodwill' gestures during the courtship, including a new motorcycle for the guard and some compensated legal work for Odom. It wasn't easy. But to answer your question: yes. It was after the failed attempt on Randy's life that Pritchett contacted my friends' firm and began trying in earnest to locate you."

The food arrived and the Rowes started in as though they were famished. I picked at my salad and felt queasy. Two years he'd been stalking me. Frustrated at his original goal, he'd taken it upon himself to frustrate all of mine.

Carolyn covered her mouth and belched into her palm, then shrugged girlishly. The color was coming back into her cheeks, and I realized that this was a woman in her element. She'd told me that she'd been a reporter in her prior vocation, and I guessed she'd likely been a fearsome one.

"I spent some time with the extended Pritchett clan while I was out there," she said now. "Not many of the people in the immediate circle are too fond of Sir Charles, and they aren't shy about sharing with strangers. New money, a couple of bad marriages tied into the family tree, is the vibe I got. There was apparently an established history of serious personality conflicts between Dad and Carrie. They got into a big fight the night before the murder. An ex-brother-in-law told me that his ex-wife said Charles had gone to confront his daughter about her lifestyle. She was enrolled in her fourth college in as many years, she kept flunking out and reenrolling the next tier down. Her record shows two arrests for misdemeanor possession. So Dad confronts her, tells Carrie she'd better get it together or he's going to cut her off financially. Most of the family members agreed that she was a little too 'carefree,' as one of them phrased it, to pay her own way. It was a big fight, Dad thinking he's just being stern, but Carrie thinking she's being disowned. Her friends said she was upset, crying, when Pritchett left the apartment." Carolyn paused, seemed to remember we were talking about a young woman. "Next time he saw her, Randy had been there first."

Everyone was silent for a moment. Duane softly said, "I got in touch with Lane Dockery's publisher and agent, trying to confirm if he'd been working on a book about Randy at the time of his disappearance. They weren't willing to give me anything. I think they thought I was working for another publisher. But I did get in touch with his sister, Jeanine, who's pretty much been losing her mind since her brother disappeared. She's sure he's dead, and she's sure there was foul play involved. It isn't in his nature to be out of contact for so long, is what she told me. She's going through the things in his office, claims she knows his system. She's going to get in touch if she finds anything."

I only halfway heard him. I was thinking about Randy. Sometimes I wondered at how long it was taking for them to kill him. I wanted him dead, and judged, and condemned to an afterlife where his soul would remain intact, hyper-sensitive and hyperaware, while his victims shredded his mind and turned him inside out over and over while he watched, helpless, not allowed to disassociate himself from it. Sentient, with no hopes for respite or redress, while they took their vengeance over and over again.

I wished it; in my heart, I demanded it. I supposed it was a sin to pray for it, but all the same I most fervently prayed that there was justice in another world. What little there was in this life seemed arbitrarily distributed, parsed out meanly and without apparent regard to who deserved what.

"It sounds to me like Pritchett doesn't believe in God," I said quietly, after the waiter had cleared our plates. "He has to take justice upon himself."

"He has the means," Duane said. "Most victims would do the same, if they could."

"None of the rest of them did," I said. "They all did the best they could to move on. I have some familiarity with denial, guys. What this whole vendetta means is that Pritchett is already doomed." I saw their eyes and said quickly, "Let me explain. In the years between Randy's being caught and now, I've tried to move on and build something apart from him, apart from what he did and whatever culpability I share in it. I haven't succeeded completely, but my son still has a chance to. I believe the effort is worth it. With Pritchett, what he's doing shows that he's never got clear of it, never got free, never let it out of his head. Imagine how exhausting that must be. You couldn't help but go crazy after a while. I can't do him any more harm."

Duane was adamant. "His type won't go crazy, Nina. His type *thrives* on it. Didn't you hear any of what his own family said about him? The guy was a prick before he ever became a victim. He wouldn't know what to do without an enemy to focus on."

I thought about correcting Duane, asking him to call me Leigh, but what was the point? I'd already been exposed in the papers; I'd been found out. *Free to be myself again,* I thought snidely.

"You're a decent person," Carolyn said. "But he means to ruin your life."

"I'm the only one who could do that."

They looked at each other and sighed. Duane closed his laptop.

I apologized. I thanked them. I bought their lunch.

CHAPTER THIRTEEN

1.

The date was August 14, 2000. It was a Saturday. Sometime between nine o'clock in the morning and one in the afternoon, under cover of the powerful thunderstorms that had been rolling across the valley since the night before, a sixteen-year-old girl named Daphne Snyder was killed in a public park less than five miles from our home. Daphne had been a week away from starting her senior year of high school. She was a nascent graphic artist, and had designed the cover of her class yearbook. She'd dated the same guy since she was a sophomore, and had

plans to join him at UCLA the following year.
Her eyes in the newspapers were cobalt
blue. The body wouldn't be discovered until
late afternoon, dumped in the public restroom at the park. It was one of those squat,
utilitarian little concrete buildings, with forest
green tiles on the roof and little wood-burned
signs for the Men's and Women's sides.
Daphne was found by some younger teens
who'd gone there to smoke.

The park was just off a main artery, the
same road Randy took to work and I took to
run my errands each and every day. Multi-
tudes of cars had passed the spot during that
Saturday, so many possible witnesses, none
of whom had seen a thing.

2.

Randy had been antsy and distracted pretty
much the entire time since Hayden's birth,
six months earlier. Now, he was the one driving me crazy. Half the time my husband was
spastic, drumming his fingers constantly on
any surface and twisting his hair and nibbling
at his nails; the other half he was uncommu-

nicative and withdrawn. I could barely rouse him to monosyllables. I told myself that he was manifesting an adjustment reaction, overwhelmed by the reality of fatherhood and the new demands on his time and attention. Of course, the truth was that he'd shown little to no inclination to actually help out with feeding, rocking, changing, or cleaning our newborn son. Except for the first three weeks, when my mother was there to help out, I'd pretty much done it all.

At this point, I knew for sure that it wasn't hormones that had been distracting me during the pregnancy. I knew it wasn't postpartum depression keeping me so vigilant around Hayden that I didn't really trust Randy to take care of him, even if he'd shown a desire. I kept envisioning him holding the baby when I just happened to do or say something that frustrated him. I saw him turning and slamming Hayden's soft little skull into the nearest sharp corner. It was absurd, but I couldn't get the idea out of my head.

In reality, I had felt something inside me going hard and unyielding the very first time Randy cradled the baby in his arms, right there in the delivery room. Three weeks later, after my mother flew home, I realized that I was frightened to be alone with my own husband. He'd avoided us during much of the time Mom was there. She'd made comment after comment, a running inventory of disapproval: *Why doesn't he hold the baby more often? Why does he act like he's pissed off all the time? It's like he can hardly stand to touch his own child.* My excuses to Mom became excuses to myself.

Then, the first night after she'd left, I awoke from a late-afternoon nap to find Randy sitting across the bedroom, holding Hayden and looking at me with an expression that was almost menacing, a hungry sort of frown that sent the cold right through me. My eyelids were still heavy and he hadn't yet realized that I was coming awake, and I saw him whispering to Hayden but couldn't understand the words he was saying. I only saw that look on his face, a sense of utter propriety more greedy than proud, more martial than paternal. Hayden seemed far too small, and Randy's forearms were too large and steely, incapable of holding such a tender thing without crushing him. I feigned waking up, yawning and stretching. Randy quickly rearranged his face; I rearranged mine to match.

3.

On the morning of August 14, he left the house at dawn, without taking a shower. He never went anywhere without a shower. I could tell from the twisted sheets on his side that he'd barely slept. He said he was going to run some errands, but he was out the door before I could think to ask where he would be. I had a throbbing headache, and felt like I'd slept too deeply. My thinking was scrambled, and I didn't really start questioning how suddenly he'd taken off until after I'd had a shower and a second cup of coffee. I fed Hayden and laid him down for a nap in his crib. I made sure the baby monitor was in my pocket when I went downstairs.

Before placing the water glass from my bedside table in the dishwasher, I found myself examining it closely, holding it up to the light, turning it this way and that. Randy had brought it up for me the night before. I realized I was looking for residue and thought: *Residue of what? Would you know if you saw it? Do you really think your husband is trying to poison you? And if so, if you're really entertaining such squalid fantasies, don't you think it's time to consult a mental health professional?*

Randy returned in the early afternoon, not too long past lunchtime. I'd made a couple of grilled tuna sandwiches and was about to suggest that he grab one from the serving board when I noticed his appearance. He was wearing his dark blue hooded rain jacket, but his clothes were wet all the way underneath, clear water dripping onto the foyer floor. His boots squeaked as he walked right past me and headed up the stairs without so much as a word.

"You're getting mud everywhere!" I yelled. I could hear the shrillness in my voice, but didn't care. I'd become something of a shrew over the past five months; it was my only defense to his nervous indifference.

No response. I heard a door slam, then the shower running. I held my hands up in exasperation, remembered I was alone, and dropped them trembling back to my sides. I went to the foot of the stairs to inspect the mess, and damned if it wasn't worse than I'd thought. Clumps of wet grass, stray slick blades, and clumps of filth were stamped all the way up to the second floor. "Randy, damn it!"

I went up the stairs in a raging fury, pausing only long enough to glance into Hayden's nursery—he was awake but quiet, ogling the spaceship mobile that spun in the air over his crib—before following the muddy footprints into our bedroom. The bathroom door was shut, the shower going full blast. I knew I'd be in for it when I opened that door, because Randy's insults were at their most lacerating when you intruded on his "personal space," but it was obvious that I'd have to spend hours cleaning the carpets and I wasn't really thinking clearly.

The bathroom was a wall of steam. His clothes were in a filthy pile on the floor, and as I stood there, him yelling at me from behind the shower curtain to get out—"I'll be done in a minute!"—I took in the condition of his outfit. It wasn't just mud that had soiled the clothes. That was blood, I recognized it, large discolored patches on his jeans and the shirt he'd been wearing. I picked up the shirt, fascinated, all my choice irate advice on his cleanliness dying in my throat. The shirt had been a sky blue button-down, light cotton, now streaked with mud and spatters of crimson, all of it mixing together from the dampness. I could smell it, that rank copper odor.

He flung the shower curtain open and snatched a towel off the rack. I stepped backward holding his shirt; when I realized I still had it in my hands, I dropped it quickly to the floor. Steam flooded out past me as I stood in the bathroom doorway. Randy was toweling himself furiously, and I saw that the towel itself was turning red now. He was bleeding from a long gash in his right cheek, and another along his left arm. He pressed the towel over his cheek and said in a low voice, "Get out. I'll tell you all about it in a minute, if you'll allow me five fucking seconds to get fucking dry first."

I backed out and he pushed the door shut behind me. I went numbly down the hall and stood over Hayden's crib, cooing to him mindlessly, blocking out every racing thought in my head. I told myself I was so scared because I was concerned about Randy's welfare. I told myself I was worried that he'd been seriously hurt.

I got into a shoving match with some asshole at Home Depot," he said, standing in

the hallway. I didn't know how much time had
elapsed. He was dressed in shorts and a
T-shirt, pressing a wad of tissues over his
wounded arm. I closed the nursery door behind me and pointed downstairs. Randy
went ahead, and asked me to bring some
bandages from the hall closet.

While I wrapped his arm in pads and
gauze, he told me about how the jack-offs
down at HD had let their inventory slide and
so they only had a couple of bags of mulch left
(apparently he'd gone out early in the pouring
rain without a shower to get . . . mulch), and
how this other asshole ("He looked like one of
those Volvo-driving cock-smokers, you know
the type.") had challenged Randy's right to the
remaining supply. They'd exchanged words
and things had escalated. "We got into it right
there in the Lawn and Garden Center," Randy
said, wincing when I patted his cheek with a
swab soaked in rubbing alcohol. "It's probably
a good thing the salesmen said they were
calling the cops, or I'd have really let him have
it. As it was, I think I might've broken his nose."

I opened a couple of Band-Aids. "This
might actually need stitches." The wound
in his cheek was so deep it wouldn't stop
bleeding, and it made me woozy to look at

it. I swallowed and held out the bandages. "Put them on yourself. If you can't handle your anger any better than that, maybe you need to—"

"What?" His voice had gone cold now as he plucked the bandages lightly from my fingers. "I need to what?"

"I think you need to see somebody, get some counseling maybe."

He grunted and went and stood in front of the mirror in the front hallway, sloppily pasting the bandages over the gash. "You are so predictable," he began, each word thick with resentment. "I get into a fight that some other asshole started, a fight where I was only defending myself, and you automatically assume the whole thing was my fault. I'm not going to let any jerk-offs push me around in the store, and I'm not going to let you talk down to me at home."

I tried to keep my words steady. "Randy, we have a child now. What if the police show up? What if the people at Home Depot got your license plate and they follow you here? What if they charge you with assault?"

"But I didn't start it!"

"The police don't always care about that.

What if you got taken in and then it got back to the HR people at work? And what if they decided that when the next round of layoffs came around and they were looking to trim the fat, that they could use any old excuse anyone had given them? Don't you think they'd come after you first? Without me bringing in any income, and with the house and the baby, we can't afford for you to be out of work or in any legal difficulty right now. That's all I'm saying." It fleetingly occurred to me how stupid this argument was, given that I knew his story about the altercation at HD was bullshit.

But if I didn't keep talking, I might start thinking.

He glared at me and then took a deep breath. "You are un-fucking-believable. I'm going outside."

He slammed the back door. I went and stood in the kitchen, watching out the window as he stalked out to his shed. The rain had abated somewhat but he still got wet all over again as he stood there, fumbling with his keys. Finally he got them out and opened the padlock while the silver drops fell past him. He looked back at the house and although I couldn't see his eyes under his pasted bangs,

I felt him marking me. He disappeared into the shed.

After a few minutes, I went back upstairs to the nursery. It seemed like I stayed there for hours, caressing Hayden's cheek, smoothing his down-fine hair, seeing his father's eyes looking up at me.

4.

Randy didn't return until it was nearly dark. We sat silently in the den, both of us mechanically eating a frozen pizza I'd made. I told him I wanted to watch the ten o'clock news to find out if the weather would clear; if so, I was thinking of taking Hayden out to the park in the morning, to get some fresh air. Randy started in right off, arguing that he wanted to watch a baseball game. He'd never shown any interest in the sport before. I thought he was being obstinate, punishing me for my inquisitiveness or judgmentalism or whatever overbearing trait he thought I'd exhibited earlier while I was cleaning his wounds. Knowing I couldn't handle another argument, I just took my plate and went upstairs and turned on the TV in our bedroom.

The lead story on all the local news channels was the brutal slaying of an area high
school student, Daphne Snyder. The police
weren't releasing many details as yet, but I
recognized the park in the footage—it was
where I'd been thinking of taking Hayden in
the morning. The cameras panned past the
swing sets and the jungle gym and the
benches by the softball fields. Reporters
stood and pointed behind them at that ugly
gray block building where the girl's body had
been found. I'd utilized that very restroom before, and I saw it now in my mind, the grungy
tiles and the skylights so filthy that you felt
like you were underwater as you held yourself up off the seat. What a lonely place to
die. I stared as the TV displayed a photo from
Daphne's yearbook, taken at her junior prom
last spring, while the anchor read off more
details of her short life. She'd been a pretty
girl, her brown hair coiffed and shellacked for
the big night but you could tell it would look
just as fine wound up in a natural ponytail. An
outdoor type of face with a kind, sad smile,
like she knew something was looming on her
horizon. Or maybe her date had just been
drunk and acting stupid. I would never know.

An uncle spoke with reporters from the

front porch of the family's home, saying that the girl's parents were in no condition to take questions, although they appreciated everyone's thoughts and prayers. An edge of hostility flashed in the man's voice when someone asked him what should be done to the guy who did it, if he were caught. The uncle declined to go into details, "Because I'm a Christian, but God will have His judgment on this monster." His voice cracked and the channel I was watching switched over to an impromptu news conference at the police station. The officer conducting the Q&A session deflected an inquiry into whether the killing might be related to any others. "We have a similar MO to some recent crimes, but really that's all I can tell you right now."

When I looked away from the TV, Randy was standing in our bedroom doorway, arms folded, watching. I jumped a little and he turned to me with an understanding smile. His look held more actual emotion than it had in a long, long time. He spoke with patience and kindness. "So, did they say if it's going to rain? Because I was thinking I could take Hayden out, if you want. I've been kind of slack, and I think maybe you could use some time on your own."

"No, that's all right. You should go see the doctor—"

But he kept right on talking, like I hadn't spoken up at all. Maybe he was so used to that that he didn't even notice it when I did. "Yeah, I'll take him first thing in the morning, and you can sleep in. We'll be back in the afternoon, and you and I can talk then. Right now, let's get some sleep."

He might've slept. At first, I know I didn't. Once Randy's breathing seemed to become regular, I got up and went to Hayden's room, thinking only of getting him out to the car and then driving as far away as possible, as quickly as possible, before I called the police. But when I got my son scooped up into my arms, Randy was right there in the hall, blocking my way. He said, "I can't sleep, so I'm going downstairs to watch some DVDs. You want to come?"

I shook my head. I went back to the bedroom with Hayden in my arms and sat there in bed trembling. When Randy came up with a glass of water for me, he stood and watched until I drank it all down. I didn't know what else to do. I kept looking at those big arms, the ropy veins on the backs of his hands . . . I drank, and before long, I was asleep. The last thing I felt was how weak my own arms had become, and how I couldn't hold on at all when Randy pried Hayden gently from my grasp.

CHAPTER FOURTEEN

1.

I came awake suddenly, to full daylight. It was the next morning, the first day Daphne Snyder's family would awake to the realization that she was gone forever from their lives. Sitting bolt upright in the bed, gasping, my head thudded with a dense pain ten times more leaden than the worst hangover I could remember. The flood of ambient light through the curtains was so sharp I could barely see. Such utter silence, the house felt abandoned.

"Oh, no," I moaned, pushing my legs off the edge of the bed. I had to use the wall to hold myself up as I staggered down the hall to the nursery. Empty.

Downstairs, I was so dizzy and nauseous that I barely made it to the sink before I threw up. I didn't know what Randy had given me, but it was more powerful than the average sedative. Puking helped clear my mind, even though it didn't sharpen my blurry vision; the edges of every object shimmered like sunlight on ice. Once I wiped the tears out of my eyes, I saw the note sitting on the chopping block, and what he'd used for a paperweight.

Hon, he'd addressed it. *Gone to take Hayden out for some fresh air and attend to some business. Be home later this afternoon. Call me if you want to talk before then. Love, Randy.*

And, placed atop the note, the key to his shed.

Not that it was labeled as such, and I don't know if I could've picked it out of all the others on his key ring. But there, sitting where it was, I had no doubts.

I almost called the cops right then. I should have. I should have called them the day before, as soon as he'd dragged himself up the stairs, bloodied and soaked. When the operator or dispatcher (or whatever those people were called) answered, I could have said: "I don't know if this will mean anything to you, say for example in the case that a girl was recently killed near my house, but . . ."

Technically, I wouldn't even have had to call 911, because we knew a cop: Todd Cline. He still lived in our old neighborhood; he'd been the one to drop all the disturbing hints about the Renault family after their murder a few years ago. Even though we'd moved, we still went to the same church—albeit much less frequently—where we often ran into Todd and his family. Todd Cline, with his requisite cop mustache and barrel chest and his soft-spoken manners. Todd Cline who'd told us that Trudi and Dominique Renault had suffered greatly at the hands of their killer, that he'd done some unspeakable thing to their eyes . . . The Renaults. Oh, God, Randy, no. I couldn't have called the cops after I saw the news last night; he was hovering like a bodyguard by then. He'd have surely intervened if he found me leafing frantically through the church directory for Todd Cline's phone number. But I could've fought, I could've not drank from the cup he proffered, I could have stabbed him with a kitchen knife and taken my son and driven all the way back home to Oregon . . .

Too late now. I picked up the key and promptly dropped it again; my fingertips were numb. More lingering effects from—*say it, you know it now, you* know—whatever drug my husband had given me. The sound of it crashing to the countertop was disproportionately huge in our empty house, and adrenaline sent an icy aftershock through me. I grabbed the key and held it in my fist and read the note again. I opened my palm. I realized, with my stomach twisting anew, that for the first time in years, my husband was trying to talk to me. He was trying to have a meaningful conversation.

2.

The backyard was still damp from yesterday's storms, but the sky was clear and the lawn sparkled, a field of diamonds in the morning light. Birds clustered around the feeder, flying off and realighting in tight orbits as I walked past them from the house to the shed. The whole world felt as numb as my

tingling extremities. It took only about twenty
steps to reach the shed, and I wondered at
the gulf that I'd always sensed yawning between the two structures. Randy's world,
and the world we shared. Now he was finally
going to open up to me.

It was your basic ten-by-ten storage building, erected by a couple of kids the hard-
ware store had sent over, hauling the entire
kit in their flatbed. Just lumber and siding
and two small windows on either end, the
glass papered over from inside. In all the
time we'd lived in our new house, I'd never
once set foot in there. I'd respected his pri-
vacy, his need to have his alone time. He'd
often reminded me of how essential it was
for his peace of mind. I put the key to the
padlock and hoped in that last moment that
maybe I was wrong, maybe it was simply a
spare from work that he'd used to hold down
his note, maybe he'd really suddenly developed an interest in being alone with our
son, maybe—but it slid right in, seemingly
frictionless. I left the padlock lying in the
grass, then turned the knob and the door
opened.

Inside it was dark. Daylight barely pene-
trated the shingle paper he'd stapled over

the windows, and I had to fumble for the switch. An overhead light came on, a naked bulb that flooded the space with a yellowish blur that somehow still left room for shadows. It smelled strange in there, but I couldn't place the odor right off. Something medicinal, chemical . . . The light didn't make the room feel any less claustrophobic. A single rolling chair on castors sat in the middle of the plywood planks that made up the flooring. I moved it to one side so I could get around. I left the door wide open behind me, and kept checking it, half dreading that Randy would come racing out the back door of our house, waving a knife and howling about Bluebeard's wife.

Nothing here was outwardly disturbing. Two big sets of shelves and drawers, blond unfinished wood with brass handles, were lined up against either wall, and then there was a full-sized closet or cabinet at the very back. Some sort of picture or drawing was tacked onto the double doors back there, but I ignored it for the moment, frightened of trying to take in too much at once. I opened the first drawer on my left-hand side, and my breath stalled in my throat. The drawer was full of ammunition, boxes upon boxes, several different caliber bullets. I picked one up and read: REMINGTON .357 HOLLOW POINT/50 COUNT. In the next drawer down were the guns themselves, six altogether, all of them holstered in leather. I didn't recognize the caliber or the brands, only the ugly black look of them. Randy had told me he went shooting once in a while with some people from work. He'd never told me he owned a gun. The next drawer contained knives, again sheathed in leather slips so polished and oiled they felt supple to the touch. I pulled a few of them out. Randy was into variety: there was one with a long serrated blade; another that was shorter and hooked at the end; still another that was notched on one side and flat on the other, sharp enough that when I laid it down gently onto the countertop, it cut into the wood. I put the knives back where I'd found them. In other drawers were other tools I didn't recognize: something like a suction cup and another silvery utensil that looked like it belonged on a surgeon's tray; rolls of duct tape; a handheld component that featured a small screen and a GPS logo; a box of rubber gloves and a hairnet; and coils of thick rope, tightly wound, and set out in symmetrical stacks.

The nausea was back. I kept glancing behind me out that open door, which seemed
miles away even though it was only a few
feet.

On the other side of the room, the first
drawer I opened revealed documents, all
neatly sorted in laminated slipcovers. I picked
up a Wisconsin driver's license with Randy's
face on it. His name was shown as Gerald
Hamby. Another ID, this one from Delaware,
was for Wilson Hamby. I dug through and
kept coming up with more: passports, bank
cards, credit cards, all in fake names. I wondered if the bank cards were valid, if there
was a monetary balance on the other end of
them. (It was revealed at trial that he had
several thousand in each account.) Randy
had always been assiduous when it came to
savings, so he probably had money to
spare. I was starting to understand why he'd
never let me in on the family finances. All his
macho crap about it being the "man's responsibility" was exactly that, but I'd never
really fought him on it. I'd always been a little
thankful I didn't have to deal with that aspect
of our lives.

Then I saw a folder with my initials on it. I
opened it and more cards slid out into the

drawer. Staring back at me from another
Delaware ID was my own face, the same
photo that appeared on my California driver's license, except Randy had renamed me
Debra Hamby. I riffled through the remaining
cards and documents until they were all
spread out on the countertop.

Inventory: five different ID cards for him,
three for me. We were the Hambys or the
Johnsons. I was Debra or Darlene. A pass-
port was made out for Darlene Johnson, the
same photo as on the other documents. I
swallowed and thought quite clearly, like a
voice was speaking aloud inside my head:
*He thinks you're going to be cool with this.
He thinks you'll go along with it. He may
think you already suspected.* My immediate
reaction, one that was purely defensive,
simply to keep me from tearing my hair out,
was to get furiously pissed. The sonofabitch
had actually convinced himself that I would
go along with whatever secret life he'd been
leading, as though it were something everyone did, some pedestrian little indiscretion
like our neighbors' indulgences, Felicity Con-
rad's fondness for Percocets or Dan Young-
blood's affair. Everyone knew these tidbits, all
the neighborhood women dished on them

whenever Felicity or Dan weren't physically present. Such missteps were accepted as the natural price for a life of entitlement, a calm serene surface with sharks trolling underneath. Sharks, our neighbors could assimilate.

But when I began to understand that Randy thought so little of me, saw me as no more than a mousy enabler who'd be just fine with it all once he'd invited me into his confidence, it was like being slapped in the mouth. Perhaps he thought that with a bit of patience and explication, I could be made to see that the situation wasn't so perverse after all, not so horrifying as I'd imagined . . .

And what, exactly, was so wretched about it? I still didn't know anything other than that my husband was a gun nut with a whole batch of fraudulent documents stashed out behind the house. I had seen evidence of nothing more.

I put the documents back in the drawer, arranging them as closely as I could recall to how I'd found them. There was still that big, wall-length cabinet at the back of the shed. As I got closer, the drawing tacked onto the double doors of the cabinet resolved into clarity, and my breath locked up again. It was one of Randy's sketches, much like the one he'd made of me when we were first dating, a thousand years ago: rudimentary and crude, pencil-drawn and shaded. But this one was of a boy who looked to be in his early-to-mid teens. The kid had a lifeless bowl of hair that lent him a mannequinlike aspect, something fake and contrived, a frowning mouth with thin lips, chubby cheeks, and a furrowed brow, as though his image had been captured at a moment of confused self-reflection. And then there were the eyes, somewhat averted from the viewer, creased with what might've been either anticipation or some secret but corrupt delight. Without coloration, there was no way to distinguish them from any other pair of eyes, except in that malefic expression. I didn't recognize anything about the boy at all, but then I started thinking about it and the answer came even as I resisted its implications. I'd seen eyes bearing that sort of gaze before; in fact, I'd seen them on my husband only yesterday. This was *his* secret look, *his* ponderous mischief, *his* projection, himself as a younger man. Then I suspected even worse: maybe I was wrong, and maybe this was what he wanted *Hayden* to look like someday. Perhaps this was our son, an unhappy future vision of him trapped in his own father's darkest shadow.

I opened the double doors slowly, pulling them out toward me, and everything went kind of sideways.

3.

An hour later, I stood pacing in the yard, muttering to myself for the pure noise of it, essentially to keep from going insane. When Todd Cline, the policeman and our old neighbor, stepped out of the shed after being inside for only a few minutes, he said, "I need to call for backup, and I need to get a warrant."

"You can't," I said. "You know he's got Hayden. You promised."

He attempted a gentle smile, but he was pale underneath. The veteran cop, shaken. "I was humoring you until I could find out what you were talking about. Really, Nina, this is something we need to handle, right now."

I barely remembered coming out of the shed after looking into Randy's cabinet, at first stumbling and then running across the backyard to the house. I was able to call up vague images of myself flipping through the church directory until I found his number. What had I said to him? That, I couldn't really remember, only how relieved I'd been that he was home. It seemed as though he'd said something about how the family usually went out for Sunday lunch, but they'd skipped it today because one of his daughters had a stomachache.

The wait between the time I hung up and the time he arrived was crystal clear in my memory. It was the worst twenty minutes of my life, up until that point.

Cline pondered a moment and continued. "Nina, I don't know what to tell you. We'll do everything in our power to ensure Hayden's safety, but first of all we need to locate Randy and get as many men on him as we can. Can you call him, see where he is?"

"I can call, but we won't know if he's telling the truth. He could be watching us right now, for all I know."

"The thought had crossed my mind," Cline admitted. He took my elbow and steered me back to the house, leaving the shed door hanging open. "Listen, I really need to call this in, though. I'll explain the situation to my

boss and we'll get some other people involved."

So I stood there, feeling like I was going
to collapse, literally, like every connective
tissue in my body would spring free of its
moorings and I'd be reduced to a pile of
quivering guts on my nicely swept and polished kitchen floor. Cline called the station
from his cell phone and spoke with some
urgency. After a minute or so he asked me
to call Randy. "I need your permission for us
to track the call. If he's on his cell, we might
be able to locate him, at least generally. Do
you think you can talk to him without letting
him know that I'm here?" he said seriously.
"I need to be sure you can do that."

I wasn't at all sure, but I had to know
where Hayden was . . . and that was as far
as my mind would allow me to go. I called
from the house phone and Randy picked up
on the second ring. Cline moved up close to
my ear, and I held the phone out a little, so
he could hear.

Randy sounded like he was smiling. "How
is your morning, Nina?"

"I feel like I'm hungover. Where are you
guys?" My voice amazingly steady.

"Well, since the park near our house was

cordoned off with the police tape and all, I brought Hayden to Wesley Park, over near the City Center complex. You know where I'm talking about?" Cool and cheery, like he'd never left the key, like he wasn't holding our son as a bargaining chip.

"I've been there once or twice." I felt my throat clenching, and swallowed quickly. "So, how is the little guy?"

"He's fine. Sitting right here on the seat beside me."

"So you guys left the park?"

"We're in the car. Do you want us to come home, Nina?"

For a moment I didn't understand him. Todd Cline was holding his cell phone up and spinning his index finger, telling me to keep rolling. I improvised. "I think I'm ready to talk, if that's what you mean."

"I've wanted to talk to you for so long, babe."

I held a hand up to my forehead, feeling the damp sweat condensing. "Don't you think you can trust me?"

The pause lasted longer than I liked, but now Cline was giving me an OK sign. Randy said, "It's kind of a big deal. I'm still not sure you understand."

"I just know I want you guys back here," I said.

"Forty-five minutes."

"That long?"

"It won't seem that way. And, babe? Thanks." He hung up.

I put the phone down and said, "Oh, God, he's going to kill Hayden, isn't he?"

Todd Cline patted me awkwardly on the arm. "I don't think so. HQ said they tracked his signal and he's about a half hour away. Not quite to City Center, but far enough that we can get things ready. I'm gonna go out front and meet the others. I'll stay where you can see me, though, and we'll tell you how we think you should handle it before he shows up. We'll run through the scenarios. Okay?"

I nodded, reeling in every sense of the word.

He touched me again, this time to steady me. He leaned me against the counter and said, "You did the right thing by calling me. You might have saved someone's life, maybe more than one."

"You were in there," I said, unable to keep myself from reaching out and gripping his shirt; I needed a physical mooring. "Was it what I thought it was? In the petri dish or whatever?"

He hesitated, then nodded. "It looked like the ones I've seen. It's always hard to tell, when they're not connected to anything else."

I retained only flash images. If I tried to concentrate on them, which I most certainly did not want to do, but couldn't help as my mind kept circling compulsively back, I got only pieces, no sense of the whole. I remembered the sketch of the teenaged boy. I remembered opening the cabinet. There was a computer monitor, silent and blank, and the keyboard tray on a slide-out shelf below. The inner walls of the cabinet papered with color photos: sometimes isolated parts of a face or body—a gashed chin, someone's bloody teeth, muscle pulled back and exposed; other photos showed scenes that seemed posed, almost tableaux, torn bodies and hanging flesh on polished hardwood floors, on soaked bedsheets. They were like the pictures in the true crime books I'd read while I was pregnant, except no part of them was blurred or pixeled out; this time I saw the faces connected with the savaged flesh. The empty eye sockets. The sockets with objects inserted where the eyes had been; smooth geodes, dice turned to sixes, tiny springs, even one that appeared to have the bulb of some flower sprouting where there had once been sight.

When I backed into the rolling chair, I'd nearly screamed. I realized I had my hand over my mouth. I'd always thought of that as an overly theatrical gesture, something you only saw in movies, but there in the shed I found it to be completely involuntary, like my body was trying to keep from breathing something in, some contamination that, if not immediately lethal, would certainly doom me to a life of quarantine. The birds outside were in a raging cacophony, sounding as if they'd gone feral and were tearing at one another, sharp hooked claws gouging feathers and beaks and black little birdy eyes. Battering wings. After I moved the chair aside, I made the door and started running. I had to find the phone, I had to call someone.

Because it wasn't just the photographs. Beside the computer was a shallow glass dish, maybe three inches deep, half filled with some milky liquid. A pair of stainless-steel hemostats propped up against one edge. Caught in the clamps, sitting in the center of the dish, was a globe the size of a Ping-Pong ball, pearly and shot through with burst vessels. A clot of tissue distended where the steel squeezed it, ropy leakage like something you'd see in an egg white. I recognized it as soon as I saw it, even though I'd never seen anything like it before. My mind simply relayed the information: *That's a human eye sitting there in whatever that is; oh, God, it's some kind of preservative.* An X-Acto knife was balanced on the other side of the dish across from the hemostats. I saw small, thin slices cut and laid to one side on the desktop, like he'd been parsing it.

Todd Cline looked at me now and nodded again. "He wants to be caught, Nina. That's what these guys do eventually, they snap and they need to be gratified and publicly recognized for what they feel to be superhuman accomplishments. A profiler came and talked to us about this kind of stuff a few years ago, after what happened with the Renaults."

I acted as though I hadn't comprehended. I was defaulting to suburban housewife. "'These guys'? Jesus, Todd, we've sat beside you in church."

"I'm sorry," he said. "But what's out there in

that shed . . . He hasn't had some kind of sudden breakdown."

And he was right.

He left me there in my kitchen with the knowledge that he was right, that this had been going on for a long, long time, maybe Randy's whole life. Certainly for most of his life with me. And then there was the thing Cline had mentioned and I'd deflected, the thing that I knew he had seen and the damning detail I couldn't seem to unsee. One of the photos on the wall, this one tacked up near the top, was right about at eye level for someone who sat at the computer and visited God only knew what sort of Internet sites. It was a picture of a small boy, his neck at an impossible angle as he lay among the dead leaves on a patch of nondescript dirt in some godforsaken unknown. The eyeless stare, the forever silenced scream, the face of Tyler Renault.

CHAPTER FIFTEEN

Randy pulled into our driveway that afternoon at five minutes past two. I was standing on the front porch, waiting, trying to hold myself together until I could get my hands on Hayden. From my vantage, I could see down the street from our cul-de-sac all the way to Maple Avenue, the main artery leading out of the neighborhood toward town, and I'd watched that intersection in agony, pacing, certain up until the very moment his car appeared that he wasn't coming back ever again. That I'd never see my son again. That I would have to bear all of this alone.

All down the street, the sense of a lazy

summer day prevailed: Tony and Sheila Johnson sat on their side deck, two houses down,
Sheila reading a magazine as Tony blabbed
on his cordless phone; across from their
house, Betsy Morrison kept an eye on her infant son as he splashed in a kiddie pool; Max
Flores labored behind his lawn mower, shirt-
less, his hairy back a target for clinging grass
and mosquitoes. Todd Cline had moved his
Expedition down the street a couple of driveways and parked by the sidewalk. When I
looked at the SUV, I could see no sign of him,
even though I knew he was there. Oblivious-
ness reigned, except in my head, where it
had counted for so much for so long.

Cline had directed me to pull my Accord
out of the garage and park in the center of
the driveway, effectively blocking it off. Randy
drove up behind my car and cut the engine
on his BMW. I heard him engage the emergency brake. I was already walking across
the yard to meet him.

He opened his door and looked question-
ingly at my parking job.

"I was thinking of washing it," I said
quickly. Tremors in every word.

His face, up until then, had exhibited a brief
instant of strange, new trust that made me

feel as if I'd been punched in my heart. As soon as he looked into my eyes, though, his expression changed to one of disappointment; a rueful, reproachful glare that said he'd expected more of me. He stood by, motionless, while I opened the back door of the BMW. Hayden was strapped into his child seat, waving his arms happily when I leaned in. The tears came hot and beyond my control as I wrestled with the straps until I had him loose and in my arms.

When I emerged, Randy was lingering there, only an arm's length away, hands clenched by his sides. He saw my tears and said, "Did you really think I would hurt him?"

I was already backing away, moving toward the house without ever taking my eyes off him. Randy's face hardened. He started after me.

Another vehicle door slammed, just down the street. Todd Cline, twenty yards away when he got out of his Expedition, called Randy's name.

My husband turned and saw the officer coming. Cline wore his service revolver in plain sight on his belt. "Hey, Randy. You mind if I have a word with you?"

I was frozen now, watching as Cline

closed the distance. I whispered in my little boy's ear, the soft, precious little ear that couldn't yet translate that I was telling him everything would be all right, Mommy was here, Mommy would keep him safe. I kissed his head and smoothed his hair. He knew something was going on, because he started to wail and cry.

Tires squealed at the end of our road, where it intersected with Maple Avenue. Three police cruisers, one after the other with only a bumper's length between them, raced toward our house. Betsy Morrison stood and moved out onto the sidewalk to watch. Sheila Johnson grabbed her husband's elbow and pointed. Randy, who'd looked back when Cline called his name, now turned back around to face me. He said, with a sadness so immense and impenetrable that for a moment it was like we were back at his apartment in the early days, me swooning from romance and mystery and all the other lies: "Nina, I thought we might have finally been able to share something again."

He was wearing those baggy khaki shorts that every man his age in our neighborhood wore during the summer. Those cargo pock-

ets so deep you could carry just about anything in them. His right hand moved into the
front pocket, and I saw the weight pulling that
side of his shorts down.

I pointed. I shouted to Cline, "He's got a
gun!"

Cline drew his weapon as Randy spun
around in his direction. He was indeed reaching for a gun, a compact .44 slide automatic
he'd been carrying in the car, but the hammer
caught on the liner of his pocket. He never got
it out. Cline didn't yell at him to drop it, he
didn't order "Hands up!" or any of that. He just
shot Randy twice. Randy jolted in place, his
right hand still fishing in his shorts. He looked
down at where the blood had instantly
soaked the front of his shirt, then dropped
over on his side in the grass. I could hear him
wheezing. Cline came up close and stepped
on his left arm, then leaned over and twisted
the right arm until it came up out of the
pocket. The police cruisers had come to a
stop, rocking on their suspensions, officers
swarming now. I heard one of them repeating,
"Shots fired, ambulance requested," into his
radio. Randy seemed unable to speak, and
instead stared up at them defiantly, bloody

bubbles frothing out of his nose and mouth. A cop fished the .44 out of his pocket and backpedaled rapidly, holding the weapon by the barrel.

Max Flores was still mowing his yard. He'd been cutting a swath in the other direction and only now did his wife come out of the house and alert him to the confrontation that was taking place behind him. The mower went quiet and finally everyone was staring.

I realized I was screaming. One of the officers came and took me by the arm and led me into our house. I was hysterical, clutching Hayden so tightly that the cop eventually had to pry him from my grasp. "You're going to smother him," he kept telling me, as kindly as he could say such a thing, but I kept twisting away when he reached for us. Finally I relented and stood numbly, staring out the front window as more and more people showed up, a regular congregation on our lawn, uniformed officers and people without uniforms who I assumed to be investigators of some kind. Soon the crowd was so thick I lost sight of Randy. The late arrivals kept clapping Todd Cline on the back, asking if he was okay. I heard Randy's awful coughing.

The ambulance was wailing in the distance, but I had the feeling that everyone was hoping the paramedics wouldn't arrive in time to save him. I don't know what I was hoping.

But they got there in time.

CHAPTER SIXTEEN

1.

After my lunch meeting with Duane and Carolyn, the rest of the week passed quietly. By Wednesday, there hadn't been a single mention of my name in the newspapers or on TV since the weekend. The last instance was a feature in the *News and Observer* Sunday edition, which focused mostly on recapping the time line of Randy's crimes, arrest, and trial, along with a few choice insinuations from Pritchett. The prosecutor who'd won the death penalty conviction against my ex-husband six years ago was quoted in the article as saying that his office never had any interest in me, nor had he heard anything in the time since then that would lead him to suspect my involvement. The reporter had contacted a few of the family members of Randy's victims, but each of them declined to make any statement, except to say that they wished to put the past behind them.

As did we all. Only Pritchett seemed to be trapped within the cycle of his grief, and I knew there was nothing I could do to salve his turmoil.

I probably should have returned to Data Managers, but by that point I saw it as an earned vacation, so I stuck around the house, reading magazines and cleaning up. It felt empty without Hayden there. Each day I watched the clock wind slowly past noon and interminably through the next few hours until it was time to pick him up from his after-school suspension.

On Wednesday, after a late lunch, I started vacuuming the downstairs. I intended to finish the living room and front hallway, then wash up and go to collect my little guy. But when I switched off the vacuum cleaner I heard a noise outside, splicing the afternoon as it edged toward the early winter dusk. Sirens, a bevy of layered clarions rising and falling in countertime, not too far away. I wondered briefly if there'd been some kind of pileup on I-40. Then I heard the television, which I'd left going in the den while I was working.

I told myself I was hearing it wrong.

When I went into the den, I was already shaking. The banner BREAKING NEWS was scrolling at the bottom of the screen. I picked up the remote and cranked the volume. They switched away from a dour anchorwoman in the newsroom, and the scene that replaced it effectively took out my knees. It was a wide-angle shot taken from a news helicopter, hovering above the grounds of Cary Learning Center. I recognized the splay of structures, the gymnasium and practice field. Several official vehicles, all with their lights spinning, were parked haphazardly out in front of a building situated to the right of the administrative offices.

"Details are still coming into News Channel Eleven," the voice-over said, "but for those of you just joining us, Cary police are confirming the death of at least one person on the campus of Cary Learning Center. This is an elementary school, just off Davis Drive. Now, officials are telling us that most of the students had already left for the day when the incident occurred, so they're asking that parents stop calling unless they have reason to believe their children might've still been on the grounds for extracurricular activities of some kind. The phone lines at the school are overwhelmed and parents are advised to call the Cary Police Department if they have any further—"

I snapped out of it. I snatched my purse off an end table and ran for the carport. The garage door was opening and I was still fumbling with my car keys when the high bark of a truncated siren bleeped behind me. The sound was so sudden and sharp, my heart nearly drove out right through my sternum. When I turned around, a police cruiser was pulling to the curb at the end of the driveway.

An officer leaned out the window. "Ma'am? Ms. Leigh Wren?"

"Is my son all right?"

The officer got out and opened the back door of the cruiser for me. "Ma'am, we've been asked to take you over to the school. We don't have any more information than that right now, but I'm sure they'll explain everything to you once we get there."

2.

I kept telling them to hurry. They used the siren and the lights. They blew around other cars as the drivers moved off to the side of the road. We arrived at the campus in a little more than four minutes, but it seemed like hours. Long enough for me to call the Rowes on my cell phone. I was doing it mostly to keep talking, anything to stall my mind, to fend off the obvious conclusion.

Duane picked up on the second ring. "Hey, Nina. We're actually over in your neck of the woods today, I had to give a depo in divorce court in Raleigh. You given any more thought to what we said about nailing Pritchett?"

"Something's happened at Hayden's school. It's on TV, and the police are taking me there right now, but they won't tell me what happened to him." I realized I was talking calmly. I should have been screaming, losing my shit, but instead I only felt a sense of deep cold, a glacial stillness as though my heart had slowed to a single beat per minute. It was like a sudden hibernation, as if I could only view the world through an aperture in my cave while events unfolded outside, beyond my volition or control.

Duane asked for directions and I gave them in a monotone. I could hear him on the other end of the line, snapping his fingers loudly; I imagined alarm on Carolyn's face as she sat beside him. "Please hurry," I said, and hung up.

We arrived at the school a moment later, the driver weaving through the vehicles lined up in the traffic circle. He parked and I started pulling at the door handle, but it wouldn't open. I'd momentarily blanked that I was in the back of a police car. The officer from the passenger's side opened my door and stood out of the way. I spotted Beasley among a cluster of policemen gathered outside the entrance to the classroom building on my left, the one I'd seen them swarming in the news report. I made a beeline for the vice principal. The officers who'd brought me followed closely behind, saying, "Ma'am, hold on, please," a couple of times before they gave up.

Beasley started saying he was sorry as soon as he saw me. The world threatened to go dark and I tried to maintain consciousness. "Where is Hayden?" I asked, and knew from the faces surrounding me that it'd come out as a shriek. I heard someone saying, "There's the mother," and I thought I might go crazy standing there. A man wearing khakis and a tie took my arm firmly and steered me toward the administration building.

"Will someone please answer me?" I pleaded.

The man holding my elbow introduced himself as Detective Justin Matthews. He was young and healthy-looking, his stark gray sideburns serving as the only indication that he'd had any experience outside of a computer simulation. I might have found him attractive, in different circumstances.

"Ms. Wren, the only way to say this is to just tell you: Your son has been abducted. An as yet unidentified assailant entered the classroom where Hayden was at the time, killed the teacher who was there with him, and then left the premises with your son in his custody. We don't know if this assailant had any accomplices, but we did get a vehicle description as they left the scene. Two witnesses saw a recent-model minivan, beige or off-white, leaving the campus. Does that sound like any vehicle you're familiar with?"

Half the parents in Cary drove something

similar. I shook my head. "He's been abducted?" It made zero sense.

Matthews continued. "We've already issued an Amber Alert, using the photograph from his school yearbook, but we're going to need some more specifics from you. Can you help us with that?"

"Abducted," I repeated. I couldn't seem to catch my breath. The world went kaleidoscopic.

The next thing I was aware of was being lowered into a chair in Beasley's office, the same chair Rachel Dutton had politely ceded to me during our impromptu conference last week. Matthews and another officer were holding me by my arms. Matthews told the guy to go find the paramedics. "Shock," he said quietly.

"I'm all right," I said. I blinked and the room came into focus: the computer terminal on Beasley's desk, his potted plants, the framed photo of him from his coaching days. I stared at Matthews hard, steadily, trying to show him I was coherent. "What do you need to know? How can I help?"

He took out a pad and pen. Another couple

of officers crowded into the room to take notes as well. One of them kept moving outside to the reception area and talking into a handheld radio, repeating what I said to a dispatcher somewhere on the other end of the line. I was familiar with the Amber Alerts, those big signs over the highway that would stream physical stats and clothing and license numbers.

I could not, even for the space of a single precious breath, believe that any of this was taking place.

They asked about what Hayden had worn to school that morning. I described his blue jeans, his tennis shoes, his light brown sweatshirt. They asked if he had scars of any kind. I told them about the slight discoloration that remained along the left underside of his chin from where he took a spill at the swimming pool last year. I had a sudden, lucid vision of a mortician lifting my dead son's face with two plastic-gloved fingers, searching for the scar. The reaction was swift and unstoppable; I turned and vomited into Beasley's wastebasket. The convulsion passed, and I dug in my purse for some mints. After I'd bitten down on one,

I held the tin out to the officers. They eyed me warily and I told Matthews, "I'm fine. Please continue. I want to help in whatever way I can."

Matthews asked if I could think of anyone specific who might want to hurt me or my son or my son's teacher.

It finally sunk in, what they'd been saying about her. "Ms. Dutton? Oh, no."

Matthews cleared the room. Once the other officers had left, he closed the door and said, "I've been following your story in the papers. We've already got someone contacting the authorities in California, to see if your ex-husband might know anything about this. Do you think he might?"

"Maybe. Except that he's on fucking Death Row, so I don't know how . . ."

"What about Charles Pritchett?"

I shrugged. "He hates me. But he can't possibly be that crazy, can he? I mean, everyone knows that he's been trying to hurt me. It would be so obvious. He strikes me as a childish, vindictive man, but I don't know if that means he's capable of something like this."

"Childish and vindictive describes the majority of the criminals I deal with," Matthews said evenly. "Especially the violent ones. Do you know Mr. Pritchett's whereabouts?"

"My private investigators know . . . I mean, his private investigators." I explained to Matthews about Duane and Carolyn. While I was filling him in, I heard Duane's voice from the reception area. He was talking to the cops, trying to find out where I was. I asked Matthews if he could come in.

Carolyn was there, too. Matthews invited them in and stood aside while Carolyn held me. Matthews said, "Ms. Wren says you folks might know where we can find Charles Pritchett. We can call the hotels but I figured it might be faster—"

"He's at the Hilton in Raleigh," Carolyn said. She pulled a couple of sheets of paper from her purse and handed them to Matthews. "There's a summary of what we've been able to find out about him. I wrote it up on the way over, so you might need me to translate some of the chicken scratch. You think he might be involved with all this?"

Matthews inclined his head toward me. "Ms. Wren doesn't seem to think it fits. But we'll certainly want to speak with him." He sized up Duane. "So you have some background in law enforcement, Mr. Rowe?"

"Fourteen years. Six in Baltimore, the other eight in Virginia."

"You see Pritchett as a possibility?"

"Can you fill me in on what actually happened? I don't want to step on any toes, but it'd help, given what we've been investigating on Nina's behalf over the past few weeks."

Matthews was cool to the idea. "Ms. Wren explained how you located her for Pritchett and then, after he went public, you guys came to her and offered your services out of the goodness of your hearts . . ."

"I wouldn't buy it either," Duane admitted. "Let me give you some phone numbers for reference."

I realized for the first time that Matthews was looking at the Rowes with suspicion. I almost wanted to scream at him: *But they're trying to help! What the fuck are you doing? Stop asking us stupid questions and get out there and FIND MY SON! My poor Hayden, oh, God, he must be so scared.* I started shaking and Carolyn asked the men to let us have a few moments alone.

The shudders passed more quickly than I thought they might. Carolyn held out a box of tissues she'd found while rummaging through Beasley's desk drawers, but I still wasn't actually crying. I told her: "If anything happens to him, I won't make it."

She didn't offer any platitudes. She said, "I know."

Matthews came back into the office a few minutes later, with Duane, Thomas Beasley, and another uniformed officer following. Matthews said, "Ma'am, if you don't have any objections to the Rowes' involvement, I don't either. I can use their background."

"I want them here."

"Okay. Mr. Beasley, can you run the surveillance footage for us again? Maybe Ms. Wren will see something about the perpetrator that rings a bell."

"You've got it on tape?" I was aghast. "I nearly got strip-searched by security when I came here last week to meet with Mr. Beasley. How did someone get into a classroom?"

Beasley looked physically ill. "The security personnel are only on-campus during regular class hours."

Everyone's faces were impassive, as though it was all simply a budgeting snafu.

But I knew; I remembered how, not so long ago, it was the children themselves everyone was afraid of. Our own children.

3.

Beasley tapped on his computer for a minute and then turned the monitor around so we could all see. I realized I was holding my hand over my mouth, and removed it by force of will. Carolyn asked Matthews if I should really see this.

"It's up to her," the detective said. "But it's only the hallway camera. There's nothing from the classroom where it took place."

Still, Carolyn held my hand as we watched. Everyone huddled around the vice principal's desk, staring pensively. Hands were busy stroking chins and there was a fair amount of shuffling. Beasley and Matthews had seen it before, but for the rest of us there was that sickening intrusive feeling that always came along with watching this kind of event unfold. Images of Columbine, that bloody kid falling out the window; panicked subway stations; plane crashes in real time. Some slightly distanced part of me understood that this footage would probably pop up on the Internet sooner or later, and sick people would watch it and rewind it and watch it again, not in order to help find my son, but for vicarious thrills. One person's queasy was another person's rush.

The angle was from above the hallway, a camera situated over the door that led out onto the school grounds. It showed a parabolic and somewhat distorted view of the rows of lockers down each side of the hall, intermittently broken by doors leading into the classrooms. Beasley tapped on the screen and said Rachel Dutton used the third room on the left for her after-school sessions. Hayden had been the only student with her today.

A figure entered the hallway and walked beneath the camera at 3:29 P.M., according to the LED display ticking off in the lower left-hand corner of the screen. I grasped at the fact that the person I was seeing on the screen was somewhere at this very moment with my child as his hostage; I couldn't really process it.

Or the fact that it only applied if Hayden was still alive at all.

The man was skinny, jeans cinched tight at

his waist but baggy around the knees. He wore a sweatshirt with the hood drawn up over his head. His face was hidden from the camera as he walked away from it, checking doorways until he reached the third on the left. He carried a backpack that seemed heavy. Matthews asked if I saw anything that struck me, but I didn't.

The murderer pushed the door open gently at first, then disappeared quickly inside and shut it behind him. The hallway was still and nothing moved. Beasley clicked his mouse and started forwarding the footage, minutes spiraling by at high speed in the corner.

"How long was he in there?" Duane asked.

"Sixteen minutes," Matthews answered. "Which is actually pretty fast work, considering that he had time to bind them both, then do what he did to the teacher."

"What did he do?" I said, and everyone turned away from me. "I mean, to the teacher?"

It was obvious from the looks exchanged between Matthews and his officers that no one wanted to say. Beasley held his head in one hand and stared silently at his computer. Duane told Matthews that I'd read about it in the papers anyway. Matthews was still doubtful, but he made his face rigid and said, "We believe he cut Ms. Dutton's throat shortly after entering the room. There were other teachers still in the building at the time, and no one heard her scream, so it must have happened quickly. He then performed a mutilation that was similar to what your husband did to his victims."

"My ex-husband," I heard myself say dully. I felt like I might throw up again. I remembered her eyes, how sympathetic and patient they were when she took my son's side after his scuffle with Ashton Hale. She'd looked me right in my face and offered her help.

"He took her . . . ?" I couldn't bring myself to say it. My voice sheered off halfway through the last word.

"We believe so, yes," Matthews said.

"Did he leave anything in their place?"

He hesitated and then said, "We think it was some kind of plant seeds. Forensics will have to identify it."

"Jesus Christ," breathed Beasley. "Ms. Wren, I know she did everything she possibly could for Hayden."

"I don't doubt it for a moment."

The vice principal had tears standing in his eyes, and he swiped angrily at them with his forearm and apologized to the room at large. Everyone told him it was all right. He turned back to the computer and lifted his finger off the mouse. The scene slowed back into real time: 3:45 P.M. The classroom door opened. The figure came out, large dark sunglasses over his eyes, a bandanna pulled up over his mouth and nose. Within that hood, only a thin stretch of visible skin. Blood all down the front of his sweatshirt, soaking the long sleeves. His hands were bloody, too; it must have been hard for him to keep hold of my son as he struggled. I felt the pressure from Carolyn's hand on mine, but all tactile sensation had gone. Hayden appeared to have duct tape wrapped around his hands at the wrists and his feet at the ankles. Another strip across his mouth, and in that moment I tasted with my own lips the bitter adhesive, I sensed the taut-ness. But my son was fighting, by God, trying to twist his way out of the murderer's hold. He succeeded, briefly, and fell on the floor. I flinched as though I'd hit the waxy tiles myself. The murderer grabbed him again, this time by the back of his shirt, balling it into a fist and hefting Hayden up. He appeared to be hissing some warning or threat from behind his ban-danna. Hayden calmed considerably.

The killer's mouth was still moving as he went underneath the camera, but now his face tilted upward, as if he were talking directly to whoever might later watch the tape. As if he were talking to me.

Hayden's eyes were so wide, so prominent, they swallowed his whole face above that mocking strip of tape. Eyes more frightened than I'd ever seen them, virtually unrecognizable. He stared at the camera, too, as they moved beneath it, then they were out of the picture and gone.

Matthew said, "I'm sure that was difficult for you, Ms. Wren. I need to know, is there anything about the suspect you found familiar in any way? Anything at all you recognized?"

I shook my head. I was afraid to speak. I knew I would need a clear head for the foreseeable future, and I didn't want anyone in this room to think I was going to be too weak to handle anything that was asked of me. Everything I could do, everything in my power, I would do. A running prayer had already established itself in my head, a mantra I returned to with every moment I wasn't taking in new information: *Please let him be okay, dear God, my God, I'll do anything you*

*want, just let me have him back, let me bring
him back home.*

Randy's victims probably prayed. Every
one of them probably asked much the same
things as I was asking now.

I told Matthews I wanted to watch the tape
again.

CHAPTER SEVENTEEN

1.

We found Pritchett having dinner in the Hilton's bar and restaurant, in the company of a middle-aged man and a younger woman. Aside from them, the room was nearly deserted; all low lights and empty tables, a single waiter running a push broom near the entrance to the kitchen. Pritchett looked up as we approached. I walked briskly in front of Duane and Carolyn, with Matthews and a pair of uniformed officers barely keeping me in check. Pritchett stood and faced me.

"I saw it on the news," he said preemptively, indicating a TV set above the empty bar. He looked dismissively past the uniformed cops and addressed Matthews. "I had nothing whatsoever to do with this. It is not what I intended to happen."

From the grim set of his mouth and his readiness for confrontation, I read two things right off: he most likely hadn't been responsible for Hayden's abduction, but he was as certain as ever that I had been involved with his daughter's murder.

I plunged ahead regardless. "You threatened my son the first night you came after me," I said. I didn't realize I was hissing through clenched teeth until Duane grabbed my arm. I was actually poised to launch myself at Pritchett, whose face was noticeably pale, if resolved.

Matthews advised me to control my emotions if I wished to stay. Then he asked Pritchett to account for his whereabouts during the afternoon. For the first time, Pritchett introduced the two people sitting at his table. They rose in concert and, incredibly, smiled politely as they shook hands with the detective. "Elliot Talese and Denise Sanders," Pritchett said. "Two representatives from my company who flew out here to consult on an upcoming marketing promotion. We've been engaged in teleconferences throughout the day."

"You sold your company," Duane said pointedly.

"I'm still on the board of directors," Pritchett fired back. He evaluated Duane curiously for a moment, then nodded as he recognized him. "I'd heard you and your wife were helping Mrs. Mosley. No conflict of interest in that, I'm sure." He shrugged him off as casually as he had the street cops, and continued to direct his defense at the detective. "Look, I didn't plan on Mr. Talese and Ms. Sanders being here. This was a last-minute issue and the company only alerted me that they were coming the day before yesterday. You can call and verify that with any number of people."

Talese and Sanders both seemed quite eager to back him up, and Matthews sent them off to another table so the cops could take their statements. Matthews told Pritchett that they'd be interested in verifying all of the phone calls and personal visits he'd made since he came to town.

"Not a problem," Pritchett said. "I'll instruct the hotel to release the calls made from my room, as well." He was still talking to

Matthews, correctly surmising that the detective's assessment would be the deciding factor in whether this was a momentary hassle or a continuing problem, but he kept turning toward me, eyes flashing. "I could never hurt another person's child. Not after what happened to mine." And then, as if he couldn't help it: "But at least now you finally know how it feels."

Duane snorted. "You been practicing that line for long?"

"I've been practicing some form of it for the nine years since my daughter was butchered," Pritchett replied, his steely sense of wounded dignity intact. "That doesn't mean I would harm her son."

Carolyn called him a sonofabitch. "At the very least you put both of them in jeopardy with your bullshit PR campaign. Even if it wasn't you, it's because of your splashing her face across the TV and newspapers that this happened."

"In that case, I'm sure you'll accept your share of the responsibility, Mrs. Rowe," Pritchett said with a smile.

Matthews suggested we wait out in the lobby.

"I'm all right," I said levelly.

Duane removed a check from his pocket, tore it into quarters, and dropped it onto Pritchett's dinner plate among the garlic bread crusts and leftover pasta. "That's our share of the responsibility. It's your payment for us finding her. I've been carrying it with me, hoping to get the chance to do that in person. Ever since you went on the air, I knew this was something I wanted no part of. And if you've made me party to the hurting of a child, if you've stained my hands with something like that . . ." He saw Matthews's warning glance and finished simply, "No matter what you do, none of this will bring your daughter back."

"And that overwrought show of umbrage won't bring her son back, either," Pritchett said. "If you want to discuss your fee, you'll have to do so through McClellan Associates. They hired you, not me personally. But I expect you know that."

Matthews sat in the chair where Talese had been. He pulled a folded piece of paper out of his pocket. It was the newspaper clipping that had been placed beneath my windshield wiper blade the night Pritchett initially accosted me, the article about the murdered woman in Tennessee. Carolyn had given it to

the detective, along with some further background details, before we left the school.
Matthews let Pritchett look at it long enough
to recognize it, then asked him why he'd left
it for me.

"That article was sent to me anonymously a few weeks before I learned Mrs.
Mosley's whereabouts," Pritchett said. He
kept calling me by my old name, goading
me to correct him, but I was determined
not to give him the satisfaction. "To be quite
honest, I think she sent it to me, perhaps
as a warning, because the people who'd
been hired to find her"—and he paused
long enough to glare at each of the Rowes
in turn—"had been sloppy and alerted her
to the fact that she wouldn't be able to keep
her identity and whereabouts secret for
much longer."

I didn't know whether to laugh or scream.
"I can understand if you still think I was a
part of what Randy did. I can't do anything to
change your perceptions about that at this
point. But you can't possibly believe that I
had my own son abducted. Why would I?"

Pritchett didn't have an answer; everyone
could see it in his face. But he maintained
his composure, even though it appeared to

cost him significantly. It was like watching an implosion of sorts, as his mouth turned down and his lips thinned. So he defaulted to his old accusations. "Why was your name on the fake documents?" was the best he could do. "Out in the shed, where he kept his trophies—your name was all over them, the licenses and passports. And your DNA—"

"Because Randy was insane, Mr. Pritchett," I said, despairing. I wished for a bullhorn so I could scream it in his face. I wanted to blare it, to force him into seeing reason. "He was crazy. He almost drove me out of my mind, and he seems to have succeeded in driving you out of yours. Maybe I deserve to pay for what happened to Carrie, but my son doesn't. So, please, if you know anything that could help us find him, *please* tell us. I'm begging you."

But he wouldn't look at me anymore. Instead, he asked Matthews to arrange a formal time tomorrow when he could come down to the station and make a statement. Matthews suggested that he make time for it tonight. Pritchett summoned his minion Talese over and instructed him to call LA. "Tell them I'm going to need some legal representation out here," he said.

My anger waned as I watched him fold his hands and stare blankly past me. When he finally managed to conjure a waiter and request a glass of whiskey, it was plain to see that he was a broken man already.

2.

Back at my place, I lingered in the upstairs hallway outside Hayden's bedroom, unwilling as yet to cross the threshold. Matthews had assigned a rotation of officers to keep watch on the house, and a couple of tech geeks had come by to put a trace on my phone. I signed forms granting them permission to track all incoming calls to the home number and my cell. Carolyn had taken two minutes to wash up and dump her purse in the guest bedroom before getting on the phone. I could hear her downstairs, tapping keys on her computer and muttering to herself about departure times. Duane had returned to their house to pack his things. He was going to fly out tonight if possible, or early tomorrow if that was the soonest he could find a flight. I'd told them I didn't know how I could pay them for their efforts and they'd waved me off without further comment. I had the feeling of being a sideline observer in a game that would have consequences only for me.

Duane's first stop would be Detroit, Lane Dockery's hometown. He'd verified with Dockery's sister, Jeanine, that she'd organized what notes she could find that pertained to our case. Duane only planned to be there for a few hours before heading farther west. If he could arrange an appointment, he was going to see my ex-husband in person.

"The prison officials have interviewed Randy, and they claim he's pretty distressed about the whole thing," Carolyn said softly behind me. I jumped half out of my skin and she laid a cool hand on my arm. "I didn't mean to startle you. I was trying to be quiet when I came upstairs, in case you were sleeping."

When I laughed at the idea, she said I'd have to get some rest at some point. But I could still hear the TV downstairs; the ten o'clock news led with the incident at the school, and they just kept going. Repeating over and over the description of the minivan that had been seen leaving the school, driving erratically, around the time of the crime.

CNN had picked up the story and we were supposedly getting coverage across the whole Southeastern viewing area, with Amber Alerts periodically scrolling across beneath people's sitcoms and reality shows and basketball games. I wondered if they would blank them out, the way I usually did.

"If it wasn't Pritchett, then it was Randy," I said. "I don't know how, and I don't know who he recruited to do it, but it has to be him. I'm thinking about those letters the warden at San Quentin told you about while you were out there. Maybe he wasn't after just Pritchett and Dockery."

"I tend to agree," Carolyn said. "We're checking all his prison acquaintances, going back for as long as he's been there. The PO box where Randy was mailing his letters will be staked out. If we could somehow connect him to the article that Pritchett left on your windshield, the one he claims was sent to him anonymously . . . Matthews says his forensics people couldn't get anything from it. But whoever killed the girl in Tennessee is likely the same person who abducted your son. We've confirmed with the authorities there that what was done to the victim in Tennessee is the same as what was done to the teacher in Hayden's school, Rachel Dutton."

"And the same as Randy did to all those others. My ex-husband has himself a copycat," I said, shaking my head. "A partner in crime to complete his unfinished business. I can understand someone wanting to hurt me, but Hayden . . ."

"Forget trying to understand. Only someone as sick as Randy is could figure out how his mind works. The police are looking into it, and so are the people at San Quentin, and so are we. But there are warrants that have to be signed by judges, logistics to work out . . . I know all that sounds like bullshit to you right now, but I'm just telling you so you understand that it's going to take some time."

I stared into my son's dark room. His bed was halfway made, or at least the covers were pulled up. If I did sleep tonight, it would be in here, on his little mattress, beneath the Backyardigans poster and his certificate of graduation from first grade, which I'd framed and put on the wall last year, even though he claimed it was no big deal. I found myself thinking about the late Rachel Dutton. *Was she married? Did she have a boyfriend? A girlfriend?* I realized that I knew nothing at all about her, not even her age. I imagined phones ringing, the police knocking softly on a front door.

"I know what Pritchett meant tonight," I whispered.

"What's that?"

"When he said, 'Now you know how it feels.' He was right. All this time, I imagined that I was hurt because Randy deceived me, and because to some degree, it doesn't even matter anymore how much, but to some degree I allowed myself to be deceived. And I thought that meant that I understood, that I had some empathy with the real victims. But it was bullshit, Carolyn, it was bullshit of the absolute worse kind."

Carolyn started to say something, but I cut her off. "No. I had some responsibility, and all this time I've spent feeling guilty and agonizing over it, I forgot the essential truth. What Pritchett meant is that now I know how it feels to have *no responsibility*, to have something done *to* me, and that's worse, because the situation is completely out of my hands and beyond my control. I'm helpless. That's what Pritchett and all the others have been living with all along."

"Will your realizing that comfort you right now? Will it help get Hayden back?"

"I don't know."

"It won't, and you *do* know it. So forget it. Focus on what you *can* do. If you can't sleep, come downstairs and help me go over the notes from Randy's trial. I ordered a transcript when we were first looking into how Pritchett went after him in prison. Maybe something in there will help."

So I followed after her, feeling like a sleepwalker. I could read the words in the transcript, but for all the comprehension that seeped in they might as well have been written in a foreign language.

All the while, a clock in my head kept winding down. The seconds ticking away my son's life while the authorities worked on getting warrants signed and coordinating logistics.

CHAPTER EIGHTEEN

I don't know exactly how they were chosen. I can tell you that it wasn't strictly visual, although that was part of it. It was primarily more of a gut instinct, like when you meet someone's eyes across a room and there's an instant attraction, that sort of sensory flash, except in this case it was only on my end. So far as I know, anyway . . . I always saw them among large groups of people, and it was like they stood out more starkly, maybe, like they were somehow more well defined. Almost like they were highlighted."

The courtroom was dead silent except

for the sound of Randy's voice. His court-appointed public defenders had entered a plea of Not Guilty by Reason of Insanity, and they'd made it clear he wouldn't be testifying on his own behalf. Randy, however, had provided the police with a lengthy and, from all accounts, exhaustive confession while he was laid up in the hospital recovering from the gunshot wounds Todd Cline had inflicted. The doctors' initial diagnosis hadn't been good; he'd lost a sizable chunk of his spleen, and one lung had collapsed. He'd been afraid that he might die without ever having made his exploits known to a wider audience. His attorneys had wanted to file a motion to suppress the confession, but rumor had it that Randy instructed them not to do so. He knew this was his moment. Although his voice on the digital recorder's playback was flinty, and he often paused for a drink or to clear his throat, every word came through clearly.

The prosecutors were playing clips from the confession throughout the trial, and on the day I was to testify they'd chosen this little tidbit. The sound was turned up too loud and rang tinny off the functional yellow walls of Courtroom #3. The room belonged to

Judge Rita Oliver, a hefty woman with slate gray hair and sharp blue eyes. She ran a tight ship; the few times when victims' relatives became demonstratively emotional, Oliver had them escorted quickly out of the observer's gallery; leading questions from the defense and prosecution alike were met with quick admonishments; she talked down to Randy on several occasions and even he seemed resentfully respectful of her. Anthony Turnbull, the lead prosecutor, a short, handsome man in his early sixties who favored bow ties and carried himself in an efficient, slightly effete manner, had warned me that I might be shaken by what I heard, as would the jury and reporters and family members gathered here to witness the trial; that was the exact intent of playing the tapes. The men and women seated in the jury box hunched their shoulders and inclined their heads toward the stereo speakers that had been placed on either side of the prosecution's table. From my spot on the witness stand, I couldn't do anything except stare at my hands while the recording droned on.

The only time I caught Randy's eye, he glared at me like some hungry animal. One of his PDs, an overstressed guy with curly hair and a beer gut named Allan Beyer, had come by the house last week and picked up a suit of Randy's dress clothes, so he wouldn't have to appear before the court in a prison jumpsuit. I'd wanted to either burn or throw away everything of his, but the prosecutors had told me there was an outside chance that some random item might be collected for further evidence at some point. So Mom and I had put it all in the garage and locked it up.

Even with a clean, pressed shirt and tie, Randy's appearance was slipshod; he'd let his hair grow and was sporting a thin beard. It only made him look more aggressive.

His tone on the playback was conversational and animated, as though he was talking to friends over cocktails. "Once I'd spotted them, once I'd experienced that initial spark, it was pretty much a done deal. I followed them from the moment I saw them, keeping a good distance, sort of drinking in the details of the way they walked, the kind of clothes they wore, how they interacted with people on the street. You know, whether they were polite or rude, if they tipped their waitress. You can tell a lot about a person by that kind of stuff, without ever speaking a word to them. If it was a woman—and it was usually a woman—I'd memorize her hairstyle, the brand of shoes she wore. I'd try to guess her sizes. That sort of thing."

The voice of a detective who'd been there during the recording intervened. "What about when they got into a car?"

"I'd be ready to keep on following them. I mean, you have to understand, these sightings most often happened at a bar or a restaurant, maybe once or twice at the airport. You watch people like I do, you get a feel for when they're preparing to leave, and by then I'd be good to go. I rented the cars through my company, because I was usually wherever I was because of work. Except for some of the earliest ones, like the Renault family."

"And Daphne Snyder. She was from El Ray, too," one of the interviewers said casually.

There was a long pause. "Yeah, she was different," Randy finally said, an air of either regret or nostalgia in his voice, it was difficult to tell which. "She was the one who brought me down. Her parents must be so proud."

Officially, this trial was for the murders he'd committed in California, and Daphne Snyder's parents were in the courtroom. I knew them from seeing their faces in the papers, and I wasn't the only one who looked at them now. Several reporters stared openly. Mr. Snyder was focused on the back of Randy's head, like he could make it catch fire by simple force of will. Mrs. Snyder, who looked as if she hadn't slept at all during the five months since the crime took place, got up from her seat at the end of the row and walked steadily out of the room without glancing back. A moment later, her husband followed.

"But with the majority of the others, it was in faraway cities," Randy reminisced mistily. "That was part of why it took you guys so very, very long to catch me. Most serial killers operate within an hour or two of their homes, a fact of which I'm sure you guys are aware. I read in the newspaper that you guys have already brought in a profiler from the Bureau. Do I get to meet him?"

"If you keep talking to us," one of the detectives prompted.

Randy laughed, knowing he was being played, relishing it. "Well, I really do want to meet him. I'll be interested to hear his impressions. But back to what I was saying. I travel a good deal for work, and I figured that

it would be next to impossible to trace someone who was picking his victims in a completely random manner. Most perpetrators
have a giveaway, like their victims are all similar in appearance, or they're all hookers or
something like that. But with me, they were
all different. I'd see these people, and I'd feel
the pull, and I'd know they were the ones.
Then I'd follow them home, and the chase
was on. I used my nights after meetings and
conferences, while all the other jerk-offs
were getting soused at the hotel bar or trying
to find an escort service that wasn't traffick-
ing in total skank, and I'd do my research.

"I'd case the home, drive around the
neighborhood, get a feel for the terrain.
These days, you can search the Internet for
any number of escape routes, but I used to
use paper maps." Directions to the homes of
some of his most recent victims had been
found on his company laptop, as well as in
the computer he'd kept out in his shed. That
PC had also revealed his obsession with a
number of unsavory Web sites, some featur-
ing surgeries or autopsies, others that traf-
ficked in S&M, and yet others that showed
photo after close-up photo of anonymous
pairs of eyes. "I'd observe the house, get to

know the family routine, like when they came and went, how late they stayed up at night. Then I'd get my kit together, you know, my tools, stuff I couldn't carry on planes with me. I'm sure you guys are familiar with all the implements my wife found in my shed at home, but on the road it was always easy to gather the knives and tape and that sort of thing from local stores. I kind of enjoyed that part of it. There was always a pond or a creek where I could get rid of the stuff after I'd used it, and I never bought it all from the same place, so your brethren could never chase down my receipts.

"And then, on the last night or the next to last night I was in town, I'd do the piece . . . And that's how I thought of it, you know, like it was a concert or a presentation. I always knew I'd take credit for it one day, and I wanted each time to be special, to have its own variations. After the piece was complete, I'd go back to my hotel and clean up. Ninety percent of the time I was on a plane heading home within a matter of hours, back in the arms of my loving wife, and no one knew shit."

"Your MO was the same, though," a detective reminded him. "The removal of the eyes and the placement of foreign objects into the sockets. Jurisdictions around the country knew they were dealing with a serial. Sooner or later we'd have traced your travel patterns, found out the same person flew into the locales where the crimes took place."

"So you say," Randy teased, his smugness obvious even on tape. "But 'sooner or later' never came. The relevant jurisdictions never got together to compare notes. You never would've caught me unless my wife had called it in."

My palms were drenched. I kept smoothing them on the chair, but it was leather, and eventually I had to pat them on the cloth of my dress. Turnbull and his prosecutorial team had advised me on my appearance, even though they couldn't advise me on my testimony; I wore a severe navy blouse and matching skirt. The prosecutor and his jury adviser said we were going for "deeply wounded but not pathetic."

"So these people who appeared . . ." The amplified sound of someone flipping through their notes raked the courtroom. " 'Highlighted' was the term you used. They always lived in suburban-type neighborhoods?"

"Not all of them. Not Carrie Pritchett. She

was in an apartment. Which actually made things more difficult, because anyone looking out their window across the courtyard could've seen me when I forced the door."

A sob escaped someone in the observers' gallery. I saw the contorted face of a man in the third row, and recognized him from some of the news coverage. It was Carrie Pritchett's father, who was rumored to have made a fortune catering ritzy affairs in Hollywood. Judge Oliver frowned at him. Pritchett's hand was over his mouth, but a few more hitches escaped before he controlled himself. He must've felt my eyes on him, because when he finally looked up he stared straight at me. It was a hard stare from a grieving man. I felt intrusive and lowered my eyes, knowing I couldn't even begin to imagine the pain Randy had brought down on him.

Anthony Turnbull stood and punched the pause button. The prosecutor affected a grave sense of historical import, as if his bow tie and dour composure alike consciously bore the weight of all past and future American jurisprudence within their mannered presentations. His slight lisp became a tool for emphasis. He addressed me by my married name, even though I was already effectively divorced; the prosecution wanted the jury to feel my intimate betrayal. "Mrs. Mosley, you heard what your husband said about coming back home to you. On any of these occasions, any of the times when we now know he had committed murder while away on these business trips, did he seem distraught or confused when he returned home?"

"No, sir."

"Did you notice him being stressed out, or in any state of emotional upset?"

"Not that I recall."

Turnbull leaned on the jury box. "And yet the defense would have you believe that Mr. Mosley is a lunatic, a man so deranged he didn't know right from wrong. I would ask the jury to consider how a man who planned these murders in detail, down to casing the areas where he would break into the victims' homes, a man who carefully plotted his escape routes, could be in a state of mental impairment severe enough to warrant his being found Not Guilty by Reason of Insanity. It is the state's contention, bolstered by Mrs. Mosley's testimony, that Mr. Mosley was not deranged at all, but rather a coherent, vile butcher. Only a cold, calculating mind,

functioning at a normal or even above average level, could carry out such acts and then
structure his behavior so as to foster a veil of
deceit so total and competent that even his
own wife, the woman who shared his home
on a daily basis, didn't suspect him to be
guilty of anything."

I thought of Randy's bruises and excuses.
I remembered all the presents he used to
buy me when we were first dating, the gold
necklace and the mix CDs he made and the
weekend trips he planned. The sketch he'd
drawn and presented me with on our third
date, how my face in it seemed incomplete,
needy, a portrait of longing that might never
be satisfied; even then he'd been trying to
control me, to offer me a vision of myself as
inadequate on my own. I thought of the way
he would cry out in his sleep at night. I remembered his listening to me for hours, like
I was the only person in the world worth listening to.

Turnbull crossed his arms contemplatively.
"Indeed, during the past few days of testimony we have established that Mr. Mosley
deceived nearly everyone in his life. We have
heard from coworkers who had no clue what
lay behind his facade. We've heard how he

fictionalized an entire life story. He claimed to have lived in orphanages and foster homes, to have suffered abuse at the hands of staff members and the families with whom he was placed. In reality, we have seen the records showing that while his mother may have been abusive on occasion and his biological father absent from the time the defendant was three, he wasn't remanded to state custody until he was nearly fourteen years old. He lived with only one foster family, who from all accounts treated him with the utmost care, as one of their own, until their untimely deaths in a house fire when he was seventeen years old."

"Objection," called out Beyer, the lead defense attorney. "That insinuation is out of line. Not only is Mr. Mosley not on trial in the deaths of his foster parents, but as the state well knows, it has never been established or contended by any law enforcement entity that a crime was even committed in that incident."

"Sustained. Mr. Turnbull, let's stick to the charges at hand." Judge Oliver, a huge looming figure in her robes, no partiality to be found anywhere in her, turned to the jury. "Disregard the prosecution's suggestions where the deaths of Mr. Mosley's foster parents are concerned."

Turnbull frowned. He obviously wanted to continue, but instead he sat back down and pushed play on the recorder again. He had little to lose by allowing Randy to do the talking.

And talk he did. Randy described in detail the killings of Keith and Leslie Hughes, who'd been found in their San Bernardino home, stabbed to death and disfigured in early January of the year 1999. "They were sleeping, and I had the Flexi-cuffs on Keith before Leslie even woke up. I'd say that one took, oh, about three hours. I bled them first. That was the one with the Christmas tree lights, right?"

One of his interviewers said that, yes, Randy had jammed small, colored lightbulbs into the couple's skulls after removing their eyes. Turnbull's deputy prosecutor, a trim, dark-haired woman in her forties named Gladys Meisenheimer, handed out photos of the crime scene while the tape ran, and the jury members glanced quickly at the glossy photos and then passed them down the line.

I remembered that a whole string of lights was missing when I packed up the decorations that year. Randy had been so excited about his upcoming business trip that we spent New Year's Eve at home so he could get some rest. I looked at him again now and he saw that I remembered, too. He mouthed the words "I love you."

The whole thing was a sham, and practically everyone in the courtroom knew it. Randy was as good as strapped down in the injection chamber, but this was his way of holding the spotlight for one more lingering moment. This way he could soak up the attention, the appalled faces of the jury, the uncontainable sounds of grief and pain that frequently sounded from family members in the audience. Despite everything I now knew about him, I had never comprehended the real depth of his sadism until then.

Turnbull stopped the tape after the description of the killing of the Hughes family. He approached the witness chair again and spoke to me with tenderness. "Nina, I know there are people who have suggested that you were somehow involved in all of this, or at least that you must have covered up for your husband. So I have to ask, was there ever any indication in your mind that he could be involved in such heinous acts? Any clue that you were sharing your home with a madman?"

I'd thought about how I would answer that question for quite some time. I started to speak but coughed instead. I cleared my throat and said, "None. At worst I thought maybe he was having an affair, but that was only because he could seem distant, and I told myself that all husbands get that way sooner or later. The only times he was away from me for extended periods were for work. He had his room in the basement, and then his shed out behind our second house, but I never went in there and I never saw anything that would've led me to suspect he was . . . doing the things he was actually doing."

"So his facade never cracked?"

The defense objected and said Turnbull was leading me. The judge suggested that Turnbull rephrase his question.

Turnbull shrugged. "I'll withdraw it altogether, if that will make the defense happy. One final question, Nina, and a simple yes or no will suffice. Before the last weekend you and your husband were together as man and wife, the weekend he came home with Daphne Snyder's blood on his clothes, did you ever consider the idea that he could've been a serial murderer?"

And it had never been easier to lie.

CHAPTER NINETEEN

1.

Carolyn woke me at ten. I couldn't believe I'd slept at all; the last time I remembered looking at the clock it had been close to four in the morning.

"Is he dead?" was my first question.

Carolyn shook her head. "No, but Duane's on the phone and he wants you to listen while he gives me the update. Jeanine Dockery picked him up at the airport and they've been at it for a few hours now."

Still wearing yesterday's clothes, I took a capful of Listerine and swished as I followed her downstairs. She'd moved her camp from the den into the kitchen to be closer to the coffeepot. I winced at the sun coming through the blinds as she pushed the speaker button on the phone. "Baby? She's here now."

"Nina. How are you holding up?" Duane was trying to sound fresh and engaged, but I could hear the lag in his voice as I leaned over the sink and spat. He must've gotten even less sleep than I'd had.

"What did you find out?"

"Well, Jeanine already had her brother's notes sorted into what she believes, and I tend to agree, is roughly chronological order. He has a system all his own, so it's difficult to tell. What we do know is that Mr. Dockery was indeed working on a book about Randy's case. Apparently it's stuck with him all these years, and he kept a file of clippings on Randy's appeals and denials. He seems to feel that time has just about run out, and that once Randy is executed it'll open up some legal hurdles that have impeded his writing the story. His first impulse was to search you out, because, and I'm quoting from some of his earliest notes here: 'Without the ex-wife's side of the story, it's just another sordid PP, and the market for that is sat.'"

"'PP' is 'police procedural' and 'sat' is short for saturated," came another voice over the line, this one gruff and terse, like a life-long smoker who'd endured one too many lectures on her habits.

"That's Jeanine," Duane said.

"Thank you for your help," I said.

"Find my brother."

Duane promised her we'd do our best. "So Dockery was convinced that having Nina's angle was the only way to tell the story. But he didn't have much luck finding you."

"That's because he didn't have us," Carolyn said smartly, and immediately slapped a hand over her mouth. I knew what she was thinking: if they hadn't been good enough to track me down, my son might not have been abducted. She put her other hand on my arm and I said, "Forget it."

"So instead he went to see Randy. Apparently they had at least one face-to-face meeting, which we found on Dockery's schedule and which I've confirmed with the authorities in California. Randy declined my request for an interview, by the way. Nina, he says he'll talk to you."

"Do you think he knows who took Hayden?"

"He still denies any involvement. I don't know. He could be behind the whole thing, and he's holding out to play it for kicks, wanting to torture you. He could really not know, but he's going to try and leverage our interest into talking to you so he can indulge in whatever satisfaction he'll get from hearing the emotion in your voice. Given his general profile, I'd say it's a safe bet he'd get something out of that. The one thing I'm fairly certain of is that he won't help us find Hayden." Duane didn't sound thoroughly convinced by any of his own theories, more like he was obliged to keep all options on the table even though he knew better.

"If there's any chance it will help, I'll talk to him." Carolyn didn't look comfortable with the prospect but I didn't care. If Randy wanted some personal time to fuck with my head, it was a small price to pay for any clue that might help me to get my son back. And I might have some choice words for him.

"Carolyn, you've got the contact number for the prison. Call them when we're done, if you still want to. But first hear me out, because I think we might have another lead worth following up. In the notes from his interview with Randy, Dockery says Randy advised him to search out a person named Carson Beckman. You guys remember him?"

Carolyn tapped on her computer, searching, knowing she'd heard the name before. But I didn't need any reminding. "The only survivor of Randy's attacks," I said.

"Actually there were two. After Randy's arrest, when his face was all over the TV, a woman named Patricia Lineberger positively identified Randy as a man who'd assaulted her fifteen years earlier. This was before he was known to have killed anyone, and the Fed profiler who later interviewed Randy thought it was his fledgling attempt. He tried to force her into his car when she was walking home from a bar near where he was living with his foster parents. She escaped, and it scared her badly enough that she filed a report. But Carson was a different matter. Randy killed the other three members of his family, in his next-to-last assault, a little less than a year before Nina turned him in. Carson was fourteen at the time, and he survived by hiding in a guest room."

"I remember his testimony. It was one of the most frightening things I've ever seen," I said, feeling the sweat pop out on my arms. "The defense team had him on the stand one of the only days I was in court. Poor kid."

"My impression is that things didn't improve

very much for him later on," Duane said. "Randy had suggested Dockery find Carson because, and let me quote from the notes here: 'RRM felt they shared a common bond of ruined childhood. Spoke like CB was important to him.' Dockery suggests that the two of them, victim and perpetrator, may even have been in contact after Randy was sentenced."

Everything inside of me went still. "'CB'? Wasn't that the signature on the letters to Randy that the warden at San Quentin was concerned about?"

Carolyn was staring at me, her mouth open. "'CB Taylor.'"

"Where's Carson Beckman now?" I asked.

"We're not sure. After the murders, his uncle on his father's side became his legal guardian. Dockery has an appointment to see them listed on his calendar, and according to Jeanine the date was only a few weeks before his disappearance."

"Two weeks to the day," Jeanine confirmed from the background.

"I've been calling the uncle's number off and on for the last half hour but I haven't got an answer yet. I left a message. But I'm way ahead of you, and I called Matthews right before I called you guys."

I was shaking my head. "Why would someone who'd been hurt by Randy . . . ? Why would they even want to talk to him in the first place?"

"We don't know," Duane said. "Look, there's no use in my going to California if Randy isn't willing to speak with me. But Beckman's uncle lives not too far outside Chicago, and Ms. Dockery has offered to drive me there this afternoon."

The cigarette voice came on again. "I tried to get in touch with them weeks ago, but they wouldn't talk to me. I have the feeling that once they hear what's happened with your boy, they might be more inclined."

Carolyn told them to quit wasting time talking to us and get on the road.

2.

The afternoon was excruciating. The police didn't want me leaving the house, in case Hayden's abductor attempted to contact me. Matthews called after we both had spoken to Duane and he cautioned us against premature conclusions. "Even if this Carson Beckman kid is involved somehow, apparently no one knows where he is. We were able to track him to an apartment where he was living up until this past November, but the property manager says he got evicted and we've got no current address. The most recent photo I've been able to find is from nearly eight years ago. He's gone from an adolescent to an adult in that time, so he won't look the same. Duane says he's going to try and fax me a more recent photo if he can get one from the uncle."

Other than that, it was quiet. No phone calls, and no incoming e-mails to my computer or Carolyn's. I paced and tried to eat. I only managed to get down half a sandwich. I kept seeing Hayden's eyes as he passed beneath the camera in the classroom hallway; so big and terrified, so helpless, pleading. And now he'd been missing for nearly twenty-four hours. In the company of a man who'd slashed Rachel Dutton's throat. A man who'd adopted my husband's habit of ocular perversion.

Carolyn tried to distract me. At first she talked trivialities, but heard the delusory tone of my responses, and moved on to possible scenarios. Carson could be the guy; Carson could be a sorry kid still wrecked from what had happened to his family; Carson could be dead himself. I stared out the window while she talked. A cop car was parked across the street, and every so often they'd come knock on the front door and ask how we were doing. I was torn between wanting to invite them in out of the cold and hating them for not finding Hayden. It was their job, and instead of being out there beating the bushes they were just sitting, waiting; it was driving me crazy.

I kept hoping that maybe this time they would actually do some good, getting Hayden's picture out there, informing people, talking to possible witnesses. Or maybe someone would recognize the vehicle, spot Hayden's abductor driving along, and call it in. Maybe by some miracle my child would be rescued by a lucky traffic cop and we would be getting the call any minute now.

Someone did see the vehicle. The police found it abandoned less than four blocks from Hayden's school, in a parking garage near an office park. A review of surveillance cameras in the vicinity caught it passing by less than twenty minutes after yesterday's assault. The driver's face wasn't visible in any frame they'd so far been able to isolate. Matthews called us with the news only a moment before it came across as a bulletin running beneath the soap operas on Channel 41.

"We assume he had another vehicle waiting. We're interviewing people in the area but so far there's nothing positive to report." Matthews sounded tired and dejected. "Have you talked to your ex-husband yet?"

"I'm calling San Quentin the minute I get off the phone with you."

CHAPTER TWENTY

As soon as Carson Beckman took his seat on the witness chair during Randy's trial, I knew I'd been mistaken about the sketch tacked to the cabinet doors in the shed out behind our house. It hadn't been a portrait of a future Hayden after all, or even Randy himself as a younger man. No, it had been this boy: there was that same thin unsmiling mouth, the rounded cheeks, and those vacant eyes. Even that bowl of fine, limp hair was the same, except that now I could discern its dirty blond color. Randy had chosen this boy as a subject for his sketch, just as he had drawn my own portrait many years before. I felt an instant and uncomfortable kinship with him.

Knowing what had happened to him, everyone in the courtroom expected him to be painfully childlike. In truth, he'd recently turned sixteen and came across more like a stooped, awkward man than an adolescent. Carson, dressed in a suit and tie that were obviously a size or two too small for his frame (every time he swallowed, the motion of his Adam's apple lifted the entire collar), sat in the witness chair and answered the defense attorney's questions in a monotone. It was surreal, the lack of inflection and emotion on display as the young man recited in short, bland bursts the story of how Randy had murdered everyone in his immediate family.

"That night, when did you first become aware that something was wrong?" Allan Beyer asked. The public defender remained seated at the defense table, so every time Carson had to look in his direction, he also saw Randy. Observing from the gallery, I wondered if that was the way I'd looked when I was up there, loath to shift my eyes toward him. Carson mainly stared off into the distance, at some fixed point above the exit signs over the courtroom doors.

Beyer was the younger of Randy's defense attorneys, and the one better tolerated by the jury. The older man, Gavin Plummer, was a bald, scowling fellow prone to lengthy ruminations and rhetorical leaps that sent eyes rolling in the gallery and more than once provoked outright scoffing from the judge. Beyer had taken over the majority of the questioning early in the day. Now he waited nearly a full minute, idly twisting the curls of his graying hair before he repeated his question.

Carson almost seemed to be smiling, lolling in place, and I guessed that he was drifting on a cushion of prescription drugs. I'd been gulping at least a Xanax a day since Randy's arrest. "When Dana woke me up," Carson said mildly.

"And what did your sister say to you?"

"She said someone was in the house."

The kid wasn't offering anything extra, but this time Beyer didn't allow the silence to take hold. "How did she know?"

"She heard Mom scream, just that one time. The only time before, I guess, he put the tape over her mouth."

" 'He'?"

"Mr. Mosley."

I had remained in the courtroom after suffering through what the attorneys had labeled a "recross." In a reversal that I found extremely offensive, but which Turnbull and the rest of the prosecution team had concluded that I could not avoid, the defense had called me back to testify again, and again it was in relation to the contention that Randy had been mentally unstable at the time he committed his crimes. Turnbull's suspicion was that the defense would assert that since Randy had left me the key to his shed, knowing what I would find within and how I would react—by taking the actions that would end his spree—that he'd actually *wanted* to be caught, tried, and executed. This, so Turnbull's theory went, would prove beyond dispute that Randy's mind was not operating in a rational manner. "A last-ditch grasp to save him from lethal injection," had been Turnbull's summary. "Novel, but something of a reach."

Worse than what they had done to me, though, was their summoning to the stand this lone survivor of Randy's attentions for much the same reason. Although the Beckman murders had taken place out of state, the defense had argued that Carson's testimony was relevant to Randy's state of mind when he committed his crimes. It had been stipulated, and noted, that the witness was testifying under protest, but Beyer and his sallow old grump of a partner had cited some archaic precedent, and Judge Oliver had reluctantly agreed to allow Carson's testimony.

So now Carson fidgeted in the witness chair, his eyes locked on empty space. An archipelago of acne traced across his chin, and his hair was flat and uncombed. His skin had a sallow cast that suggested months sequestered in the same bedroom, leaving to attend school but not much else. The aunt and uncle on his late father's side, who'd taken legal guardianship of the boy, were seated not far away from me in the gallery, but I found that I couldn't meet their eyes.

Beyer tented his fingers and leaned forward at the defense table. "What did Dana tell you to do?"

"She said we should go across the hall and hide in the guest room," Carson said. As though a switch had been tripped, he suddenly became more animated, and began to speak in a rush. "She was talking about climbing out the window. But we were on the third story, and I don't think she was thinking clearly. I was scared so I followed her, and while we were in the hallway we could hear that something was happening in our parents' bedroom, but the door was closed so we couldn't see anything. When we got into the guest room, though, we could hear our parents' door opening and then a voice called her name. It wasn't Mom or Dad. I couldn't look back, because she was pushing me ahead of her, and when I got into the room she slammed the door and that was the last time I saw her until it was over."

The room was dead silent except for the sound of Carson's quickened breathing. Judge Oliver asked him if he was all right to continue. She told him he could have a break if he wanted to. Carson shook his head curtly and gave her what was, under the circumstances, an oddly charming smile. "I'd prefer to get it over with," he said.

Beyer continued his examination and Carson told the story: how he'd been too frightened to move or to turn on the light, so he'd huddled in the guest room in the dark and listened. His sister had screamed once after closing the door behind him and that was all. Carson described the sounds of a struggle. He said, "There were . . . damp sounds, like when you walk through a puddle. Someone beating on a wall or maybe the floor, I don't know." Few in the courtroom could look at him while he was saying these things, but I did. I couldn't look away. A shadow of some prurient intensity, a pale sort of transport I associated with deep and abiding trauma crossed his face before the dead flatness returned.

"How long were you in there?" Beyer asked.

"The police told me later that it was over an hour, but I don't know. I wasn't wearing a watch."

"When did you come out of the guest room?"

"After he told me it was okay."

Beyer didn't have to look up from the desk to note the stark shift in everyone's attention; it was palpable. "Who told you? Mr. Mosley?"

Carson nodded, then leaned toward the microphone mounted on the witness stand. "Yes."

"So he knew you were hiding in there?"

Carson had gone ghastly, and for a moment I thought he might faint and slide sideways out of his chair. But he stayed in place, face frozen, his lips barely moving. "I was sitting on the floor with my back against the door in case he tried to come in. I had decided that I was probably going to die. I heard someone coming out of my parents' room and down the hallway, and I had my hands over my mouth, I remember that, I was trying not to let him hear me breathing or anything. There weren't any more sounds and I started thinking maybe he was already gone and I should get out of the house or try to go and help Dana and my mom and dad, but I was too scared. Too much of a coward."

Beyer said, "Son, no one is suggesting that you could've done anything to prevent what happened to your family. It wasn't your fault. You should be thankful to be alive."

"You'd think so, wouldn't you?" Carson snapped suddenly. We were all watching him intently now, leaning forward in our seats as he glared first at the patronizing defense attorney, then finally over at Randy. "He knew where I was hiding the whole time. He knew. He was standing outside the door, right on the other side of me, and he just started talking, like it was a normal conversation. He said, 'I know there was a boy in this family, I just can't seem to find him anywhere in the house. I'm going to have a son myself, soon. My wife doesn't know it yet, but I think it will be a boy, I can sense it.' And then I must have made some kind of sound because he went, 'Shhhh,' and then he told me to wait another few minutes before I came out. He said not to look for my parents or my sister, but to go straight downstairs and call the police. Then he left and I waited and I did what he said."

Beyer shifted his focus to the jury. "In all his years of committing the most appalling of crimes, Mr. Mosley had never before been in the habit of leaving survivors. He even spoke to Carson prior to leaving the Beckman home, fully aware that Carson would be able to identify his voice to the police, which he in fact did, over a year and a half later. We would ask you to consider whether these are the actions of a sane person acting in his own best self-interest, or rather those of one who was deranged and functioning with an impaired reasoning capacity, as evidenced by a clear wish to be apprehended." Randy saw that his lawyer was ready to let it go at that, and he whispered harshly in Beyer's ear. The public defender was obviously reticent, but did his client's bidding. He turned again to the witness stand. "One more question, young man. Can you offer any explanation other than insanity for *why* Mr. Mosley would have spared you, after what he'd done to your family? Can you think of any sane reason for him to have left you alive?"

The judge looked at Turnbull, expecting his objection. The prosecutor had even risen to his feet when Randy spoke up from the defense table, aiming his words directly at Carson Beckman, who sat motionless and pale on the stand. "He knows," Randy said.

Carson stared at him as though he could make him disappear. His voice was adamant. "No, I don't know."

Judge Oliver told Randy to hold his tongue unless he wished to be sworn in. Beyer and his partner frowned and Beyer put a hand on Randy's arm. But Randy was still watching Carson, and he mouthed the words silently this time, the same as when he'd mouthed that he loved me while I was on the stand: "Yes. You do know."

Turnbull's prosecution team led me out a rear exit from the courthouse, so I could avoid the cameras and questions from the gauntlet of reporters staked out on the front steps. The exit led into a private parking garage reserved for court employees and witnesses who'd been summoned to testify; it was a cold and shadowy concrete structure that I imagined could bring out the paranoid or claustrophobic tendencies in even the most stable folks. Turnbull promised me that this would be the last time I'd have to come to court, unless I wanted to be present when the verdict was read, which he expected to be sometime the following week.

"Is there any chance they'll find him not guilty?" I asked.

"There's always a chance," Turnbull said, fidgeting with his bow tie. "But I think the jury will see through the insanity defense. What they did with that boy today bordered on crass, and juries typically don't respond well to such tactics."

"Then I don't need to be here," I said.

I'd turned to my Accord when I heard one of the entrance doors to the deck opening behind us. I looked around and saw Carson Beckman coming down the aisle of parked vehicles, flanked on either side by his aunt and uncle. I had fully intended to get in my car and drive home as quickly as I could, but seeing him there, a diminished-looking figure between his older guardians, I don't know what possessed me. I couldn't help myself.

They stopped by a big silver SUV, and Carson had one of the rear doors open when I approached to within a few feet and cleared my throat. He turned, as did his uncle, a distinguished- and harried-looking man with snow white hair and a three-piece suit. They both stared at me. "I'm so sorry to disturb you," I said, hearing the tremor in my voice, but determined to overcome it and say what I needed to say. "I'm Nina Sarbaines, I used to be Nina Mosley. Would you mind if I had a quick word with you, Carson? It won't take a moment."

His uncle seemed about to intervene and politely ask me to go and leave them in peace; in fact, I could almost see the words forming in his head, but Carson nodded and quickly walked a little distance away from them. I followed him and when he turned around I couldn't help reaching out and placing a hand on his arm. He flinched and I drew my hand back.

"I just wanted to tell you that I'm sorry," I said in a rush, almost stammering. And of course that wasn't all I wanted to say, but my throat closed up on me and I couldn't continue. I'd meant to tell him that I understood that what my husband had taken from him was irreplaceable. I'd wanted to tell him that although I knew my situation was different, Randy had taken a lot away from me, too.

He stared at me curiously a moment, not obviously offended, but not comforted either. After a pause that lasted long enough to make me question my impulse to confront him, he said in a voice quiet and hollow: "I don't feel right. I don't feel like I'm supposed to feel." Like the lack of emotional response on his part had frightened him. "There's something wrong with me."

"Don't say that," I pleaded. "Don't even think it. That's exactly what Randy would want, and we can't give him one iota more satisfaction than he's already taken from what he's done to us." I couldn't find the words to express what I really wanted to share with him, that I knew what it was like to repress something great and horrible; it was like a solid block in your chest, a state of shock that seemed never-ending. But the level of my presumptuousness in pulling him aside was weighing on me, the sheer indefensible audacity of it.

"You'll feel better eventually," I managed, hearing the dull weak sound of this serviceable platitude. How patronizing I must have seemed, trying to impart some insight to this young man whose entire family had been erased by my husband while I was blithely pretending there was nothing wrong. I was trying to convey to him the feeling of something unlocking, a great unburdening to which I so desperately aspired but of which, in reality, I had no understanding as yet. In my head I was crying out that I'd been cheated, too, but of course what he'd been cheated of was so much greater. Finally, I finished lamely, "You can't let anyone else tell you how to grieve. It'll happen at its own pace, whenever you decide you're ready."

"But I don't even *want* it to happen," he said, and now there was that twinge of terror and uncertainty that had surfaced momentarily on the witness stand. It was like he was begging me for something, some reassurance that he would eventually feel what he was supposed to feel, that he would make contact with something in himself that was essential and elusive.

I realized now, too late, that I had absolutely nothing to offer him by way of apology or reassurance. His uncle was coming across the garage toward us, and I felt a surge of gratitude at any excuse to be released from this proximity to Carson's desperation. I reached out and squeezed his cold, unresponsive hands one more time before walking briskly to my car. I couldn't bear to look back.

CHAPTER TWENTY-ONE

1.

Matthews pulled into the driveway a few hours after we'd last talked to Duane. He didn't have the siren on, but as Carolyn and I watched him hurry up the sidewalk to the front door, the urgency in his step was obvious to us both. I held the door and he nodded at us in turn as he came in.

"We need to talk," he said, dumping a briefcase on the couch. He immediately set to rummaging through it, pulling out reams of papers, scanned photographs, and official reports, then separating them into stacks as Carolyn and I traded anxious glances. Finally, he opened his laptop and placed it beside Carolyn's.

"Did you get to speak to your ex-husband yet?" he asked.

"The people at the prison said they'd get back to me by this afternoon. We're still waiting. Carolyn thinks they wanted to take a crack at him themselves. Is there any word on my son?" I said.

Matthews shook his head. "Sorry. But I've been on the phone with Duane and a variety of Detroit-area police departments for most of the last couple of hours. Duane apologizes for being out of touch with you guys, but he thought it would move things along more quickly if we were getting this information firsthand. He's been sending us stuff via e-mail pretty much the whole time. I'll get to everything, but first I want Nina to see . . ." He trailed off and flipped through some papers until he found what he was looking for. He held up a grainy reproduction of a photograph, obviously scanned through a computer or fax machine. I recognized Carson Beckman's thin mouth and his dark eyes, but this was a very different portrait from the boy I'd last seen in court. His features were more drawn and the cheeks were missing their former fullness, as though his skin had lost its surface tension and lapsed into a loose mask. It made him appear stupefied, an animal facing the sluiceway. He wore three earrings in the right ear, two in the left. An untidy soul patch on his chin added to the general air of unchecked self-disregard. "Have you seen him recently?" Matthews asked.

I shook my head, uncertain. "I don't think so. It's hard to be sure."

Matthews spoke excitedly, as if he was trying to compress everything into a concise summary but knew it was hopeless. "That's Carson's ID card from his last known employer, a delivery service he worked for up until about six months ago. The picture is over a year old, so he's probably changed his appearance to some degree since then. However, we did send a copy of it to the Murphy Police Department in Tennessee, and they said it matches their witness descriptions of the suspect in Julie Craven's murder." He brought out another photo, this one of a college-aged girl. He handed it to me and watched my mouth come unhinged.

"My God," I said.

"Looks a lot like her, doesn't it?" Matthews agreed.

"Who?" Carolyn said.

I set the photo down with trembling hands. "My son's teacher. Rachel Dutton."

"Doesn't necessarily mean anything yet," Matthews warned us. He finally seemed to have his things in the order he wanted them, and he leaned back on the couch and took a deep breath before continuing. "But compulsive killers, especially early on, are often driven to seek out victims that share certain physical characteristics. So, along with everything else we've discovered over the last few hours, it adds up to the most solid lead we've got. Okay. So, after the Beckman family murders, Carson is remanded to the custody of his paternal uncle, a man named Joe Beckman, and his wife Laurie."

"Duane went to see them," Carolyn said.

"That's where he was calling me from. Apparently, Lane Dockery's sister had been trying to contact them for a while now, ever since her brother went missing, but they wouldn't allow it. Either their original interview with Dockery didn't go so well, or Carson told them not to communicate with anyone else about it, we're not sure. But when Duane told them about Hayden, they relented. Carson lived with the aunt and uncle from the time of the murders up until two years back, when he moved into an apartment across town. They thought he was still there until about six weeks ago, when the Realtor called them and said that the apartment was being repossessed because of nonpayment. There were a few boxes there and the aunt and uncle had cosigned the lease, so they picked up the boxes and stowed them in their garage at home. They claim to have had no contact with their nephew since then.

"Duane got part of the story from them and I followed up with the local police, but the rest of this stuff is straight out of Carson's own possessions." He held up pages of handwritten notes. I swallowed thickly, recognizing the handwriting. "Jeanine Dockery says she found her brother's watch among the items in Carson's boxes. It's engraved with Lane Dockery's initials. The aunt and uncle had been fairly reticent about the whole thing up until that point, but Duane said the sister kind of lost it on them and the aunt started spilling while the uncle called his lawyer. Duane convinced Joe Beckman that later on he might want us to consider him to have been a help, rather than a hindrance. The poor people sound like they've been at their wit's end with the whole thing."

I put a hand on Matthews's arm. I could feel his hot skin, the racing pulse. "Start at the beginning, please."

He took another deep breath and said, "Okay, okay. Carson basically had problems from the time he moved into his uncle's house on through the time he left."

"Which is to be expected, after what had happened to him," Carolyn said.

"Agreed. But when you've been in the business as long as I have, you can't help but notice how often the victim becomes the aggressor. I'm sorry, but it's a fact of life. Take Charles Pritchett, for a relevant example. Duane says the aunt kept repeating how Carson was in one kind of therapy or another the whole time he was living with them, and how they couldn't have been expected to do any more than they had. Their own children were grown and moved out of the house, with families of their own, and all of a sudden they have a troubled teen living under their roof. Their kids tried to make Carson feel welcome when they were home on holidays or whatever, but Joe Beckman claims that the more they tried to include him, the more he withdrew. Finally it was basically an arrangement of them providing food, shelter, and an allowance to someone they felt to be a stranger. They intimated some trouble with the authorities but Duane said they wouldn't elaborate. That's why I called up the local guys. Carson is old enough now that any juvenile records should've been expunged, but that doesn't always happen in our own office, so I figured it was worth a shot. I got to one of their records' guys and explained the situation and that a child might be at risk, and he found what I needed."

Matthews slid a few papers out and let us look. They were official police reports, one showing a charge of minor battery against a female. Carson was listed as the suspect. "This is from when he was sixteen," Matthews said. "Only a few months after his testimony at Randy's trial, he attacked a girl at school. She wasn't seriously hurt, but she was scared enough that she and her parents pressed charges and the school kicked him out. The judge in the case felt some sensitivity to Carson's past and suspended the sentence, and he was allowed to finish high school at a private academy." He showed us another incident report. "No conviction on this one, but Carson was brought in and interviewed as a suspect in a series of Peeping Tom complaints in his uncle's neighborhood. I think what we're seeing here is ample evidence of a young man going off track in a real way."

I shifted the papers and found one that had caught my eye before. I held the letter out to Matthews and said, "What about these?"

He nodded. "From Randy. There are quite a few, and it looks like Carson held on to most of them, which suggests to me that he wanted them to found at some point. They've been in contact for years. That's why I asked if you'd talked to Randy yet."

Carolyn was shaking her head. "Why would Carson Beckman want to correspond with the man who'd killed his own family?"

"He wasn't stable," Matthews said, shrugging. "I mean, I can't pretend to know for certain, and we've only got Randy's end of the correspondence. I imagine you were correct in surmising that the prison authorities in California were taking their own shot at getting information from Randy. I've already been in touch with them and they've searched

Randy's cell but haven't found anything. He knows they were reading his mail, all prisoners know it, so I imagine he tossed all of Carson's letters as they came in, or at least before all this blew up." He met my eyes. "We need to call San Quentin back and have them put you in touch with him, right now."

"Not yet," I said. "I need to know the rest about Carson. He's at large and Randy's not."

"Well, like I say, he'd graduated high school and worked a series of jobs in and around the area. No real record of any extracurricular activities, but that's not unusual for a kid his age. We haven't been able to track down any friends or acquaintances, so the Detroit cops are starting with coworkers at his most recent employer. He was in infrequent contact with the aunt and uncle until the Dockery interview, after which he disappeared. They didn't hear any word on him again until the apartment supervisor asked them to pick up his things."

He laid out a series of papers, copied versions of Randy's letters to Carson. "These are in roughly chronological order, as best we can tell. The first one appears to be from just over two years ago, right after New Year's.

Randy makes reference to Carson's 'resolution,' which Duane and I agree must've been some internal prompt that compelled Carson to make contact. He would've been twenty-one years old then, and most severe mental illnesses often manifest their onset between the late teens and early twenties. Then there's this: Randy writes, 'You say you've tried to put it all behind you but the dreams keep coming. You tell me they won't stop, and that Dr. Vale and her pills don't help either. I suggest you ask yourself why you would contact *me*'—and that's Randy's emphasis—'out of all the people in the world. The answers you seek are already there inside, if you have the courage to face them. I cannot give you the answers, but I can offer whatever help I can—I owe you that much, at least. Some ground rules, though: I'm sure you know that all incoming and outgoing mail here is read before being forwarded. The best I can do is set you out a map of sorts, a way to navigate to your own answers. My advice for you right now is to quit taking those pills. Drugs will only dull your soul and obscure the truth.'"

"Jesus," Carolyn breathed.

Matthews showed us other letters. "Notice

how Randy starts addressing Carson by the time they've been communicating for a few months." We saw the dedication line: *Son*. I remembered how Randy had tried to contact us after he'd first been sent to prison, how he'd addressed his letters to Hayden. I swallowed and felt sick. Matthews continued. "Their code wasn't very sophisticated, but it didn't have to be. Unless they're otherwise instructed, prison censors can only scan for overt mentions of criminal activity. The reason the warden initially became suspicious was when Randy mentioned 'the caterer's house' in the aftermath of Pritchett's attempted hit on him. For two guys with very little chance of owning their own homes anytime soon, we see a lot of reference in their correspondence to real estate. From Randy: 'My suggestion is that you start with something much older. A fixer-upper no one else would want. The risk is much lower, since such structures often stand alone and isolated from more crowded neighborhoods. I know they don't hold the same attraction or romance as what you referred to as your "dream home" or your "ideal place" but I strongly advise you to begin with something more rudimentary. Otherwise, the idealized home could prove more than you're yet able to handle.' Randy talks about checking the area beforehand. He tells Carson to 'be sure to familiarize yourself with the other possible buyers who'd have an interest in your acquisition.' He says to check for 'lines-of-sight.' We think he's referring to family members and neighbors."

"Guidelines for how to stalk someone," I said.

"Sounds like it. And it's not long after these letters that we start seeing reference to 'the caterer's house.' The chronology coincides with the failed attempt on Randy's life."

"He sent him after Pritchett?"

Matthews looked at us. "We can't say for certain, can we? But Carson apparently wasn't up for the job, and some of Randy's most recent letters are pretty testy. This one says, 'For all your pages and pages of unseemly smugness about how well it went with the place in Tennessee, and how maybe since that was your first house it could be the best house and you might not want to move again, we both know that isn't how it works. If you ever want to have serious assets, you know you have to build an entire portfolio.'"

"It's him," Carolyn agreed. "Randy must have sent him here after Pritchett exposed you."

"Actually the last letter we have is from right after Lane Dockery came to see Carson, just before Carson dropped off the map. Randy says, 'So you see that I can send you the right prospects. The *writer's house*'—my emphasis—'opens up whole new avenues of revenue to you. We are connected now by more than our shared past, we are connected by a living present and the foreseeable future. You are my hands.'"

They were both looking at me when Matthews let the final page fall to the table. I set my teeth. I told Matthews to call the prison and get things moving.

2.

That voice.

It was amazing; even though I would have told you I'd blocked it completely from memory, as soon as he came on the line it was as though I'd been hearing him speak in the back of my mind every day since I last saw him, smug and corrupt and for one final time on display in court. Once we'd dispensed with the niceties of the prison authorities and the setting of recorders, he was right there in my ear, like we were together again in the very same room.

"Nina? Is this you?"

Matthews and Carolyn were hovering at my shoulder, listening in on the speaker. The detective had coached me on what to say; how to restrain what would undoubtedly be reactions of fear and hatred on my part, to allow Randy his perception of control over the situation, and to glean from him every piece of information we could get.

I kept Hayden paramount in my mind. I said, "Hello, Randy. It's me."

"My God, you sound terrible. I can tell when you've been holding back your tears, trying to be strong. I've seen some studies that say denial can give you cancer. The physical body simply chokes on all that emotion, and poisons itself. You should let go, at least once in your life." His glee was forced, and I tried to savor his failure to deliver the scorn he so obviously wished to impart, but it was difficult over the rushing pulse in my ears.

"Randy, you know why I called. Someone

took our son. I need to know what you know about it."

"Time out," he said, and now the sneer came quickly and unchecked into his tone. "I haven't spoken to you in six years and in all likelihood I'll never speak to you again, so we're going to make this count. You are going to listen to *me*."

And I was stunned to hear the desperation in *his* voice. Had he lain awake nights, down the years, imagining this conversation, trying to find a way to inflict more pain? If so, I was ready to take it. It didn't mean anything at all. "I'm listening, Randy."

"You and a whole room full of cops, no doubt." He seemed to regain some footing and his voice steadied. "I think the last time I saw you was in the courtroom, where you put on your act about how stunned you were to discover the truth about me. I have to ask, did they coach you on that?"

"No. They weren't allowed to."

He scoffed. "If you say so. Please don't bore me, Nina, because I am already ever so bored. I have nothing to tide me over here except the thoughts of you and what you must be going through, so do share."

"I'm dying," I stated, as plainly as I could.

. "Ah, at last," he said. "The ring of truth. You aren't stupid, Nina. You never were. You knew some things about me long before I gave you the gift of the key."

"It didn't seem like a gift, Randy, it seemed like a curse. It seemed like you meant to hurt me from the start, and you did it with lies and your secret life. And when you couldn't do it with those anymore, you did it with the truth. You're a sadist, Randy, and you're right that I knew it somewhere inside. But I never wanted to believe that I could be living with someone as monstrous as you."

Unbidden, the memory came of him and me sitting on the couch in his apartment, the night I broke down and sobbed for half an hour over my ex-boyfriend, Brad. It was melo-drama squared, a horrible display, especially since Randy and I had only been together a few months at the time. But he sat there and rubbed my shoulders and wiped the moisture away from my cheek with gentle fingertips. The giddiness, the thrill that ran all the way through me when he said, "I can take care of you," the admission that he knew I wouldn't love him like I had this other absent shadow, but that he would love me regardless, without condition, and how much the tenderness of it swept me away. I thought I needed taking care of, then; I couldn't conceive of surviving, after being all alone.

"What we want to believe and what we do believe are seldom the same," he said now. "I know you won't believe this either, but I never hated you. I never felt sadistic toward you. I felt as much connection to you as anyone I ever knew. I even thought of sharing it with you before then, before the Snyder girl." His voice climbed, edging toward rhapsody. "You can't imagine it, the intensity of it when you have another human being at your mercy and—"

"I don't imagine it. Where's Carson Beckman?"

"She rises!" Randy gave a laugh that turned into a cough. After a moment he collected himself and apologized. "Sorry, there's not much to do in here except smoke, and I do so with gusto. Now, since this conversation is being taped, I don't want to hold anything back, okay? I want you to be able to go back over it and sift for details and hidden messages. But I'll tell you now, and for free, that there won't be any. My appeals are nearly exhausted, and after this current affair I'm sure they'll set an expeditious date, even in this craven state. So I don't want there to be any more lies between us, Nina, nor anything that won't be independently verified for you in what will most likely be a painfully short period of time. I know you're suffering now, but there may soon come an hour where you wish for the luxury of uncertainty. Sometimes knowing the ending is worse. I'll tell you the truth now, Nina. Ask away."

"Where is Carson Beckman?" I repeated.

"I couldn't begin to guess. I haven't communicated with him, by phone or mail, for a few weeks now. Not since we first heard about you on the news. Initially, he was supposed to be going after Pritchett, but Carson is a boy of limited means and stilted experience, and he never made much progress. I believe that as far as he ever got was sending a suggestive article to the old fool, a way of bragging about his own nascent exploits and unnerving Pritchett at the same time. I thought it was a nice touch but certainly not the payback I'd have preferred. But then Pritchett found you, and now I've got the crown. I realize that you and your police friends may imagine that I have Carson under some diabolical thrall, mind control or some such horseshit, but I assure you that the young man is an independent operator. I didn't make him into what he is, I merely recognized it."

"What is he?"

"He's the same as I, of course. A natural killer, a sociopath, whatever brand you wish to tag him with. You can't imagine the impact when I discovered him. I'd always ascribed to the notion of a godless universe, entropy as the prime mover, only the self to answer to. But after Carson, things started to change, because I realized that for me to have found him, out of all the targets in the world . . . Well, that's a bit much to write off as coincidence, isn't it?

"I first saw his mother and sister walking down Ashland Avenue and they were both highlighted. That had never happened before, two highlights in one sighting, but at the time I wrote it off to chance, mere luck or a possible evolution in my taste. I followed them, I staked out their house per my usual MO. While I was watching, on my second day of surveillance, shit, I'll never forget . . . It was a clear day and the air crisp and cold. No one else was home when young Carson got off the school bus out in front of the house and then ten minutes later he's sneaking out the back door, carrying something cradled in his arms, like it's the biggest secret in the world. It was a burlap sack, like potatoes come in. He left it lying there in the yard and I watched him go back inside and return with a shovel, then he dug a deep hole near the rear of the property, close enough I'd have worried about his seeing me if he hadn't so obviously been consumed with his task. This wasn't the burial of some favored pet—that much was apparent from the way he kept looking around behind him at his house, checking to make sure no one came home while he was busy. He was mostly hidden from the neighboring yards by the trees, which was one of the advantages I was figuring on for my own entry. Once the hole was ready, he upended the bag so that the cat's corpse fell out, and it was in several different pieces. I saw his face when he did it. He stared a long time, reminiscing, and I could tell he was aroused by whatever images came to mind. He balled up the bag and covered his little hole and went inside without looking back.

"I had almost forgotten to breathe. I saw him. I *knew* him."

"And that's why you let him live?"

"Well, of course. I can't claim total foresight—I never imagined he would get in touch with me. I simply wanted to leave him untethered and loose in the world, and to savor the idea that I'd probably prodded him along, given what happened to his dear, clueless family. What I did to them would drive even a normal person to extremes later in life, most likely. With him, it was practically assured." He stated it simply, like an academic rumination. "When he did contact me, at first I only thought of it as an exercise, a mentor/pupil type of relationship. Maybe I could pass along some information that would keep him from making some of the same mistakes I'd made. It got me off, I won't claim that it didn't, but I really didn't consider using him as an extension until Pritchett's ham-fisted attempt on my life. That came only a few months after the initial contact with Carson. Again, I took it as a sign from some greater power, that I'd been offered this tool, blunt and unformed though it was. I believed the boy might have uses, but he is, alas, in many ways too raw for remote control. If he ever can manage to exert some channeling of his impulses, he'll eclipse my numbers. But as of now, there's no telling what he'll do. Quite honestly, I meant for him to kill the both of you, straightaway. I'm not sure what all this kidnapping and such is about. Perhaps the boy has been poisoned by Hollywood scenarios, thinks he can bargain with someone."

I couldn't indulge Matthews's restraints anymore. I said, "My God, Randy. Hayden is your son, too."

"He'll never forget that, now," Randy shot back. "And neither will you."

"Good-bye, Randy."

"Nina? If he does contact you, I suggest you take him seriously. Whatever becomes of Hayden, I don't think Carson will be able to let this go without addressing you personally. I believe that, across the years of our communication, I did manage to transfer a bit of that obsession to him."

"When do you stop hurting me? When do you stop hurting everyone?"

"My damage lasts generations. You can ask any of my victims' surviving families. And in your case, my damage ends generations."

I couldn't help but laugh at him, but it was the kind of sound I knew I'd never want to admit to having made. "You're pathetic, Randy. I mean it. I hope you feel it when you go, when they push the needle in. I hope it hurts." I slammed the phone down.

Carolyn put her arms around me. Matthews wouldn't meet my eyes.

Chapter Twenty-two

Carolyn drove to the store late that night to buy some groceries. I hadn't left the house now for two days straight, and what little remained in the fridge was paltry and unappealing: half a two-liter of flat Coke, some cheese slices, and a couple of frozen dinners; salad dressing and grapes gone mushy. I lay on the couch while she was gone, thinking about Hayden and Carson and all the rest of it. Matthews had left hours ago, with assurances that he'd call if he heard any news. On TV, a sitcom babbled and droned, and I found the canned laughter, normally an irritant even on my favorite shows, soothing, like waves on the beach of some alien sea.

I didn't realize I'd fallen asleep until the front door opened. Carolyn stood there holding my door key while I blinked and sat up. Her color was high and she wasn't carrying any grocery bags.

"What now?" I said.

She looked behind her, a brief glance out the open door toward the police cruiser parked by the sidewalk. She turned back to me and closed the door. "I'm trusting you to do the right thing here," she said. "Don't make me regret it. This was on my windshield when I came out of the store." And she pulled an envelope from her coat pocket.

Her hand was already shaking and I noted the clear tremor in my own as I took it from her. It was a plain, white envelope, letter-sized, just like the one Pritchett had passed along to me in a similar fashion. The same sort Carson Beckman had sent to him. Inside, on a single sheet of paper, were block letters written in Magic Marker: FOLLOW THE DIRECTIONS AND BE HERE TOMORROW AT NINE O'CLOCK. NINA ONLY. NO COPS, NO FRIENDS. IF YOU AREN'T ALONE, THE OTHER ONE COMES OUT. After the text was a list of street directions, rights and lefts that I recognized would lead me about a half hour west of Cary, into Chatham County. It was one of the few rural areas remaining in the Raleigh/Durham/Chapel Hill area, mostly farmland punctuated by small communities and encroaching developments. The rare sort of place where the residents still fight Wal-Mart.

My hands were shaking so badly I couldn't hold on to the page. I placed it gently on the coffee table beside Carolyn's laptop. I turned to Carolyn. "What 'other one comes out'? What does that mean?"

She said, "I wanted you to read it first. I think that was the intention. And I think we should sit down." Then she handed me the other folded piece of paper that had accompanied the letter.

On it was a scanned photograph. The picture showed my son, duct tape around his wrists and ankles, posed on a plaid couch whose pattern might have been fashionable in the 1970s. A stark, empty wall behind him, a cellar or basement; gray concrete blocks, no visible windows. Hayden wore another strip of tape across his mouth, just as he had in the surveillance photos from the school camera. Except now there was a black, crudely fashioned patch of gauze held over his left eye by another swatch of gray tape.

"Oh, God." One hand clamped over my mouth—again, like all those years ago standing in Randy's shed, that involuntary sealing off. *My baby's eyes.*

Carolyn sat beside me, gently prying the photo away. "We need to walk out that door right now and tell the police. They'll call Matthews. He can have a SWAT team out there in an hour and we can bring Hayden home tonight."

"No." My response was immediate and adamant. In my mind, I could already see them unloading a Hayden-sized body bag out the front door of some nondescript hovel. Scenes of hostage standoffs on the evening news replayed in my mind. The outcomes were rarely good. And Carson was totally fucking insane, at least as insane as Randy and maybe a good bit more. I took back the photo and made Carolyn look at it. "You see what he already did to one eye. If this bastard could do that, to a child, then do you think he'll have any trouble killing him? Look."

Carolyn tried reasoning with me. "If you go alone, he'll just kill both of you—"

I realized I was barely breathing. It was like there had been a rushing, consuming roar in my ears and my head for years, but now things had gone quiet. Still, and calm and clear. "Maybe not," I said. "Maybe he wants me more than Hayden. I mean, that's what all this is about, right? You heard Randy on the phone. He's using Carson as his last chance to finish me off, his last opportunity to work his will on me. If Carson wanted Hayden dead, then he wouldn't have sent this message, he'd have just killed him and buried him and then come back for me another time."

"He might have done that already," Carolyn said, as softly as she could. "We don't know when that picture was taken, or what's happened since."

"Don't make me take a chance on my son's life, Carolyn. You can't."

She knew well enough that I was serious, but she tried one last time. "At least let me call Duane. Carson has to have been in this vicinity within the past half hour. He had to have been watching the house, and followed me to the store to leave the note. It's possible he's still watching us, right now."

I shook my head and held up the directions. "Then he's been watching us for longer than the past few hours. He knows the police are here. If the police haven't noticed him in all that time, what makes you think they'll be able to track him now?"

"There must be security cameras in the parking lot at the grocery store. Maybe we can find out what kind of vehicle he's driving, and—"

I put both hands on her shoulders. "Carolyn, stop. If I have to, I'll find a way to duck you and the police, both. Carson isn't demanding any ransom, he isn't asking for anything. He doesn't intend to let us live. I know that. But you remember what Randy said? He said I should take Carson seriously, and I think this is what he meant. This is my chance to do something, and I need your help, but I can't risk anyone else fucking it up. You've already given me more than I ever could've asked you for, but this is the single most important thing you could ever do for me in either of our lives, the thing that will erase your helping Pritchett find me and everything that's come about because of that. Help me save my son. Don't tell anyone. Not Duane or the cops."

She hung her head and I saw tears falling, but she didn't make a sound. Finally she went to her overnight bag and pulled out a handgun that looked as though it must weigh fifty pounds. "If you're determined, you're taking one of these. And I'm going with you, at least until you're at the house. I can wait by the end of the driveway if you want, but I'm going. That's not negotiable."

"I want you to go," I assured her. "But right now we need to go unload the groceries from your car before the cops realize something's wrong."

CHAPTER TWENTY-THREE

1.

If you insist on going through with this, I insist on you wearing it," Carolyn said. "Duane and I both carry them in our cars, in case of confrontation. After what happened to him . . ."

As part of her efforts to keep me from going through with answering Carson's summons, she'd spent a good deal of last night telling me, in lucid and excruciating detail, about how Duane's career as a cop had ended. He'd been a detective by then, after serving his time on the street in a patrol car. He and his partner had gone to arrest a crooked councilman; the councilman had been tipped that they were coming; he responded to the knock on his door by politely inviting the men in, then shooting them both from three feet away. Duane's partner was killed instantly; Duane sustained wounds to the chest and head; the councilman then turned the gun on himself. That was how Duane Rowe had left the Reston, VA, police department with a full pension plus disability, and how he'd had the cash to start his own business. She'd met him while covering the story for the local newspaper, and the rest, as they say . . .

Carolyn reminded me of grave details now as she pulled the straps tight across my ribs and buckled the sides. She made her point with numbers: Duane sopped up nearly twenty pints of blood in the ER, underwent eight different surgeries over a period of twenty months, and endured four years of painful physical therapy during his recovery. The hair never grew back over the entry wounds in his scalp and that's why he favored a baseball cap to this day.

I let my arms fall back. The Kevlar vest was bulky and uncomfortable, and I'd told her I didn't want to do anything that might make Carson suspicious, but she wasn't taking no for an answer. "His note didn't place any specific restrictions on you protecting yourself," she advised me, for the umpteenth time.

There was little point in reminding her that we weren't dealing with a person who would be likely to consider whether or not I'd breached the prescribed etiquette; she knew. She was feeling impotent and frightened, because this wasn't how she'd have scripted it. She wanted SWAT teams descending from helicopters, snipers in the tree line. I only wanted my son safe and alive in my arms. It was my responsibility to get to him, even if it was only so that neither of us would be alone when Carson made his final move against us.

Carolyn helped me put my coat on and then she stepped back and appraised me. "If he frisks you, he'll know right away."

"But it won't matter, because you'll be watching out for us." I realized, dimly and remotely, that I had no expectations of survival at this point. Hayden was all that mattered.

"That's the plan," she said with a sigh. "You know, we're doing all this without really knowing what we're walking into. Every one of our assumptions could be wrong. He could be working with a second party. There could be booby traps at the house, he could see me when we drive in—"

I stopped her. "You're right, we don't know. So we better get moving with what we've got." It was seven thirty. The drive would take between a half hour to forty-five minutes, and I wanted to have plenty of time in case we hit traffic or any other impediments.

Carolyn wore one gun in a shoulder holster, and another on her belt. She had a short knife clipped onto the belt as well. I carried the revolver she'd loaned me in my right front coat pocket.

She inclined her head toward mine and we stood there touching while her lips moved silently. When she said, "Amen," I said, "Amen."

We'd spent part of last night searching the Net and then going over satellite photos of the property Carson had specified in his directions. It was a small house in the middle of five acres of land, the title still owned by the bank but the mortgage held by one Mr. Abraham Locke. We found his number in the phone book. Carolyn included it, and directions to the house, along with a summary of our intentions, in a note we left behind for the cops to find, in case things went bad. We were operating on the assumption that Mr. Locke wasn't a party to the kidnapping; he was most likely out of town or dead. Locke was seventy-eight years old, a widower for more than a decade. His one grown child lived in Florida.

The blueprints available online gave the impression of a small, cozy house, albeit one with few hiding places. There were closets and a workroom, but the whole place was just the single ground floor and a basement. Carolyn thought the basement was the most likely place for Carson to be holding Hayden; the photo had certainly been taken there. I agreed, but I couldn't look at that picture for more than a few seconds at a time without feeling sick. Carolyn kept forcing me back to it. She asked what I saw. Where were the possible exits? How would we get downstairs and find Hayden and get him out? We went through scenario after scenario; all the outcomes seemed hopelessly bad.

But now there was no more time, so we went into the garage and I didn't lock the door behind me. I told Carolyn I planned to bring Hayden back home before the day was out.

2.

She stopped briefly and got out to chat with the cops parked on the street. "I'm going to get her car serviced," Carolyn said, leaning on their cruiser and talking through their window. "She set up an appointment for a brake job before everything happened, and I need some fresh air anyway. Don't bother her, though, unless it's important. I made her take a Xanax. The lady needs sleep."

After we'd driven out of the neighborhood, I crawled up from under the blanket where I'd hidden in the rear floorboard. "I hate that you had to do that," I said.

"I do, too."

It was a cold, cloudy morning, overcast, right on that frosty verge of heralding either a cold rain or a wet snow. Traffic on the interstate was fairly heavy, typical for a weekday. I stared out the window at the commuters in their cars, babbling into cell phones or crooning along with whatever song was playing on their radios. I thought very clearly: *My*

God, they have no idea. No idea that I may be on my way to see my son for the last time. No idea that traveling this same road with them was someone like me, who'd once been among their cheery and clueless ranks but was now fighting for the very life of the one she loved most. I wished I could tell them all to slow down—didn't they know how easily accidents happen, all the unintended consequences that could come from taking your eyes off the road to answer that phone or adjust the station? I wanted to warn them to hold the people in their lives extra-tight, especially the children, to overlook those nagging everyday nuisances and celebrate each moment they shared. I'd come up short with Hayden, hadn't watched over him as closely as I should have, hadn't encouraged his passions, hadn't memorized his eyes or his laughter as he grew. You do all those things when you're a new parent, but as time goes on, you forget that they're changing and every day is one less day you'll have with them. Oh, God, my dear sweet son.

I prayed for him to be all right. I prayed that all these rushing motorists, who appeared to me as clever imitations of the living, closed off from everything outside their

speeding vehicles, would get smart and become more diligent, so that they'd never feel
this gnawing terror I felt inside. How many of
them were at this very moment suffocating
from denial of unspoken suspicions, some
vague unease perhaps driven by the behavior
of someone close to them? How attentively
did they watch their own children, and how
many were hiding their own secrets? A part
of me wanted to envy them in their oblivious-
ness, but now, at this late stage, I recognized that impulse as the most dangerous
of seductions. It was my own resolute refusal
to face reality that had led me to this very
moment.

As soon as we got off I-40 and wound our
way past Chapel Hill and into Chatham
County, the number of cars dropped off and
the roads became narrow two lanes thread-
ing through the rolling fields and forests. I
kept checking my watch; last night, it felt like
time was moving so slowly that it was mad-
dening, but each second elapsed far too
quickly now.

We followed Carson's directions onto Old
Lystra Road. An empty, crumbling farmhouse, overgrown by kudzu, marked the
turn. Just over a mile farther on, we saw the

border of Abraham Locke's property. A beige metal mailbox stood among the trees at the end of a gravel driveway. Carolyn drove past it at speed and continued down the road until we found a suitable side road where we could turn around. The landscape out here was thick with dense stands of trees, and all the homes seemed to be set well back from the road. Only a few miles behind us, sprawl was eating away the countryside, but out here the natives were so far holding fast.

Which was too bad for us, because once we turned down Locke's driveway, we'd largely be out of view from the road. Carolyn put the car in park and we traded places. She lay down under the same blanket that had hidden me as we left my house. My hands felt cool and clammy inside my gloves, even though we had the heater blasting. I reversed out of the turnaround and started slowly back down Old Lystra toward Locke's driveway. It was ten minutes before nine. I kept telling myself I'd have Hayden back soon.

"One more time," Carolyn said from behind me.

We'd been over it more times than I cared to count, but I recited what I knew she wanted to hear: "If he comes out to search the car and Hayden isn't with him, you'll shoot him right there and we'll hope for the best." I couldn't help but sound skeptical of our half-assed contingency plan. "Otherwise, I go in alone. You'll wait ten seconds after I've entered the house, and then you come in behind me. If Hayden isn't within Carson's reach, I'll say, 'Where is he?' loudly. You'll go around and check the basement door, which should be accessible from the backyard if the blueprints were accurate. But Carson will most likely have Hayden with him if he means to negotiate his release."

"Which he doesn't, or he'd have indicated it in his note."

"We don't know anything for sure."

Carolyn decided it was time for tough love. "Yes, we do. He means to kill you both. I won't move in until we know Hayden is alive, but if either of us gets a clear, unobstructed shot at Carson Beckman, we need to take it. Don't shoot to wound him. Aim for the dead center of his chest or forehead. The chest area is a much bigger target, so go for that if you can."

She'd made these points over and over. "What if he's wearing a Kevlar vest?" I asked.

"Then aim for his fucking eyes." Her voice was flat and cold and exactly what I needed to hear. "Is your safety off?"

I checked for the third time. I told her I was good to go. In a lifetime of lies and denial and willful blindness, it was among my biggest ever.

3.

At five minutes until nine o'clock, I took the turn into Locke's driveway. It was as though we could hear each individual shard of gravel grinding beneath the tires. The narrow drive bent slightly toward the right, then the house came into view. It was exactly as we'd imagined from the blueprints; a one-story ranch with trees close in the yard, in some cases with their branches brushing the weathered shingles. The driveway terminated in a two-car garage. A Toyota Land Cruiser and a Lincoln town car shared the bay. Carolyn, still hunched down in the rear, asked me what I was seeing. I described it to her through tight lips.

"Lane Dockery owned a Land Cruiser," she recalled.

"Carson must've changed the plates, then."

I cut the engine and tried to swallow but my throat only clicked dryly. I took off my gloves, put one hand in my pocket, and took hold of the pistol grip. A door was visible in the garage past the Land Cruiser, or I could take the brick walkway leading around the garage to the front door.

Carolyn asked, "Do you see him?"

"No."

"I'm sure he can see you. Get moving."

I finally managed to unlock my muscles and climb out of the car. My breath streamed past my face and I thought I might be sick. Stillness shrouded the world, with only that impersonal, arctic sound of wind moving the tree branches high overhead, the brittle creaking and clattering as the boughs bent and scraped together. I walked stiffly around the garage, down the walkway out front. The curtains were tightly drawn across both sets of windows I could see. Off to my left there was only a thick encroachment of trees, intermittent views of the road fifty yards away. No cars passed.

At the unadorned front door, I lifted my hand to knock when a voice came clearly from the other side: "Who were you talking to out there?"

"Myself," I answered without hesitation.

"Come in with your hands up, where I can see them." Tremors all through the words, like whoever spoke them was as frightened as I was, although I didn't think that was possible. I was so intensely terrified that I felt high, removed from my physicality, liable at any moment to disintegrate into a clutch of ghosts.

The front door opened onto a dim hallway, with a large living room off to my right. An absence of lighting and the drawn curtains cast the scene in an underwater gloom, and it took my eyes a moment to adjust. But the smell was rank and immediate. As the shadows resolved themselves in the dimness, I saw a body lying in the hallway that led back into the confines of the house; it was wrapped in a clear plastic tarp, so I couldn't see any features, but it was man-sized, not child-sized. Blood coagulated along the edges of the liner, and a pair of yellowed feet with long, curling toenails was exposed at the end of the roll. I briefly wondered how Abraham Locke had died, whether Carson had simply knocked on the door and greeted him with a slashing fury, or if he'd broken into the house during the night. Had the old man come awake in time to see the blade descending toward him? And had he retained his eyes, did they still peer out from within that opaque shroud?

I remembered Randy's letters to Carson, advising him to prey on the old and weak because they were isolated and more likely to go without being reported as missing for much longer than a younger, more connected person. Locke had probably met his death for no more reason than that his home was far enough off the beaten path to suit Carson's designs.

The floors were hardwood, the walls papered in a pale beige pattern that might have been cheery in the years before it had faded to a dingy jaundiced cast. The stucco ceilings showed water stains and cobwebs clung in mossy strands in the high corners. It was chilly in here, the temperature not much warmer than outside. Somewhere back in the farther rooms of the house, a clock ticked loudly.

I turned to my right and saw Carson Beckman seated in the living room, perched on a worn faux-velvet easy chair in front of a cold, empty fireplace. He was watching me with rapt attention in the gloom, evaluating the degree of my fear, and a flash of pleasure tightened his face when I gasped at seeing him there. A sizable bass was mounted above the mantel behind him, a twisted silvery fish shape with gaping mouth and empty marble eyes. Framed family photographs on the walls, Locke with his late wife and child, all dressed in the fashions of an earlier decade. A couch underneath the curtained windows, an old gray blanket or quilt stretched across the cushions. Carson wore a body harness and my son was strapped across the front of him. It was obviously a makeshift contraption, as Hayden was too large for it, but as Carson stood up, it became apparent that it was also effective; my son's body moved in concert with his captor's. Hayden's hands were taped together in front of him, and he was wearing the same tape across his mouth. Both of his eyes were covered in gauze. His feet were free, though, bare and kicking, and a soft involuntary moan escaped me at the sight of his utter vulnerability. Hayden heard it and started squirming, screaming against his gag. Carson carried a sawed-off shotgun, which he now leveled at me.

I kept my hands up. Carson beamed, a shark's smile from the bottom of the black ocean floor, and gestured with the shotgun. "I can't buy one of these in Illinois, because of my mental health background. Good thing the homeowner kept this one in his closet. I fired it a couple of times yesterday, out in the backyard. Thing will cut a tree in half. So don't fuck with me."

I couldn't look away from Hayden. He was struggling and Carson wove an inch or two to either side, trying to keep his balance against the fifty pounds of child trying to pull away from his chest. "Oh, God, baby," I breathed. "Mommy's here."

This was not the same Carson who'd been in court the last time I saw him. Not the same even as the haunted loner on the ID badge Matthews had shown me. He was more gaunt, lankier, reduced somehow despite his height, like he'd been eaten away at the center and might snap in two if he tried to bend over at the waist. He wore jeans so baggy they threatened to trip him up, and unlaced hiking boots too large for his feet. Probably he'd found them in the same closet as Locke's shotgun. His face in the shadows was ravaged, lined and pitted with traces more pronounced than those of men twice his age. Blackened pouches surrounded eyes that held entire dead worlds of swirling ash. He stared at me, a sad, serious smile spreading across his face like the fissure in a mountainside giving way.

"Let him go," I demanded.

Carson aimed the gun at me. He said, "He's going to be so proud of what I've done."

That was when I knew he was going to kill me. Instinct took over. I flinched sideways as I moved toward him, trying to reach Hayden. Not a good idea, since the Kevlar protected my front and back but didn't extend to the sides, where there were only the canvas straps and buckles. The blast from the shotgun was huge and somehow flat, like a stone wall collapsing onto a marble floor. I took the full force in my right rib cage, and slammed off the wall in the entrance hallway. My legs went out and I sprawled facedown. I couldn't breathe. I heard his footsteps approaching, and rolled over onto my back. My right side was completely numb; I couldn't move that arm. The pistol was in that pocket. My chest heaved, trying to inhale against what felt like a metric ton of pressure squeezing the air from my lungs.

The ringing in my ears nearly blocked what Carson was saying as he came and stood over me, smoke still trailing out of the barrel he'd fired. The other one was less than a foot away from my face, and I could feel the gun's heat.

"I was going to kill you both, last week," he said, smiling in a remote kind of way now. "But then I followed you to school when you went to pick Hayden up, and that's when I saw the teacher. That lady was *exactly* my type. She got highlighted and I shifted my plans. I bet your husband was sort of pissed about that. Still, it was only a postponement."

I tried to say, "my ex-husband," but it was impossible with no breath.

I didn't hear whatever it was that he heard right then. But his head snapped up and he turned quickly, with surprising agility for a man with another person strapped to his chest, and fired his second barrel through the front window. The curtains blew apart and glass shattered and I saw Carolyn's hand flailing as she went down. She'd been approaching the front door, crouched over, but he'd heard her coming. I tried to scream and breathed fire. Hayden was still shrieking against his gag and Carson slapped him on the side of the head before turning back to me.

"No fair," he chastised me. "You were supposed to come by yourself. Not that I expected you to. But that one's down, and I'm ready for however many more you've got coming. God, isn't it great to *feel*?" He knelt and smoothed a hand over my hair. It came away bloody and he showed it to me. The world spun and Hayden's kicking foot brushed my arm. I tried to grab hold but Carson pushed my hand away as he stood and broke the breech on the sawed-off. He chucked the empty cartridges and pulled two more shells from the pocket of his jeans.

"One thing I can tell you that might help," Carson said. "I couldn't kill your boy. Randall told me that harvesting a child was special, they see special things, and it was like a delicacy. He thinks I'm just like him, but really I'm not. I couldn't do it to a child. I didn't even touch his eyes. That was just to get you out here. I tried but I couldn't do it. He's too much like I was, back before all this started. I want him to have a chance, away from you and his father both. I'll take him with me. He's my brother."

I was gasping like a landed fish. I thought

of the bass mounted above the fireplace, how it must have died straining in the filthy shallow bilge water of some flatboat.

"Your husband is the only one who ever recognized me for what I was," Carson said quietly, rolling the shells between his thumb and fingers. "If anyone else had known, they'd have tried to lock me up, but Randall understands. He knows what it's like to live completely alone, with no one there who could possibly know you, the reality of what goes on inside. All those years, ever since I really started to grow up, I knew something was wrong with me. I dreamed of doing things, awful, ugly things to people, and I knew it wasn't right. I knew I couldn't tell anyone. So I hurt other things instead. But then Randall Roberts Mosley came into my home and even after he left me alive he never really *left.* I kept dreaming of all those things I wanted to do, but now I dreamed about him, too. I thought about contacting him for years and years before I actually did it. That was the bravest thing I ever did in my life, just putting that first letter in the mail. When he wrote me back, when I realized he understood, even though we were writing in code . . . That was when I knew I could really *do* the things I'd always dreamed. He gave me the strength to quit fighting it, to accept who I was and seek out the face from my dreams."

"He's . . . a piece of shit," I managed.

Carson looked at me sadly. "I know," he said. "But so am I." He loaded the shells into the breech and tried to snap the shotgun shut, but Hayden kicked out again and this time his small, tender foot wedged between the stock and the barrels. He screamed. Carson laughed and moved his foot away. The front door opened. Carson turned as Carolyn shoved herself into the hallway, laid out on the floor, both hands on her gun and aiming steadily as she fired twice. The shots were tiny plosives in my ringing ears. Carson's head snapped one way and then another, blood and tissue exploding as his face disintegrated. I screamed for Carolyn to stop, certain that Hayden would be hit. Carson twisted and fell over on his side, facing me. Hayden flailed in his grip and blood cascaded down across both of them.

Carolyn set her gun carefully on the thin carpet and looked at me. I saw that her back had been torn open by the buckshot, a large swatch of bare and bloody sinew above her waist. Blue smoke choked the air and she said, "Called . . . I called the cops before I got out of the car."

I couldn't answer her. I pulled myself across the floor on my fingernails. I made it to Hayden and Carson, tearing at harness straps and the strips of tape binding my son. He screamed when I pulled the tape off his mouth: "Mommy! Mommy!" I asked him if he was hurt but he just kept crying. I worked the straps until they came loose and he tumbled into my arms. He got the tape off his own eyes and blinked at me. I saw the full blue of his irises and that's when I really lost it, screaming and crying along with him.

Finally he stopped sobbing and managed to say, "M-mom, you're bleeding. Are you okay?"

I didn't tell him that it was getting more and more difficult to breathe. I looked over at Carolyn and said, "Hayden? You need to go get that blanket off the couch and put it on her back, okay? Hold it there as tight as you can."

He didn't want to leave me but he did it. Carolyn made a painful sound when the blanket touched her skin, and I wasn't sure it was the most sanitary course of action, but she was bleeding a lot more profusely than I was. She hadn't been wearing a vest, and there'd been nothing to absorb the blast but skin and bone. She stared at me now, looking more exhausted than anything. I supposed she was in shock, and her next comment removed all doubt.

"I give you the vest and you manage to get shot in the one place it doesn't cover you," she said, sounding somewhat puzzled and amazed. "I'm probably going to be in some trouble for not calling the police sooner. You'd damn well better live long enough to explain all this to Duane."

EPILOGUE

1.

Randall Roberts Mosley's execution was scheduled for March 10 at six o'clock in the morning. It was still twilight when I arrived at the penitentiary, passing by a small cluster of death penalty opponents who hefted placards and candles as they marched outside the gates. I knew from the news coverage that some of Randy's victims' families were among the protesters; I admired their sense of forgiveness and idealism, but I could never stand with them. Not for Randy.

I sat in the observation room with eleven other people, mostly relatives of the victims, and a couple of witnesses from the press.

None of Randy's lawyers showed up. The warden came in and introduced himself and briefly summarized what we were about to see, and the rules of behavior. Warden Jenkins was a small man in his sixties, informally dressed in a collarless shirt and khaki jacket. He advised us to try to contain any overt displays of emotion, although he understood how difficult that might be. He said that, under normal circumstances, the prisoner would be given a chance to say some last words, but that Mr. Mosley wasn't handling the situation very well and wouldn't be making any statements.

Randy had tried to get in touch with me several times during the past year, since the ordeal with Carson Beckman. I'd ignored his requests. I was glad he wouldn't have the chance to speak today. I felt like I'd given him ample chance to say anything he had to say. Two years of dating, four years of marriage, and then another seven when I'd suffered alone; I don't think I'd have ever again listened to so much as a single word that came from his mouth.

We watched as he was brought into the room at five minutes before six, fully restrained, with two guards holding his legs and another couple holding his arms. I was momentarily taken aback by how fat he'd become, an extra hundred pounds at least since the day he left the key for me. He was bald, too, and it made him look even more pathetic. It didn't help his fearsome image that he was twisting and fighting every inch of the way. Several of the people in the observation room shifted uncomfortably, and I understood; movies had trained us for a solemn occasion, informed by quiet gravitas from the condemned and honorable satisfaction from the maligned. But Randy, as ever, seemed determined to spoil it for everyone. He screamed through his rubber mouthpiece and pushed at the guards as they strapped him onto the table. Canvas straps secured his arms and legs, and I couldn't help but think of Hayden and Carson Beckman.

I'd left Hayden back east with the McPhersons, who'd started speaking to me again once I became a celebrity of the acceptable sort. And imagine, all it took was my getting shot.

Seated on my right side was Dennis Hughes, the younger brother of Keith. Keith and Leslie Hughes had been murdered less than a year before I found out I was pregnant with Hayden. On my left were Paul and Katherine Zimmerman—their daughter Jane was killed shortly after Randy and I were first married, while he was on a business trip to Minneapolis.

Dennis held my right hand, tightly. Katherine Zimmerman held my left.

The majority of the impacted families had declined their invitations. Despite the many who'd gone on the news to express their opposition to the sentence, most were satisfied with it, but felt no compulsion to see it carried out in person. Charles Pritchett was in the observation room, seated behind me and to the right. I saw no reason to speak to him, and he finally afforded me the same respect.

The surgeons had dug over forty pellets out of my side. The force of the impact broke two ribs, and I wouldn't ever be sleeping on that side again. I lost part of my liver, and was later told that I'd been within minutes of bleeding to death when the paramedics had arrived at Abraham Locke's house. The liver is a regenerative organ, I was pleased to discover, and grew back. I spent two weeks in the hospital and countless hours being interviewed by Detective Matthews and other policemen, all of whom were uniformly displeased with me. None, however, was as angry as Duane Rowe, who hadn't spoken more than a few words to me in the entire time since, despite the fact that his wife and I had kept in touch. He was initially so furious with Carolyn that he might've divorced her, if he hadn't been so happy to have her alive. Her wounds weren't as serious as mine, but she'd undergone multiple skin grafts, and spent several months recuperating.

I had rejected the book and movie offers, but given the Rowes my blessing to accept the same. From what I read in the papers, they'd sold the rights for a healthy six figures. Lane Dockery's sister was writing a book of her own.

When Randy was finally strapped down, all the fight seemed to go out of him at once. The medics tipped the table where he was splayed, and it canted upward slightly so that he was able to look at us. The glass separating the observers' gallery from the injection room wasn't mirrored, and the warden had told us he would be able to see us clearly. He granted his final regard to each of the witnesses in turn, his face pinched and twisted. I heard Pritchett cursing him one last time. Then Randy's eyes settled on me.

He tried for a menacing grin, but with the rubber guard jammed between his teeth he just looked ill.

I smiled for him, though. As the medic hooked up the IV and pushed the plunger on the first syringe, the one with the drugs that would sedate him, I kept looking right into his eyes. I wanted my face to be the last thing he ever saw.

The terror and sorrow he experienced at the end were clear in his expression, until the drugs hit his nervous system and his features went slack. Then the medic fed the other drugs into the IV line, the ones that would paralyze him and finally stop his heart. A few minutes crept by before his chest quit rising and falling. A minute or so after that, a doctor pronounced him dead.

2.

Two months later, I sat in Pullen Park with Jeanine Dockery, watching the children play in the mild midmorning sunshine. Jeanine had flown in that morning and was leaving the next day to meet with her publishers in New York. The hard glare reminded me of how I'd first met Duane and Carolyn Rowe in this very same park last winter. Too much had happened since that meeting, and I didn't see Duane anymore, and Carolyn only rarely. The press surrounding the Carson Beckman affair had made it difficult for them to continue with any anonymity in their chosen profession, so they'd shifted their duties from fieldwork to managing a small workforce of other private investigators, consisting mostly of former police officers that knew Duane personally. Carolyn had told me Detective Matthews had retired from the Cary police force to take a job with their firm.

"They do good work," Jeanine said when I updated her. "And they were helpful in writing the book." Jeanine looked better than I'd imagined when I only knew her as a voice on the phone. A slender, soft-featured woman of fifty-eight with hazel eyes and auburn hair, she was slightly stooped from an early onset of osteoporosis. The wrinkles that bunched her face when she smiled were an attractive feature rather than a distracting one. But her voice was still that gravely, throaty rumble, and I enjoyed listening to her as she told me about the publication schedule for her nonfiction book. She kept referring to it as "Lane's book," but I knew from Carolyn that Jeanine had done almost every bit of the work.

"I'm sorry I wasn't more helpful with that," I admitted. "I needed to forget about as much as I could."

She waved a hand dismissively and took a bite of her ice cream cone, careful not to drip it on her pink pantsuit. She looked over toward the swing set. "Thank you for letting me come and visit with Hayden," she said. "I needed to see the life that was spared. I needed to know Lane's death helped save someone in some way."

In one of Carson Beckman's final letters from Randy, there'd been mention of "the final disposition of the writer's property." Randy said the view sounded spectacular, but that Carson probably should have "made it farther from your own property line." After Carson's death, Jeanine and a swarm of Illinois state police had combed over the city blocks surrounding the apartment Carson had rented before being evicted. They found nothing. They tackled the suburban grid where his aunt and uncle lived. Three miles from their home was a proposed development that had been abandoned when a group of environmentalists successfully sued to keep the builders from fouling a lakeshore bird sanctuary. Some of the land had already been bulldozed and foundations dug. In one of the empty cellars, among the pipe shafts and fallen tree limbs, the body of Lane Dockery was found underneath a pile of construction debris. Dockery's throat had been cut, his eyes removed, rolled up scrolls consisting of pages from one of his true-crime books placed into the sockets. I'd read the news with sorrow and regret. I remembered the vindictive part of myself wishing ill to Dockery, when all along he'd only wanted to tell what he saw as a fascinating story.

Apparently, the reading public agreed. Jeanine's version of the Randy Mosley/Carson Beckman case wouldn't even be released for another two weeks, but it was already a bestseller on Amazon and some other prerelease retailers. She informed me of this without great pride, but as a sort of warning that the publicity might be rough on me for a bit longer. Despite what I'd said to her about needing to forget, I was long past the point where forgetting was an option. I couldn't outrun it, and both of us knew it.

"He does seem to be doing quite well, given what he went through," Jeanine said, still looking over at Hayden.

"It wasn't this way at first," I assured her. "He wasn't really hurt, but they had to keep him in the hospital for a few days until the shock wore off. He's had nightmares, and we've both been in counseling." I didn't know if the sessions with the shrink the hospital had recommended were doing me any good, but they seemed to help Hayden. He was back in school, making up the classes he'd missed while I kept him home during the rest of the winter after his abduction. Right now, he and Caleb McPherson and some other boys were taking turns pushing each other far too high on the swings. I called over for them to be careful, and Hayden shouted back, "Sure, Mom!" and promptly ignored my admonition, swinging higher than before. It looked dangerous to me and I rubbed my hands together nervously.

Jeanine Dockery reached over and laid her cool hands across mine. They were steady, calm, reassuring. "It's a good sign he's not scared," she said.

I wanted to believe that. I wanted to embrace the power of simple bravery in the face of a world where there was so much to be scared of. But I'd ignored the core truth that sometimes fear was telling you something you needed to know, and it had cost me, had been costing me for years and years. I told Jeanine, "I'm trying to find the line between a healthy wariness and paranoia. It's kind of tough going."

"No shit," she answered brusquely, and we both laughed a little. "Most people walk through their lives oblivious, and for most people that works out fine. Hayden and you both know more about the real dangers of the world than anyone should have to. But danger isn't everything. Look around you. Think about the fact that you're here and alive and you've recovered from your physical wounds. All of those things are blessings. Your boy is a blessing. Now it's up to you to make something good out of what's been granted to you. Scars and all."

These were the kindest words anyone had said to me since the whole thing started, and I teared up despite my best efforts. Jeanine, who I was starting to recognize as a true class act, fished a tissue out of her purse and politely excused herself while I wiped at my eyes. She walked over to the swing set and told Caleb to sit in the swing next to Hayden, and then she took turns pushing them both. I thought it was a fine thing that she'd finished her brother's work.

My cell phone started ringing and I took it out of the front pocket of my shorts. The caller ID showed that it was someone from Data Managers calling, even though I'd taken the day off from my job. I knew what that meant. Jim Pendergast, my boss, had pushed his formerly lukewarm romantic overtures into a new phase during the time since I'd returned to work. We'd even been out to lunch a few times, and he was angling hard for a dinner date. I kept brushing him off, telling him it was too hard to find a sitter for Hayden, but in truth I hadn't been prepared to leave my son alone. Now, watching him push his legs back and forth in the swing, arcing up across the sun like he might take flight and not care about ever looking down, I decided it was time to answer my phone.